Mehmet Eroğlu

The Disenchanted

Translated by Alvin Parmar

Milet Publishing
Smallfields Cottage, Cox Green
Rudgwick, Horsham, West Sussex
RH12 3DE England
info@milet.com
www.milet.com
www.milet.co.uk

First English edition published by Milet Publishing in 2013
Copyright © Milet Publishing, 2013
ISBN 978 1 84059 766 0

First published in Turkish as *Düş Kırgınları* in 2005

Funded by the Turkish Ministry of Culture and Tourism TEDA Project

Mehmet Eroğlu

Mehmet Eroğlu was born in Izmir in 1948, and studied civil engineering at Middle East Technical University in Ankara, where he was president of the students' union. After the military coup in 1971, he was put on trial and sentenced to eight years in prison and two years in exile before being amnestied in 1974. On his release, he worked as an engineer and started writing. His first novel, *Issızlığın Ortasında*, won the Milliyet Press Novel Contest in 1979. However, in the wake of the 1980 military coup, he remained unpublished until 1984. He now devotes his time to writing and teaching writing. Eroğlu has also written screenplays, including the screenplay for *80. Adım*, which was awarded Best Film at the 1996 Istanbul Film Festival. *The Disenchanted* is his ninth novel and the first to be translated to English. He lives in Ankara.

Alvin Parmar

Alvin Parmar was born in England in 1976. After studying French and Arabic at Cambridge, he spent ten years in Istanbul, where he learned Turkish and got involved in literary translation. He has over ten published translations to his name, including, along with *The Disenchanted* by Mehmet Eroğlu, *Something Funny to Write About* by Deniz Kavukçuoğlu, *Kind-hearted Sinners* by Cezmi Ersöz, and *A Midlife Dream* by Erendiz Atasü, and eleven stories in *Europe in Women's Short Stories from Turkey*, all published by Milet. Two plays that he translated have been performed in New York.

Editorial Notes

Throughout this novel, we have retained the Turkish for several types of terms, including personal names, honorifics and place names, among others. We have used the English spelling of Istanbul, rather than its Turkish spelling, İstanbul, because the English version is so commonly known. For the Turkish terms, we have used italics in their first instance and then normal text for subsequent instances. We have not italicized the Turkish honorifics that form part of a name, such as Bey and Hanım, to avoid splitting the name visually with a style change. A list of the Turkish honorifics that appear in the book follows, along with a guide to Turkish pronunciation.

Turkish Honorifics

Bey: A respectful term of address used after a man's first name.

Efendi: A title of courtesy, equivalent to the English 'sir', literally meaning lord or master.

Hanım: A respectful term of address used after a woman's first name.

Guide to Turkish Pronunciation

Turkish letters that appear in the book and which may be unfamiliar are shown below, with a guide to their pronunciation.

c   as j in 'just'

ç   as ch in 'child'

ğ   silent, but lengthens the preceding vowel

ı   as a in 'along'

ö   as German ö in 'Köln', or French œ in 'œuf'

ş   as sh in 'ship'

ü   as German ü in 'fünf', or French u in 'tu'

Contents

Do we speak about ourselves, to make us believe that we exist?
If that's the case, I'll keep quiet . . .
—Kuzey Erkil

INTRODUCTION

Author's note, November 2004:

"If art is the conquest of divinity, then the artist is the leader of this holy war . . ."

The date: May 20, 2004. The place: the wide terrace that looks out over the sea, in the old stone house where I spend six months of the year. It must have been almost seven o'clock. On the one hand, I was looking out to Domuz Burnu, taking deep breaths; and on the other, I was busy with the final lines of an article I had promised to send to a magazine in Istanbul by the weekend. I wondered if I should say "discovery" instead of "conquest," or if I should use the two words together to soften the challenge thrown down to God? I was trying to overcome the anxious attention to such details that don't have too much meaning or importance, which takes possession of the writer as they near the end.

And right then, just as I was focusing on quelling my indecision with the now cold coffee I had left sitting on the table next to me, onto the terrace—which the lifeless sea breeze blowing inland from the middle of the channel had not been able to cool—came a woman wiping the sweat from her forehead. I had never seen her before; I was not expecting anyone either. For a few seconds, like two predators of different species who meet by chance in the darkness of the night, we waited, sizing each other up in silent discomfort. The woman leisurely took in the surroundings, and then began to walk decisively toward the corner where I was sitting. I hastily put the coffee I'd just picked up back down on the table as if I was going to stand up. But I didn't stand up: my indecision had been replaced by a lackluster sense of surprise. The reason for this needless surprise that imprisoned me in paralysis was not the woman's sudden appearance on the terrace—which, since I spent most of my time there, had turned into my own private room—rather, it was the strange, diaphanous strip of fabric wrapped around her face and hair like a head scarf. As she approached, everything became clear: either the skin of my uninvited guest was radiating light, or her limpid face was absorbing the slanting early evening light around her. She was in fact tall, but she had temporarily put on a few pounds that hadn't yet settled into her figure, and these caught the eye.

The woman, glowing like the phosphorescent fireflies that I encountered some nights in the field next door as they made their mating calls, began to speak as soon as she got to the table, without feeling the need to introduce herself. She was as unabashed and reckless as she was strange; this was clear from her tone of voice and from how she looked into my eyes with the belief that she would get what she wanted.

"I came here to ask you to write a story." These were her first words—or, taking her behavior into account, her first order. But then, in contrast to her quick, bossy opening, she fell silent before completing what she was going to say. Like me, she was out of breath. She must have reached the house by climbing the path from the direction of the sea, not by the tarmac road. If this was true, she couldn't have come by car, but must have come up from one of the neighboring coves by motorboat. "His story," she mumbled when she had caught her breath. "A madman who turned his life into the poem of his sorrow."

And then, so that I could meet the madman she'd mentioned, she put the photograph she held in her hand on the table.

Things were getting stranger and stranger. I felt like snapping at the woman, but instead I turned in silence to the picture on the plastic table. It was a photo of a man standing beneath a decorative cast iron streetlight: he was more than six feet tall, with a body that had not broadened at all, shoulders that stuck out slightly, mousy hair, colorless eyes that were large but had no spark, from which a traceless look spilled out, and a face that didn't betray his age.

"Love, the troubled adolescence of our soul . . . Would you agree?"

It was a good definition, good enough even to make me wish I'd written it myself. Who'd said that? The man in the photograph? Love, the reason for our existence, the immortal seed of our soul . . . I angrily paused when I noticed that, spurred on by an irrepressible desire to find metaphors, I was looking for a piece of paper. I was troubled by questions: who was this woman who was challenging me like this? Had she read any of my books? Where had she found the nerve to come to my house unannounced, to leech into my privacy? Then, I was startled by the most unsettling question: where had she gotten it into her head that I was going to write a story to order, as if I was some kind of second-class hack?

The luminous woman answered this vital question like she'd read my mind: "He's important . . ." She waited a moment and then uttered some words whose effect she was sure of, a sacred code that would break my resistance. "He's in the Register as well, just like you."

The Register! As soon as I heard these two words that for the majority of the peninsula's inhabitants were taboo, and for some of them a magical and mysterious key, I understood who had sent her. Haplessly, I tried to control my body, but I was reeling like I'd taken a punch. It was obvious who had sent her: the secret master of the peninsula, the strange sea creature. Had he decided to make the first move after all these years? As these things were going through my mind, out of the corner of my eye I sneaked a look at the man on the table: we were equals, relatives even. Now I knew who he was. When the woman began to speak again saying, "His name is—" I raised my hand and silenced her.

I had heard her name and the name of the man in the photograph before. For months, all of Karaburun had been abuzz with gossip about the Karayel Hotel in Burgazardı. I think I made up my mind there and then. If I was to write, it wouldn't just be their story; it would also be the story of the peninsula and, naturally, of the fish god. My breast was wracked with a slight pang: yes, behind it I was going to conceal my own story, like a shadow in the mist—the story where I entrusted my fate to a dolphin.

I smiled at the woman—actually, at the one who'd sent her—with a look of obedience that made it clear I'd acquiesce. I pointed for her to sit down on the swing seat opposite me. Then I started coughing; my lungs hadn't been able to cope with the excitement.

After that evening, when she promised to be open about everything and to not hide anything, we started meeting two, sometimes even three days a week. She told the story in chronological order. When events got bogged down in details that would only interest a lover, I would break the flow of events with a coughing fit, and deliberately ask her annoying questions she thought were unnecessary. We were both tense at the beginning. By the first week of June, once our meetings had become routine, due to that powerful glue that gets rid of differences and habit, we were more relaxed. She didn't ask me why I was immediately willing, without the slightest objection, to put down on paper the story she told. And I didn't mention to her the real reason why I'd agreed to write. She told the story without stopping, and by the end of June I'd accumulated enough notes. Whenever I felt overloaded, like a fuse about to blow, I'd recommend taking a break from our meetings for a while, so that I could outline the plot and rest a little too.

If youth is when we exaggerate our successes, then old age is when we learn how to come to terms with our failures. Throughout that July, I often reminded myself of this fact as I thought about the novel I was going to write. My life, which could be summarized as a listless and aimless wallowing in my own laziness, had been coming to these terms for a long time . . . July was also the month of complaint on the peninsula. The sun bakes the surroundings; old women prophesying doom beat their breasts, saying that the earthquake that will destroy everything is nigh; fishermen, saying that because the well-fed fish, plump and full of eggs, had swum straight to the open sea this year instead of coming downstream, they would not be able to catch even a gray mullet the size of a penknife before the beginning of August, made bets with each other that ended up in fights. As for the source of the story, she would phone at least twice a day to remind me that I was late.

They were difficult and troublesome days. The heat was busy

melting away what was left of my lazy lungs, which had been giving me slovenly service for the last ten years. For this reason, I would almost never sleep at night. In the morning, I would get up at the hour when the dawn, opening like a hesitant flower over Foça, recreates the peninsula from scratch. I would stare until sunrise into the channel, which lay between the peninsula and Foça, often looking like a sleepy river, as if it contained the answers I was looking for. And sometimes—probably when I was seized with desperation—I would go out onto the treacherous rock, Gazep Kayası, watch the bottom of the sea in the hope of seeing the god of the dolphins, and get lost in thought . . . While the love stories I had planned to write were growing tall and blossoming before drying out like spring flowers, where was I? What was I doing? Had I ever met, even by chance, any of those three people who were enchanted by the heart's most exquisite fluttering? I couldn't remember. A drama, no matter how much it might burn, is only an internal fire that roasts its hero; no one notices it until the flames it kindles are transformed into black, sooty smoke. Everything had happened a few kilometers on the other side of this terrace that had become the focal point of my life, but we hadn't noticed anything. Sorrowful love songs, lust-filled screams, an Iraqi mother's screams, happiness or unhappiness, the way my equal cried on a large woman's breast, cunning killers—we hadn't heard a thing, not even the barking of the dog that was the child of two lovers.

In August, I met the others. When I had come to the end of the interviews—or statements, as Sami called them—that I had on tape, I had enough material to go on. But how was I going to start? This was still an unanswered question. First of all—leaving my own story to one side—there was not one, but two stories floating around, and between them, there was something like a five-year gap that would create problems for the plot, and that would stretch the internal weave of events. But then, one morning when I noticed the sharp earthy smell that rose like the scent of flowers from the neighboring vegetable garden, uniting death with life, I realized that those five years didn't separate the dramas from each other; on the contrary, this gap brought them closer together and made them whole. I finally knew how I was going to start the story, which I was going to adorn with literary flourishes and the sorrow of which I was going to try to dilute: with the diary—itself well written enough to make a writer jealous—of my equal in the Register. No other beginning could tell the story, its tone and its intensity like what was in those three paragraphs. Wasn't the fourth page, like a piercing scream, the key underlying an important piece of music?

"O irreparable sorrow of our existence, o savage emptiness of my nothingness, o fate!"

From the diary of an itinerant drunkard, page 4:

The dead do not die . . . And that is their only superiority when they are compared with the living.
—Friedrich Nietzsche[1]

O irreparable sorrow of our existence, o savage emptiness of my nothingness, o fate! Leave and abandon me to my drunkenness. O raucous redness of the sunset, o ill-omened squalls of the coastal waters, o western wind, o dry northeastern wind; o lascivious songs of the cicadas . . . Leave me.

Why is there no volcano nearby that, with its lava, will bring hell right up to our feet? Lustless sea breeze that caresses my hair, diaphanous barrier that seals off my inside from my outside, rivers that I have not stepped into, that I have not washed in, swamps that I have not sunk into, peaks that I have not climbed, shallow seas that I have not drowned in, carnivorous women . . . Leave me.

O drunken veteran of wars that you have not fought in! Arise, it is time to go: prepare yourself for the great return that stretches from year to year, from city to city, from embarrassment to embarrassment, from woman to woman, prepare yourself for your sacred journey . . . Do not be afraid, you are not alone: on long journeys like this, death, the traveling companion, will be at your side . . .

O death, my death, do not leave me . . .

---

[1]   Nietzsche, quoted in Kuçuradi, *The Tragic in Max Scheler and Nietzsche*

CHAPTER I

Life is the carnage of a few dreams; it is the graveyard of a few infringed, betrayed, sold, abandoned, forgotten dreams . . . What a waste . . .
—Pierre Schoendoerffer, *Farewell to the King*[2]

---

[2] *L'Adieu au Roi*

Am I going to die today? If I am, I'm ready; my last words are on my lips. When the time comes for last words, you should definitely have something to say. As Kurtz was breathing his last, twice he said, "The horror! The horror!" My last words will be, "I've drunk, I've drunk so much." What better proof could there be that I haven't wasted my life?

Since we can forecast the moment of birth, how meaningless the randomness of the moment we shall migrate to nothingness is. That inevitable end that we've spent our whole life preparing for depends on the dice fate will throw, not caring which numbers come up but with resolve nonetheless. The uncertainty of this moment, when I comprehend that I've passed beyond the bounds of doubt, that my life has been a defeat, must be the revenge God has been brewing all these years to take one day. Who said that God does not play dice? Which numbers will come up today? That's the question du jour.

I have other questions on my mind too. As I get ready to die, will I be able to save myself from the life instinct's brazen claws? Maybe the wish to die is simply the desire not to suffer. No, while whining as if I've lost all hope, I shouldn't be unfair to myself: I'm not afraid of pain; mine is only the impatience of a delayed meeting.

I haven't died yet; I'm in the embrace of death's little brother, sleep. I'm rocked in a happy unconsciousness that swathes my body like a second skin. But now I have to open my eyes slowly, get ready for that tiresome return known as waking up, and get my bearings once more in my dingy labyrinth.

Although my bearings may be uncertain, I know what awaits me at the end of the road: an unsettled, roiled silence. Somewhere in the distance, Schoendoerffer's dog will be howling bitterly; downstairs,

Mücella's anxious footsteps, as she gets ready to sweep the terrace; at the end of the headland, the cough-like noises the sullen motor boats make as they return from bringing their nets from the channel . . . Wind! I can find the evening breeze, hung over, skulking in its nest in Çandarlı Bay. And what about the ruler of the peninsula, its real God? I prick up my ears; since the cicadas have not started making a racket yet, even though he's appeared, he must not have risen yet.

The semi-darkness, fluttering like a gray scarf, is unfolding, winding and crumpling with me. I'm halfway there . . . The odd voice here and there. I listen: No, they're not voices, but faint, lifeless heartbeats dripping from my breast to the bed, like water. My poor, stubborn friend is beating like a torn drum today . . .

And here, if I die face down in my bed, where shall I go? This too is uncertain. My destiny and I haven't reached a decision yet about the direction. To heaven? I'm not sure. The worst thing about heaven is that you only get to go there after you die. And, while it's brimming with things that beckon us toward sin, like houris, a climate that breeds indolence and narcotic bliss, there's no alcohol. What's that all about! So, what about hell?

The semi-darkness is pierced . . . Am I in hell?

"Wake up!" It's Sami! What nerve . . . he'd been lying in wait for me in the corner. In the gloom, I tried to pick out his voice, which hid his friendship. "Şuayip has been waiting on the terrace for half an hour."

I'm no longer waking up, I'm sobering up . . . When would he accept this? I pulled my eyelids open and turned over. The whole place was illuminated with a broken light. Sami, at the foot of the bed, looked like one of those toys that turns somersaults on crutches. I was in my room, at the mouth of hell. That must have been why it was so hot. "I guess I'm not going to die today," I said.

"What's so strange about that?" asked Sami. "'The dead do not die . . . And that is their only superiority when they are compared with the living.'" I yawned lazily. He must have pinched that saying from somewhere. Or had he been reading my diary? I didn't dwell on it; it was good news I was dead. As I reached out my hand, he said, "You've finished the bottle."

His voice still wasn't friendly. I swung my feet down. Like he said, the bottle was empty. Could I get up? Just as I was about to try, I paused. Perhaps I should have waited a little longer.

"I want to be alone," I said, stalling for time. Sami raised his eyebrows, and I raised my voice. "Didn't you hear me?"

He had. "Solitude is for wild animals and kings," he hissed. "Which one are you?"

"I'm not going to rise to your bait," I said. "I'm just going to have a shower, and then I'll be back."

"Just so you know . . ." He took a deep breath, came close and gave the first diktat of the day: "There'll be no drinking until three o'clock. And don't even think about forcing or threatening anyone to give you alcohol, because I've got all the keys to the cupboards."

Evil bastard! I just looked at him. "What time is it now?" I asked.

"Eight."

Seven hours! Impossible! In despair I mumbled, "You're forgetting that you work with me."

He shook his head. "Just a resident," he said. "You're forgetting that."

"Well, in that case, remember that I saved your life," I replied shamelessly.

Sami looked at his crutches, and spitefully continued his sentences beginning with "just:" "Just my top half . . ."

I must have made him angry. I could tell not from his spite but because instead of wandering off, he was still there, scrutinizing me. Or was he trying to work out whether or not I could stand up? I paused. Just when the silence seemed it had come to stay, I asked, "What have I done now?"

"You embarrassed the captain," he started. How? I wondered. "You went right up to him and sang marches the whole night in that terrible voice of yours. What's worse, it was the same march over and over again, like a broken record."

Which march was it? I decided not to ask and waved my hand. If I'd asked, I'd have heard all about it. And to bear my embarrassment before I'd completely sobered up would have been stupid; I could have fallen over. "I'll find an opportunity to apologize," I said. "He's an unarmed soldier, anyway."

As Sami left the room, I looked up at the ceiling fan. The wings weren't moving. Fucking electricity! Another power cut. That must have been why it was so hot. I'd gotten my hopes up for nothing; I still hadn't been able to get to hell.

I went into the shower; the water was turning into steam before it touched my skin. In front of me was another day that I'd get through like I did yesterday, the day before, and the day before that. A day when I wouldn't have a drink for seven hours. I turned off the shower and got out. I waited for a while. I wasn't going to bother shaving; it was too difficult when sober. I was trying not to look in the mirror, but it was no use; in the end my eyes found their counterparts looking back at them. When had the face staring back at me given up on looking like me? Two, three, five years ago . . . Skin: the litmus paper of our health. "You look terrible," I said to my twin. And I was right: there was a typical drunkard's face looking back at me.

Back in the room, before I got dressed, I sat down on the bed and lit the first cigarette of the day. When she'd been here, I hadn't been so bad. How long had it been since her face had faded in the alcoholic haze that clouded my memory? I looked at my fingers; I wasn't going to count. Water running down my face dripped onto the bed. I dried it with a towel. It dripped again; I guess I was crying. When I hadn't had a drink, I'd cry. At this rate, I wasn't going to be able to make it until three o'clock. If only I could remain frozen inside this semi-darkness and thaw out at three!

I got up and opened the blinds. Outside, it was the sort of day I'd hoped for: the sun, still in the first steps of its long climb, had managed to get three fingers above the low mountains of Foça. On the right, I could see Alman Koyu, under a parasol of silence; directly behind it, Delikli Burun, looking like an index finger dipped in the water to see how hot it is; four miles farther along, the impassable Domuz Koyu, waiting at the entrance of deserted coves to the south. In front of me, the channel—transformed in the oblique daylight into a silver tongue extending toward a vagina—between the mainland and the peninsula, which advanced thirty miles from north to south and plunged into the bottom of the gulf. Below the hill, two islands—like a semi-colon placed on the sea—completed the picture: low and crocodile-like Küçük Ada, where not a single plant grew; and more to the left, in the north, in front of Mytilene, Büyük Ada, which had puffed up its back like a seal getting ready to mate. In the straits between them, as if to make up for the pain of the wind that had been beating Değirmen Dağı for three days, as many as ten sailboats that had only now launched themselves into the calm waters were busy furrowing the sea . . .

If I'd been inclined to live, I would have lived here and maybe believed in God too . . . I stubbed out my cigarette.

Şuayip was on the terrace. He was so thin that he looked like a skeleton wearing clothes. He had a tie on too. I always felt embarrassed of what I was wearing when I was with someone like Şuayip who believed in being well dressed. As soon as I stepped onto the terrace, he scurried over. He must have been hurrying so he could catch the nine o'clock minibus leaving for town. If he missed it, he'd either have to wait for the eleven o'clock or else walk two and a half miles uphill in the heat.

"Good morning, sir." I used to object to it at first. But now I knew that whatever I did, I wouldn't be able to make him believe I wasn't a sir, so I'd pretend I hadn't heard it. I answered his greeting with a quick nod. Taking this as a cue, Şuayip immediately said, "A motion for adjournment to give to the taxman."

The respect he showed was sincere, enough to make you embarrassed even. I signed the papers he held out and gave them back. We looked each other up and down without speaking. I had to find a question to show I was interested: "How much is it now?"

"Almost thirty-five billion," he said in a voice that had the air of someone who knew the figures and wanted to be trusted.

He paused a moment for a second question; then, when he realized I wasn't going to ask anything else, he went off with rapid steps, as if he was worried I'd take back the pieces of paper he was holding tightly. To see him walk, you'd never have believed he was almost seventy.

I found Sami beneath the bougainvillea-covered pergola, grappling as ever with one of his crosswords to the sound of classical music. The four newspapers in front of him were also open on the crossword pages. I perched next to the man whose legs and manhood I hadn't been able to save. The breakfast tray covered with a muslin cloth that Mücella had prepared was waiting for me on the table.

I listened to the music, intense with its dramatic weave, and amused myself with the bread for a while. Sibelius? I coughed. Sami paid as little attention to my cough as he had to my existence; he had no intention of putting down his crossword.

"This is it," I said. "In October this'll all be the taxman's. Adieu, Karayel Hotel." He nodded his head without lifting his eyes from the newspaper in front of him. I made another move: "Poor Şuayip will be more upset than us."

"Yes, because then he won't have any excuse not to go back to his wife."

I knew he was saying that just for the sake of saying something. He didn't care about Şuayip or the hotel.

"He's from Yozgat, isn't he?" I ought to eat a piece of cheese as well. If I didn't touch the cheese, Mücella wouldn't consider breakfast to be finished and wouldn't take the tray away. "I don't think Şuayip is the sort who can live in Yozgat," I said.

"What's wrong with Yozgat?" he asked.

"It's cold," I said. "Thin people feel the cold."

"'Cube,' Arabic . . ."

I carried on as if I hadn't heard him: "I suspect that Şuayip gave Şükrü and Mücella their salaries last month out of his own pocket. Has he said anything to you?"

After a long silence, Sami said, "*Kaaba*."

"What do you mean, 'kaaba'?" I asked.

"'Cube' in Arabic," he replied. He was never deaf when it was something to do with his crossword. I was just getting ready to swear, but he got in first. "He hasn't said anything. Maybe he did. I'll ask him if you want."

I knew what he was insinuating. "I've done what I could to find some money," I said. He hadn't said I hadn't. Ah, if only I could have had a beer. "I asked Salim. What my mother left has run out."

Sami didn't reply, so I continued, "He's expecting me to ask him for a loan."

"Of course. He is your big brother, after all."

"But that's not enough for him; he wants to be my lord and master too. He's been trying for forty years."

Sami lowered his glasses and turned off the CD player, as if he wanted to listen to the crescendo when he was alone. Then he said, "Don't exaggerate. You might be tall, and you might have strong arms, but you're getting on. Who'd want a slave in their fifties?"

"I don't care if I lose this fucking hotel," I said. "I'm not asking him for a loan."

"Is there anything that you do care about?" I was about to say, *A bottle of beer*, but he quickly added, "Apart from alcohol." I should just go back to my room! "Eat something," he continued. "You didn't eat anything last night."

Do you want something to eat, comrade? The first time I met Sami, thirty-one years ago in Heidelberg, in that Lebanese restaurant on Hauptstrasse, he'd talked about food too. Back then, he stood on his own two feet without crutches, and at night he had an Italian lover who made him happy. He was very handsome. If I'd told him he was coming with me to Amsterdam the next week, what would he have done? He'd have laughed.

"What are you thinking about?"

I returned from Hauptstrasse to Karaburun, from 1972 to 2003. "That you used to be handsome," I said.

He didn't care if he was handsome or not anymore. He pointed to İzmir Burnu on Küçük Ada. "That's the handsome one, over there."

I looked over. Out by the island that looked like a crocodile lying in ambush, there was a faint shadow stirring between the rocks in the shallows extending into the gulf. One more person drowning in their own loneliness . . . "Captain Emin!" He shook his head.

"I promise," I said, abandoning any thoughts of befriending him. "I'll apologize. Maybe I'll even mention the dog to him."

"Leave the dog out of it," said Sami. He was getting stressed.

Annoying bastard! "We used to love that dog," I said. "You, me and her. The three of us. Or have you forgotten?"

"It's not the same dog," he replied. "No dog can survive out there in the wild for two years."

"Did you know that apparently dogs and horses judge us depending on our ability to love? If a dog loves you, it's a sign you're a good person."

"What? So now animals are the measure of how good or bad we are! Don't make me laugh!"

"You know," I said, "I've had it up to here. After thirty years, I'm this close to hating you." Sami didn't look at the time I'd squeezed down to a few weeks between my fingers. He was looking at Küçük Ada, at Emin. He opened his mouth like he was about to say something, but for whatever reason, he changed his mind. Then I thought the rumors doing the rounds in the hotel about the captain might be true. "He shouts at night as well, doesn't he?"

At first, Sami didn't seem to want to answer. Then, with a shrug, "Sometimes," he said. "When he's feeling sad." Sad! He's a Schoendoerffer soldier. Abandoned in Bingöl or Hakkari instead of Borneo. "You don't hear him," he mumbled afterwards.

Because you've passed out by then. That was what he wanted to say. But he didn't. He was suddenly feeling sorry for me. He shook his head and said, "I guess you're both crying . . ." in a voice that trailed off. "Him out loud, you silently."

I was mistaken; he wasn't feeling sorry for me. Since I'd begun drinking, he'd changed too. At least as much as I had. "I miss her more and more," I said.

Our eyes met. Was he going to put his hand on my shoulder? He seemed to have mellowed, and I trembled with joy: maybe he'd say yes to a bottle of beer. Just as I was about to ask, I closed my mouth in shame. I was a filthy drunk; I was about to sell the most precious thing in my life, my sacred pain, for a bottle of beer.

"I know," said Sami.

What did he know? That I was a drunk or that I missed her? "Which one?" I asked.

"Come on, have something to eat!" he said, again.

I had a bit of cheese and a bit of bread. I didn't touch the tea or the coffee; if there'd been any alcohol, I'd have had a drink. Any other liquid gave me an upset stomach. As nine o'clock approached, first the cicadas in the pepper tree started; then, marches poured down the hill; they were sung by the soldiers of the anti-aircraft unit deployed in Değirmen Dağı in 1975 to spit fire at the Greek planes that were supposed to come and bomb the Aliağa Refinery. On the other side, over Foça, the sun, which had been loitering all morning, was getting whiter and whiter and climbing the stairs one by one. To the northwest, in the open waters off Kanlıkaya, a ship laden with containers had broken through and steered around behind Büyük Ada to enter the gulf. Behind Değirmen Dağı, the magnificent white cliffs of Akdağ—the backbone of the peninsula—were reflecting the sunbeams downward like a mirror. As the shadows shrank, the heat was going to intensify.

Sami leaned back over his puzzle, and I went back to my sorrow. The dog still hadn't howled; would it be able to make it safely through today as well? "Whether you like it or not," I said, "he's family. I'm going . . ."

He didn't say anything at first, then he hung his head as if he wasn't going to stop me. "Whatever you say. But a dog isn't a wild animal."

"Still, I want to be alone," I said. "If I'm not going to have a drink, maybe I'll have a swim."

"Okay. But be here at one! Handan and Erica are coming for lunch." A troubled expression spread across his face. "Apparently they want to talk about the elections."

The bloody local elections again! I was going to shake my head, but just then I had a flash of inspiration. "First a couple of beers," I said. I was feeling more like my old self. "Or else you'll be listening to the two of them for hours on your own."

Without looking up from his crossword, Sami made me eat my words. "You're the one they want to talk to."

"One bottle?" I parlayed.

Shaking his head came so easily to Sami. "You call one of them mother, and you're sleeping with the other," he said. "You should be ashamed of yourself. You're not getting a drop until three. Whether you come or not."

"It's been a long time since I've slept with anyone," I said.

He was surprised. "Do you think we're all blind? Whenever Erica's here, doesn't she go to your room once a week?"

"We just hold each other," I said. "So you see, there isn't that much of a difference left between us."

If it had been any other time, he might have laughed. But not this time. "What, you mean things are even more serious than they seem?"

"Don't bother," I said. "There's no point trying to deny it. We're from a generation that's officially impotent."

"Leave everyone else out of it."

"Okay, I will."

Sami paused for a moment. He was thinking. Then he told me what he'd been thinking. It was something that rarely happened: he agreed with me. "You might be right. We couldn't manage to have a revolution; we couldn't manage to be good lovers. We couldn't manage to love women like they're supposed to be loved . . ." For the first time that morning, he was looking into my eyes. "And now we can't even have sex."

He was on the verge of saying we'd wasted our lives. It didn't bother me when I was drinking, but when I was sober, the dramatic emphasis in his voice got on my nerves. I put my hand on his shoulder. We both needed comforting.

"Someone intelligent once said that people take sex more seriously than they should, and I think he was right. Look at nature. Birds, for example. They get the job done in a couple of seconds flat. And some species, scorpions I think, don't even touch each other."

"You're not a bird," said Sami, ignoring my long-winded explanation.

I wasn't a bird, but was I a human? I didn't ask. There was only one thing standing in the way: saying good-bye to beer. "I've never been that obsessed with women anyway," I said.

"If you ask me, that's just proof that your will to live is weak," replied Sami. He broke off as if something had just occurred to him. "And maybe that's why you're so rash." I scowled. "What? Didn't you like that?"

"I'd have preferred you to say 'brave' instead of 'rash,'" I said. "Not that I care though, but still I'd have wanted you to say that."

He shook his head. He must have believed bravery was something different. I was surprised, but if I hadn't been sober, I wouldn't have been. All these years we'd been together, and we didn't even have a shared definition of our most distinctive trait. I laughed. He frowned. "You've been spending too much time talking to İhsan Hoca," I said. "Is that freak coming to lunch too?"

"Just like you can't have a party without music, you can't have a meeting around here without philosophy."

"What? We're going to be listening to a speech on the theory of the purity of what you may call it . . . what was it now?"

Before going back to his crossword, he said, "The purity of goodness." I hated it when he spent the whole day going after words like that without even looking up. "Seven across: Explorer? Arabic." He looked up. "It's come up before, I remember; I think you knew it."

I could have said Arafat, but I said I didn't know. "How am I supposed to know?"

He leaned back. "Didn't you go to Palestine?"

I stood up. I wasn't going to tell him. "A few months, that's all," I said. "And anyway, I couldn't hear anything through all the gunfire."

I took out a cigarette and went over to the garden gate, leaving him alone with his puzzle. He was right: we hadn't managed to have a revolution, we hadn't managed to be good lovers, and I somehow hadn't managed to turn my diary into a book of stories. They called us the generation that knew how to die, but I couldn't even manage that. Drinking and making friends, that was the sum total of all I'd managed to do.

I left behind the ever-increasing racket the cicadas were making, and walked toward the dusty, primrose-lined path that went down to the rocks opposite Küçük Ada. Practically each step I took, a grasshopper would leap out into the air and land in front of my foot, as if it wanted to be crushed. Suicidal grasshoppers! It reminded me of how weak my own will to live was!

If that was true, shouldn't I have died after she went? That question, like a hand grabbing my arm, stopped me in my tracks. Maybe Sami was right; maybe I had died, just like he said, and because I was so stubborn, I was refusing to lie down. I walked on, leaving my voice and the grasshoppers behind.

There was no one on the concrete sunbathing platform on the rocks, which had been made by the holidaymakers from the big, smart houses at the bottom of the slope. I took off my T-shirt and jumped into the narrow strait between Küçük Ada and Değirmen Dağı. Two hundred meters. If only I could have swum right to the bottom. Maybe one day . . . In the end, fate would keep throwing snake eyes.

Ten minutes after I got to the island, Emin came out from the hole he was hiding in and appeared at the top of the rocks. He might have retired, but the instincts that kept him alive in the mountains were still functioning. When I waved to show I was a friend, he came down to the shallows. He had a bag in his hand.

When he reached me, I said, "Sorry about yesterday evening." He didn't reply. I took the towel he offered me to dry myself. It was difficult to make out what he was thinking from his face, which had the look of a bust carved out of hard rock. "I go off the rails when I drink a lot." When he noticed I was looking at him intently, he shrugged his shoulders as if he wanted to prove he was a living being. "Which march was I singing anyway?"

Before answering, he offered me a cigarette. Sami was right; he was handsome. I took the cigarette. His was a dark, reflectionless handsomeness; not even the sun had been able to dispel the shadow on his face. One of those men you'd be afraid of even if he was smiling. It was his eyes, which always had a distant look, that gave this impression. He withdrew into a long silence as if he had said and exhausted everything he was ever going to say. "'Gendarme, We're Communists,'" he said, after a long time. "I believe that was the march you were singing."

We lit our cigarettes. Then we both laughed. Or rather, when I started laughing, he had to join in.

"You were lucky, Captain," I said. "Because that's the march I sing the best. And it's my favorite. I sang it for the first time on June 15, 1970, together with the workers who were besieging Istanbul in a pincer movement. So don't think it's just an ordinary march; compared to the others it has a special place, you see."

In a voice that didn't give away whether he liked the workers or not, he said, "You must have been pretty young back then."

"I was eighteen," I said. "It was a tense day. The working class had finally woken up from its deep sleep. The police, like rats, were looking for a hole to escape into. A hundred, maybe two hundred thousand people were in the streets. The revolution was well within our grasp, an arm's length away. In Kadıköy, when the gendarmerie units cut us off, we were right at the front, leading the workers with marches, and that was where I sang it for the first time. Repeating after a girl called Leyla."

I was just about to say she was beautiful, when he broke in: "I understand."

I didn't know what he understood. But I could remember. "As we were yelling, 'We're communists!' one soldier had his fingers in his ears, like he thought he was going to catch communism from hearing us."

If Emin had been there that day, he might have shot us. That's what I thought; then I stopped worrying about it. This time he laughed first, and I joined in. The seafront had become crowded. Now there were a few windsurfers too, along with the sailboats. The soldiers had finished their morning drill and Değirmen Dağı had fallen silent. The old windmills—now used as headquarters—that had been painted khaki when they were repaired were like lighthouses that had been removed from their rightful place by a playful giant and planted on the mountaintop. As we stood there smoking, I tried hard not to mention the dog that had managed to live on its own away from human contact for two years. But he was the only person who'd be able to work out where a lone dog could be hiding on the rocky peak opposite covered only with scrub and olive trees. Mücella's grown-up son had seen him a fortnight ago, just after he moved into the hotel, inspecting the terrain, investigating every nook and cranny one by one, like a warrior who wants to identify the points where an enemy could attack.

It was already hot. I put my feet in the water. "I guess the breeze isn't going to pick up," I said. "We're going to roast."

Emin nodded. He looked as though he'd gotten extremely cold while he was fighting in the mountains, and had missed the heat. As I was thinking about asking him if he had any beer, he said, "That old man, what was his name now . . . you know, the one who's only got a few teeth left, the tiny fisherman who brings fish to the hotel."

"Fındık İbram," I said. He repeated it over to himself, and nodded when he was satisfied. "If you ask me, he's the most interesting man on the peninsula."

"Yes, he must be," Emin said. "He does strange things at night at the bottom of the pepper tree around the back."

To call what Fındık did strange! That was more polite than could be hoped for from a soldier. "He pisses on it," I said. "To dry it out. And last year, he tried to chop it down, but he wasn't strong enough."

I looked into his face; he wasn't surprised. "Why?"

I couldn't wait any longer. "Have you got any beer with you?" I asked.

He shook his head again. "Just water. Why does he do that?"

"He calls that tree a brothel. You'd think all the cicadas on the peninsula go there to screw and breed. If we get rid of the tree, he says, the unruly insects will migrate to Chios or Mytilene, and we'll make life difficult for the Greeks."

Emin seemed a bit confused. "He mustn't like the Greeks," he said.

Did he really not have any beer? Or had Sami warned him too? "He doesn't," I said. "In 1922, when he was still in his mother's womb, Greek soldiers escaping from the advancing Turkish Army bayoneted his father to death because he wouldn't give them his boat. So Fındık, every year on the 17th of September—" without being asked, I added, "the 17th of September is the date 'round here was liberated—he jumps in his motorboat and goes to invade Mytilene, but each time he does, someone catches him on the other side of Büyük Ada. In 1976 though, they lost sight of him, and he got all the way to Mytilene, a flag in one hand, a hunting rifle in the other. He was in prison for three months."

Emin smiled without nodding. "That's a good story," he said.

Was he telling the truth? "Just water, eh?"

"Yes," he said. "Would you like some?" I shook my head. "And how does someone like him catch all those fish, those lobsters?"

If he'd had any beer, maybe I'd have told him that Fındık İbram could live at the bottom of the sea. But he said he hadn't, so I said, "It's luck."

He stood up; I didn't. "I'm going to Çeşme for a few days," he said. "Can you look after my things somewhere until I get back?"

"Of course," I said. "I wouldn't even bother emptying out your room. We don't have any reservations anyway."

"Thanks," he replied.

There was nothing to read on his face: no joy, surprise, anger, irritation; there was only that shadow. Why was he going? "Ahmet said you'd be staying two months."

"Yes. You never know, I might even stay six."

"Two months at the most. The hotel closes in October. Maybe

Ahmet can find you somewhere to rent for then. There must be empty houses up there in the teachers' complex."

This time he shrugged his shoulders. "I'm happy with the hotel. It's close to İhsan Hoca. I promised him I'd help out with the philosophy seminar." I laughed. "Why are you laughing?" he asked.

"Do you know how many years he's been planning that seminar?" How was he supposed to know? I continued, "This is the fifth summer. If you ask me, that seminar isn't about to be held any time soon."

"Why?" It wasn't his face that betrayed his disappointment, but the indecision in his voice.

"No one knows." I put out my cigarette. "And no one feels they can ask İhsan Hoca."

"If only I'd gotten to know someone like him earlier." Why earlier? I looked into his face, into his eyes. Both were silent. If he'd known a bit about philosophy, would he have retired so young? "What do *you* think of him?"

"He's honest," I said. "You can tell because he's so talkative. Most honest people are talkative."

Emin nodded. He seemed happy with the answer he'd got; then he pointed at my back. "Those scars, cigarette burns, how did you get them?"

"It's all in the past," I said.

Then, for some reason, he reached out his hand; I thought he was going immediately. I shook it. He carefully placed his things in his plastic bag, and went into the water. He had a silent swimming style that was attuned to going long distances. I looked at Değirmen Dağı, as if I was going to see the dog that hadn't appeared for two days.

To curl up in the shadow of a rock and go to sleep. I couldn't think of any other way to use up the beerless hours. I looked at the wild fig tree fifty meters away. We'd made love on this island, and we'd slept. I didn't drink as much then. And I hadn't died. My eyes stung; I opened and closed them. Tears or sweat? I didn't put my hand up to check. Being caught between a lone dog and drink makes you lose your curiosity too.

Toward half past, I went back up the slope beneath the sun, burning like a white brand, to the hotel. The grasshoppers were gone now, as though they had committed mass suicide. Sami was looking after the Germans, who were shouting songs—maybe they wanted to drown out the cicadas—at three tables that had been pushed together at the north side of the garden, which was still in the shade. I didn't waste any time and made straight for the kitchen. Double six: the drinks cabinet was wide open. I shouldn't be ungrateful. From time to time, God did throw good dice. I took one bottle from the shelf of beers and walked toward my room, but then, halfway there, I turned around and swiped another one. "From now on, I'll always make sure I've got a reserve in the room," I vowed to the mirror, offering prayers of thanks to the Germans. When I was about halfway through the first bottle, I turned the fan on. The heat was unbearable; if the wind didn't pick up for another week, the grapes would dry out on their vines this year.

Twenty minutes later when there was a knock on the door, I was brushing my teeth. It was Mücella to say that the guests had arrived. I threw on some clothes and went out onto the terrace with a face that the beer had stretched to both sides. Erica and Handan were about to come in through the garden gate. İhsan Hoca had arrived and was even sitting at the table Sami reserved for respected customers—the ones who ate fish in the moonlight and so wouldn't object to paying a hefty bill. I went past Sami, hiding my face from him, came down and gave the two women a hug and a peck on the cheek. Handan was tender, Erica was generous; when she kissed me, she pressed her body against mine and chose a spot very close to my lips. There was something lopsided about Handan's dress: it sat on her, not looking like it had been put on, but like it was about to be taken off. We went out onto the terrace. While they were saying hello to Sami and İhsan Hoca, I sat down at the table.

Handan was one of those women who had never given birth but could be everyone's mother. I had become her son while crying in her arms. I remembered it well, that night five years ago when Fındık and I returned from the sea: her big breasts turned into a sponge, a huge sponge that absorbed pain and tears. She was maybe 100 kilos, but she was looking younger than usual. What kind of woman had she been in her twenties? Her cheeks, which overflowed from her face, suggested that she'd gotten fat later in life.

With the shame of the secrets we reminded each other of, we smiled furtively. If İhsan Hoca drank two glasses of wine, Handan could get a new offer of marriage this evening. Her broad, chubby face was as fluid as ever. The outlines of her face had stretched downward and were distended, resembling a drop that was about to fall. Her face was held in check by her lips, which looked like a dam that would stop the water. I turned to the side. İhsan Hoca, desperately moving his lips like a puppy torn away from the teat, had already started dishing out compliments. I watched them for a while. Why—in spite of all those snide, bookish remarks he made—did I put up with this old man with a mind that came and went like the tide? It was a stupid question. I knew the answer: because he had a door that opened onto madness. The same reason I put up with Fındık. Besides, for some reason, I liked the muffled rhythm that his half-falling-out false teeth made as he was speaking.

As for Erica, who was pressing her leg against mine, she was on my right and living proof of how healthy a forty-year-old woman could be. Tiring trips between Germany and Karaburun, coping with a load of mostly old women for three weeks, and those long walks at the top of the mountains; I guess that was why I couldn't sleep with her. She was full of life. The incompatibility of the living and the dead: we were going in opposite directions.

While we were waiting for the food to come, Handan spoke—continually wiping away her sweat—about the Friends of Karaburun Association. The number of active members had reached seventy-five. For the elections next March, they were thinking of bringing in at least a hundred people who had summer houses here and who returned to Izmir, Ankara and Istanbul in the winter. One hundred votes was a number large enough to affect the outcome of the elections in this small district. Even though I didn't believe it, I nodded, pretending I thought they actually could do it. They seemed determined to overthrow the current chairman, who thought protecting the seals was lunacy. While Handan was talking about the seals, she looked at me out of the corner of her eye. But I was watching the bread crumbs in front of me, seemingly oblivious to the seals and the past. What's more, the chairman of the local council was thinking of widening and shortening the narrow thirty-five-mile coastal road that connected us with the Çeşme motorway. I scowled as if I'd forgotten that if the road was shortened, more tourists would come to spend the night and that would be good for business, as if the very thought of it turned my stomach.

İhsan Hoca didn't like the chairman because he had asked him to vacate the hovel he lived in. Erica didn't get involved in the conversation, but was gently nodding and blinking. At one point, when Sami was looking the other way, I leaned over and whispered to her to order a beer. Just as Handan was about to tuck into Şükrü's mouth-watering *imam bayıldı*, she finally got to the point: the association needed quite a large room to hang their signs and hold their meetings. They hadn't thought of going to any of the other hotels because they didn't have a single penny to pay for rent.

I looked at Sami. He was going to say no to avoid the wrath of the chairman of the local council. I preempted him and said okay.

Throughout the meal, I took sneaky mouthfuls of the beer Erica had put between us. Near two o'clock, the wind still hadn't picked up. The heat was spreading down from Değirmen Dağı like mist. At around half past two, Şuayip came. He was looking glum. When Sami got up from the table to speak to him, I finished off the rest of the beer. The numbness, just like the heat, was spreading over my skin. There was half an hour left until I was allowed to drink again; then that long happiness would last until I passed out . . . At one point, Erica brought her freckled face close to mine and whispered that she was going to Germany the day after tomorrow. Instead of telling her not to come, I smiled invitingly, in honor of the second beer. Finally, İhsan Hoca tapped his glass with his knife. Obeying his wishes, we stopped talking. He had finished his second glass; the philosophy lesson was beginning . . .

"The time has come for our brains to conceive." I always found that he had a strange turn of phrase. Shakespeare apparently used to put uncommon words in the mouths of his heroes. And İhsan Hoca believed he was following in the footsteps of the great master. "Today's topic is morality," he said, looking at Handan. "I want an opinion from everyone." I leaned back. It would generally start off like this, but often he wouldn't give the floor to anyone. "You, Handan Hanım, how about going first?"

It wasn't actually that bad. At least we didn't have to discuss the incarnation of God or the power of the Good.

Handan placed her small right hand—like a white rose—onto her ample bosom, unhidden by her black dress, and burst out laughing, which made her seem even younger.

"Why me?" she asked, but had no objection to being the first; she liked to speak her mind without being influenced by anyone else. "I agree with the concept of morality found in nature. Especially when it comes to immorality. If we believe in love, if we respect it, we must also believe in eroticism, and renounce puritanical repression."

Did that count as a philosophical answer? I didn't know. Even if it wasn't, no one minded. Sami returned to the table with a long face that he'd caught from Şuayip. It was Erica's turn; although her Turkish was good, she gave her answer in German—it must have been out of respect for philosophy—and Sami had to translate what she had said: "The reconciliation of good and evil, or else the soul's persecution of the body."

İhsan Hoca applauded. He had a look in his eyes that said he couldn't decide if it was the definition of morality or the woman who gushed health from every pore that had pleased him more. I was sure that if Handan hadn't been there, he'd have declared his love to Erica and tried to carry her off to his hovel.

"What about you? Lord of the Compass, Kuzey Bey!"[3]

"I'm on the side of immorality," I said hastily. "Call it loving literature, if you want."

"True," ventured İhsan. "A lot of literary masterpieces are nothing more than nobly shameless displays of sin and immorality, like a magnificent feast."

He stopped speaking and directed his gaze at me, waiting for approval. Knowing that I would have difficulty even reading a sentence like that, never mind defining literature, I said, "That's exactly

---

3   *Kuzey* means "north" in Turkish.

what I was thinking. We're taught how to use weapons, but not how to use our bodies."

After İhsan Hoca had finished his long speech, they all left at a quarter past three. Erica said good-bye with a look in her eyes that told me she was going to come back that night; Handan hugged me tightly as though to tell me not to drink. I kissed them both. The wind was blowing out at sea but somehow couldn't get down the channel to the shore. "There must be a storm brewing," I said to Sami.

Sami, landlubber that he was, answered without even looking at the sea. "Why did you say yes to them?" He was looking for a fight. "Now the chairman will come down on us like a ton of bricks."

"This time he'll lose the elections, just you wait and see," I said. "Didn't you hear? They've found a hundred people."

Sami shook his head. He looked convinced that the man wouldn't lose. "It's still that sob story about the seals, isn't it?"

"It's not because of the bloody seals," I sighed, since he had nothing to add. "It's because he poisons dogs—that's why I don't like the guy." He was still shaking his head. I wasn't going to waste my time on him; I pointed at my watch: "You owe me fifteen minutes. Give me the keys to the cabinet."

"You're taking the piss." Maybe I was, but now I was going to have a drink. "Aren't you curious about what Şuayip has done?"

"There's life in that old dog yet," I said. "At least five years, mark my words, maybe even ten."

He tried to put his hands up, like he was giving up, but that's a dangerous movement for someone whose legs can't hold him. He changed his mind when he started to totter. "Will it be that much, I don't know, but I bet he'll live longer than you."

He seemed to believe what he was saying. If I'd held out my little finger, he'd have taken the bet. Then, presumably because he remembered he was my friend, he leaned toward me on his crutches. I moved back without letting him get any closer. I didn't want him to feel sorry for me, at least not now. While talking of dogs.

"Let's not fool ourselves," I said in the decisive voice of someone who defied his own death, someone who believed in the future. "The hotel's finished. You'll need to find yourself a new job."

"The head of finance said we'll see." I grabbed the key. He shouted after me, "You're on reception between five and seven!"

I took the bottle from the cabinet and walked to my room. The fan was still on. I lay on the bed. The cicadas were rustling the silence like gravel. Fındık was right; it was such a den of whores, the pepper tree. Then the question I asked at least once a day came to mind: Who am I? I took a long swig from the bottle . . . A desolate emptiness, an empty heart and now a tipsy head. No one would be surprised if I said that.

* * *

I went back to the terrace at half past five. I had a two-hour stint at reception, but just to be on the safe side, I'd had four hours' worth to drink. The silence, which had dissolved the song of the cicadas, had fallen across the whole garden like a shadow. There was no one around. The Germans had gone down to the sea, and the staff was taking the opportunity to nap. When I leaned back, I noticed Emin sitting at the table in reception. He was motionless, watching the sea. The heat had sprinkled a skittish, dust-like haze over the middle of the channel. There was a yacht anchored in the bay at Büyük Ada. I looked for the sailboats; they had disappeared like the grasshoppers.

For a while, I occupied myself with the newspaper. In Baghdad, the Turkish soldiers who'd had bags put over their heads when they were arrested by the Americans in Sulaymaniyah in Northern Iraq had finally been released.

Just as I was about to swear, I saw the two women in front of the garden gate. They must have come from the blue BMW sports car parked at the edge of the road. They looked to be about twenty-five; they were both wearing sunglasses. The one in front was a lively blond, with hair like corn stalks; the one behind was a brunette. The brunette's body, which she generously displayed, was spectacular. The blond, classically beautiful, seemed younger. They were both wearing shorts.

I watched them for a while. Then I suddenly got an itch in my nose. There was at least thirty feet between us, but from where I was I could smell something that bothered me. There was a trace of it in my memory, but still, it was a smell that I couldn't quite place, and I could have sworn it was wafting from the two of them. I gave Mücella a sign. She met them and brought them to reception. The blond's face was familiar for some reason. We must have met somewhere before, but while I was this sozzled, try as I might, I just couldn't work out where. So I decided not to worry about it unduly. Cowering personalities: anxious looks at their environment, as if something was going to pounce on them, and expensive handbags on their arms. Then that little bell inside my head went off and everything became clear: what pricked like a thorn and smelled was wealth! They weren't our customers; they'd come here by mistake; they should have turned off onto the road below. Thank God.

"You've come to the wrong place," I said. "The Turkuvaz Hotel is down there."

"This is the Karayel Hotel, isn't it?" It was the blond speaking. She had a bright, oval face and a pointed chin. Her smooth skin was milk white. She seemed serious. I nodded. "In that case, we've come to the right place," she said.

That may have been so, but I hadn't taken to them. I really didn't like rich people, and certainly not the ones who gratuitously insisted on smelling, even though they tried not to make it obvious they were rich. And not without reason: whenever I met rich people, there would always be a problem. I shook my head and insisted, "This hotel isn't right for you. Why don't you go to the one down there?"

If Sami heard I'd turned them away, he'd blow a fuse. And Şuayip? He'd have fainted, the poor thing. The thought of Şuayip fainting, in his suit and tie, which he always made a point of wearing, even in July, made me laugh.

"Really, darling, whose side are you on?" asked the brunette.

I turned to her and smiled. "I'm on the workers' side," I said. "I'm a communist. The gendarmes are close to us, but you're far away." Our eyes met for a moment, then we both laughed. I was just about to sing the march when I noticed Emin was watching us. I pointed him out to the women. "Ask him if you like."

"Very amusing," said the blond. The soothing softness of her voice didn't match the seriousness of her face. "But we want to stay here."

"Our water and electricity keep getting cut off, and we don't have a generator," I said.

"And rooms? Do you have any rooms?" If it had been up to the brunette, they'd have left immediately. It was the blond who was the stubborn one.

"Oh, and right behind us, over by that tree, there's a brothel too." If I hadn't mentioned the brothel, they would have continued. But that shut them up. While they were trying to make their minds up, I pointed to the car. "Is that yours?" The blond nodded. "Well, I'm afraid BMW or Mercedes owners can't stay at this hotel. It's a management policy we've been diligently applying for years."

The brunette gave a blatant laugh: she didn't even feel the need to hide the insult it contained. "Çiğdem, I think this man's drunk."

"That's right," I said. "You're in a bad hotel adjoining a brothel, *and* you've got a drunken receptionist, one who sings marches at night too."

"We're determined to stay," said the one who answered to the name of Çiğdem. "Can someone bring in our luggage, please?"

She had a politeness that kept her clean, that set her apart from other people, that covered her body like a second skin, and that matched her voice too. Just as I was going to tell them there was no one to bring their luggage into the hotel, the brunette, whose name I didn't know, gave a start and let out a scream. We all looked down at her feet in the direction her horror-filled eyes were pointing. Fındık, with four lobsters in his two hands, was slithering across the floor toward the kitchen.

"Don't be afraid," I said.

The legendary creature had appeared at just the right time. "What's that man doing?" Çiğdem muttered after Fındık as he passed by and went inside.

"He's swimming," I said.

Her voice was trembling, and so was my jaw. The hairs on the back of my neck were standing on end.

April 1998:

She has a long nose with a big mouth beneath it. Her bottom lip is longer and fleshier than her top lip. Her center-parted light brown hair, which comes down to her pointed chin, clings to her face on both sides like palms. And she's very young: like she's waiting for her turn in life to come. She's looking at Fındık İbram, who is at her feet, and as she does, her already large eyes have become even larger out of fear and hardly fit beneath the arc of her eyebrows.

"Don't be afraid," I tell her.

She's afraid, but trying to control herself. "Who is that thing?" she asks.

Thing! She's right. Who, what is that strange thing? I could say a lot of things. I decide to tell the truth. "He's a dolphin man," I say. "Half fish, half human. He can live at the bottom of the sea and on land. His name's Fındık."

There's a light rain outside. Neither of us says anything; we look at the creature slithering off toward the door. I'm smiling. The interesting thing is, although I've seen him hundreds of times, I still find Fındık strange. When the old dragon has disappeared from view, she says in a voice that's trying to calm herself down, and without taking her eyes off the door, "It caught me off guard. I don't normally scare so easily."

She has an ardent voice verging on a contralto. She's not exactly what you'd call a careful dresser. The floral patterns on her thick dress, which descends to her lace-up boots, look funny. Her coat is on top of her bag. There are raindrops in her hair and they look like flower buds. She's sizing me up too. I shudder with an irrational feeling of embarrassment. "He always tries to intimidate people he's meeting for the first time by doing that," I quickly add, "because he's very short; he couldn't scare anyone standing up."

"Why does he . . ." she's going to say slither, but remembering that Fındık is a dolphin, she says instead, "swim?"

Our eyes meet. I suddenly understand. I'll love her eyes and love looking at her. It's a nascent thought, an unlabored prediction. And just as natural as the rain falling or the wind blowing. When I remember her question, I say, "Well, one of the reasons he goes along the ground like that is because he's carrying all the secrets of the peninsula on his back."

She doesn't say anything for a while. Throughout the silence, I watch the strong body in front of me, radiating vitality. Broad shoulders, a narrow waist, curvaceous hips and good posture. Her skin is the color of wheat.

I'm watching her; she's thinking what kind of secrets could be hidden on a little, tucked-away piece of land like ours. Finally she tells me not her thoughts, but the reason why she's come. "I'm here to investigate the seal that was found dead in Foça on the 7th of April."

A beginning that could not have been any stranger. But an interesting coincidence too, her meeting a dolphin while on the hunt for seals.

As these two magical sea creatures are going through my mind, Sami says, "This is Karaburun." He was behind me; I'd forgotten he was there. Before the girl arrived, we'd been arguing, about Sibelius. Because he wasn't able to get the better of me, his voice quivers like a knife that's been stuck into a piece of wood. "We're precisely eleven nautical miles from Foça."

First, a dolphin that swims on land, and now a man on crutches who can barely stay upright. I'm sitting down. The girl replies in a troubled voice, as if she's given up hope of seeing anyone who can walk on their feet, "The seals can swim up to Chios and back to feed. It's been proven." While talking, from time to time she looks over to where Fındık has disappeared. "I'm investigating the role of fish farms in the seal slaughter. We know there are quite a few such facilities on Karaburun Peninsula. There is evidence to suggest that seals are being poisoned by farm workers because they eat their fish."

Sami gets his own back by telling her we're closed. "We're not open for the season yet. You should look at the hotel in the next cove along. They've even got central heating. We've only got stoves."

"They're redoing it," says the girl, interrupting Sami. "And Handan Hanım said I'd be able to stay here. She's the one who sent me."

Just the excuse I was looking for! "We can't say no to Handan Hanım," I say, standing up. "But because we haven't opened for the season yet, we don't have a cook, so you shouldn't expect dinner or breakfast." Sami advances toward the cupboard, striking the ground like he wants to plunge his crutches into it. He's fuming. I turn to the girl before he can. "My friend will give you a key. His name's Sami, and mine's Kuzey."

The girl says, "What, Kuzey?" She smiles. "So it looks like we're neighbors then. I'm just to your left, in the east, mornings only, of course." Then she gives her name: Şafak.[4]

"Your room's upstairs. We're downstairs. So we're only distant neighbors."

She takes the key Sami's holding out, and beams at him without letting what he said earlier get to her. "Thank you. I can pay up-front, if you want."

"What make is your car and what's its registration number?" She stops, presumably out of surprise. "The police want to know," I explain. "An anti-terrorism measure, apparently."

---

[4] *Şafak* means "dawn" in Turkish.

"I bet the PKK hasn't heard of this place."

"This hotel is better known than you'd think," I say. "It appeals to the middle income bracket."

She's still laughing. I write down the registration number she gives. Then it's time for the make of her car. "A Citroën," she says. "A tiny 2CV . . ." She pauses a moment, then asks, "If it had been a BMW or a Mercedes, wouldn't you have let me stay?"

"Spot on," I say. "We wouldn't have. This isn't a place for rich people."

"Don't you like them?"

"I don't like the way they smell," I say. "It seems strange to me."

Just as she's reaching for her bag, she stops, and before she focuses—as if something has just occurred to her—her smile lingers for a moment. "This dolphin man, what do you think, would he help us?"

When she speaks, there's a slight hollow in her cheeks, and her cheekbones become more pronounced. And her mouth is big. So what is it that makes her beautiful? When she turns back, I realize what it is. The way she looks at me. Her carefree, generous eyes. And her presence is as prehensile as a hand.

"I'll ask," I say.

Is she going to go? No. "Do you think it'll keep raining tomorrow as well?"

"No, it won't," I say. "It's a dying rain."

When my next-door neighbor who comes to the window every morning at daybreak heads to the stairs, Sami mutters behind me, "First Handan and now this one, so now we've got two eco-warriors."

I know why he's grumbling. "Weren't you the one nagging me about our occupancy rate needing to go up?"

"We were going to have the top floor painted, or have you forgotten?"

I don't reply; I leave him and go out so he can listen to Sibelius in peace. I wasn't wrong; it's a decrepit rain that'll meet its end on the hill soon enough before it gets past the little fortress rock, Hisarcık Kayası. Drizzle doesn't last very long here if it hasn't got the wind behind it. I find Fındık under the pergola, looking out at Büyük Ada.

"It be no good," he says as soon as he sees me. How tall is he? I wonder. He can't be more than four foot seven. Is this the man they say can unleash storms and destroy the mainland with floods when he gets angry? I bend forward so I can hear what he's saying. "Cut 'im down bevore 'e gets too big." It makes me laugh because I know why he doesn't like the pepper tree. When he sees I'm laughing, he changes the subject. "If a zeaworthy bwoat zuddenly turns up, 'ow long would it take us to get there?"

So it wasn't Büyük Ada he wasn't looking at, it was Mytilene. Thirty-two nautical miles. "Two hours at most," I say.

"A modorbwoat like thine?"

He takes the cigarette I offer him. He's not going to like the answer. "Ours can't go out to sea," I say. "It's got a flat bottom. When you're on the open sea you've got to take the waves head on, you know. And when we take them head on, we'll slow down. And get a soaking for free."

"Makes no difference even if it be driftwood," says Fındık. "I be a man 'o's gwone to Foça and back, even in that bwox of thine."

Is he really a man? The question makes me laugh. Maybe he's just a guardian. The last descendant of the family who've kept the book where the secrets of the peninsula have been written for centuries. "The lobsters be thine," he says when he gets to the end of his cigarette. "That 'eathen woman do be ask'n, but don't worry, I don't be giv'n 'em to 'er."

"Erica?" I ask, pretending to be curious.

"Erica, Jessica—what do I know?" he says. "That mad woman vrom the Alman Koyu. Thee do know, the one 'o 'as the wold volk on 'er arse at daybreak and do gwo up the mountains." He gets on tiptoe and leans toward my ear. "I twold the gendarme commander, this woman do be a spy I zaid. She do be wander'n around after me. A Greek spy!"

"Okay," I say. "I'll have a word with her and she'll leave you alone. But you've got to give up this Mytilene business."

He nods his head. His lips gathered around the cigarette have made his mouth disappear. How many teeth has he got? I suddenly realize that he never opens his mouth while talking. Fish don't use their lips or tongues when they make noises. The thought turns into a guffaw and shoots out from my mouth. "Şükrü the cook's bastard son," says Fındık, not paying any attention to my laughter, "Ahmet. When do 'e be do'n 'is milidary zervice?"

"I don't know," I say. "Maybe next year."

"Good," he says. "If 'e don't get 'imzelf killed by the Kurds, and if 'e comes back, 'e can bring one of them rifles back vor us. When we gets there, let's be armed."

I lean forward and put my hand on his shoulder. It's wet and slippery. Is he really a fish, like Şükrü says, this strange creature? Then a question pops into my mind.

"Why do you give us the lobsters for free? You could make a fortune on them from the Germans or from the hotels down below."

He smiles. He has a strange smile too. What did I expect? How else can a fish smile? "I do give them to the army too," he says.

I know he takes care of the gendarmerie. When I repeat the question, he says, "Because thee be mad. It won't be long bevore I writes thee down in the book too."

To be recorded in the Register. Should I be angry? No. It's

synonymous with being immortal. At least it is on this peninsula. I lean over and kiss him on his bare head. My lips sting. His skin is covered in salt like he's just come out of the sea. It must be true that he can live underwater. How else can you explain someone of his age being able to catch and bring up lobsters whenever he wants, when everyone else has been searching high and low for them for the past ten years without coming across any? Yes, he's a dolphin.

"'O be that girl?"

That makes me laugh too. He's a nosy dolphin! "Have you seen any seals recently?"

He turns and fixes his eyes, which go dull when he's on dry land, onto my eyes—as if I'd told him to tell me his secrets. Or are dolphins and seals enemies? He asks for a cigarette, but gets no reply. My neighbor will be disappointed. Then, before disappearing, he asks as he always does, "'As they gwone?"

"Yes, they've gone," I say.

He shakes his head and makes a sign with his hand. "Gwone, my arse! They'll trick thee if thee lets them. Let's take a look at the moon this even'n." He points to Delikli Burun. "That's where they'll come out vrom, over yonder."

I know he'll get angry if I laugh. "Okay," I say, without laughing. "I'll take a look."

July 2003:

"He's swimming?" said Çiğdem.

"Yes," I replied.

"A brothel on one side, a drunk who sings marches on the other, and now a horrible creature. What are we doing here, darling?"

I turned to the brunette. She was one of those women who feed their egos solely on their beauty. What about her brain? It would have been foolish to hope that God had given a brain to someone who justified her existence with her body. When our eyes met, "'Gendarme, We're Communists.' That's my favorite march," I said.

"And a communist madman as well."

She was stupid, but her instincts were keen. "That's right," I said. "I'm a madman, and that's why I'm going to be in a three-hundred-and-fifty-year-old book."

The one who was called Çiğdem said, "We'd like two rooms," apparently placing no value on immortality.

"Two?" I asked. She nodded. I explained: "There are three beds in each room."

"And?"

"One room is more than enough for the both of you," I said.

"Two rooms and two lobsters," she insisted. "And have the lobsters ready for dinner, if possible. But we'd like the rooms now. And I hope you have no objection to us drinking white wine."

The blond was intelligent. I could see that from her quick-wittedness. And it was probably she who was rich. Still, I heeded Sami and warned them. "It'll cost you."

Emin had approached. The brunette looked at him smiled. "Don't worry, Pavarotti, we've got money." Then she turned to Çiğdem and said, "You think he's a tenor too, don't you?" Then she sniggered.

"But a drunken tenor."

"Rana!"

So I was Pavarotti and she was Rana. Maybe ten years ago I'd have thought about screwing her. But now! Oh, it gave me the creeps! That must be what happens when you get old.

Just then Rana turned to Emin, who had come right up to the reception desk, and reached out the key that she held in her hand. "Can you bring in the luggage from the car, please?"

"Now you've done it," I said to the girl I hadn't thought about screwing. "You've just insulted a captain of the Turkish Armed Forces, a gendarmerie captain."

Emin took the key. "It doesn't matter." His face was still shadowy.

Sami appeared a few minutes after the girls had gone upstairs. Mücella must have only just managed to tip him off about what had happened. He was angry. As soon as he came up to me, he asked, "What have you done now?"

"I've just sold two girls a grand total of six beds and two lobsters. And don't worry, they've got money. They came in a BMW."

He wasn't happy; I hadn't been able to find anything to make him happy for a long time. He came closer. His eyes seemed sunken, as they do when he's embarrassed. His voice was the same too: distant and devoid of hope. "So why are you crying then?"

Was I crying? Fucking hell! I had died, but I still had my tears and this bloody memory of mine. "I cry every time I see a twenty-five-year-old girl," I said. "Didn't you know?"

When the words ran out, we looked at each other. He was going to give me a hug. It wasn't pity I wanted, but an end. I walked briskly to the kitchen. Maybe I'd catch Fındık before he disappeared. Had he dived where he'd promised to? If he'd gotten some news, I was going to keep my word and cut down the pepper tree.

Fındık was nowhere to be seen. It was surprising he could move so quickly on dry land. I didn't bother asking Şükrü, who had an enraged look in his eyes, where he had gone. If I had, he'd have said, "To the depths of hell, I hope!"

I went back to my room. I drank two more beers, one after the other. Then I lay on the bed until it got dark without thinking anything, just watching the ceiling fan—not counting the two times I got up for a piss. I couldn't seem to pass out. When the sun disappeared, the cicadas shut up and their mating screams were replaced by a strange, deepening well of silence spinning whirlpool-like on its own axis. It was confusing. Maybe it was my head that was spinning. That's what I thought. Just as I was about to lose my way, the cheery din of hungry Germans coming out from their rooms for dinner filled the well and destroyed the silence.

At half past nine, I sneaked out of the hotel without being caught by Sami. If we'd run into each other, it would have been the same game we played every evening: he would have nagged me, telling me to have a bite to eat. From next to the pepper tree, I went onto the path behind the hotel, and from the steps that had been hollowed out down to the soil, I went down to the tarred road. The night was hot and noisy. In Burgazardı, bare hillside thirty years ago, there was now an area that clashed with the fabric and the past of the region, where the rich holidaymakers—mainly from Izmir—with showy houses on top of the rocks could congregate. As I approached the neighboring cove, toward the pier, it got louder. Everything had come to a standstill in front of the Turkuvaz Hotel because there were cars parked on both sides of the road. I looked over to the pier from the slope. The footpath was roughly half a mile long, and it was already crowded. There seemed to be no empty places in the fish restaurants at the edge of the sea and in the cafes that sold beer.

Without getting sucked into the crowd, I wandered off down the back way, parallel to the footpath that extended along the shore like an illuminated necklace slipped around the neck of the sea. Değirmen Dağı, in shadow, stood like a fist about to descend upon the cheerful crowds. After a hundred feet I turned left again, toward the isthmus—which used to be sea—between the hill and the mainland. After another couple of hundred yards I was there, at the mouth of a pit surrounded by four or five olive trees where rubbish was dumped. I stopped and took a look around. I must have been too late: the rubbish had been collected. There wasn't a single living creature around the pit, where first the dogs, then the cats, and finally the seagulls came to fill their stomachs.

Still, I waited as long as it takes to smoke a cigarette. The farther you were from the sea, the hotter it was. From time to time a car would pass along the road, with headlights shining like a razor, cutting the night and separating the gleaming coastal strip from the shadowy plain. I put out my cigarette, and looked over the dark hillsides that gently slope down to the orchards on the plain. It was strange—the air smelled of earth, not rubbish. This smell made my thoughts green: if only I had been born here. You can't choose where you'll be born, but what about where you'll die? I'd have wanted to be buried in this earth . . . Slowly I knelt down, but as soon as my knees touched the ground I shot upright as if I'd touched fire. It was a stupid wish; why was I forgetting that Fındık would select the site of my grave? That was when I noticed my tears. My sorrow was like snot; I didn't seem to be able to stop it from flowing. So I gave up trying to fight it and cried and cried at the mouth of the pit. *Love is our heart's most exquisite fluttering.* By the time I remembered she had said this, I was sobbing.

On the way back, I joined the footpath from the bottom end in the hope of finding a gentle sea breeze. As I went along, the earthy smell that makes thoughts about your fate grow like a seed yielded its place to the smell of fish and burnt oil wafting from the restaurants. The night was fertile; I deduced that from the crowd dividing and multiplying like a single-celled organism. Young people—perched like seagulls on the rocks that had been placed on the side of the footpath closest to the sea for protection in winter against waves that could get as high as ten feet—were cheerfully singing and drinking beer. When I got to the top of the slope, I heard my name and stopped: someone was calling me from one of the tables that leaned against the small harbor building.

Halit! The man who'd gotten up and was waving at me was one of the few well-known people in the region. I waved back. He was the general manager of a bank whose name escaped me. It had its head office in Istanbul; that was all I could remember. That and his surname: Paşalar.

I walked toward him. He was alone at a large table decked out with *meze*. He must have been waiting for someone. Whenever we met when he came back for the summer, for some reason he'd always act like I was an old friend. When I got closer to him, I was startled to see he was like a giant standing up with open arms. We hugged. "How are you?"

Instead of telling him that I couldn't stop crying, I told him I was fine.

"So, you're a hero now? What are you up to?"

He offered me a seat and I sat down opposite him. He was smiling, and more importantly, drinking *rakı*. "Just out for a walk."

"Will you have a drink?" He must have known I would; he must have known I wouldn't turn anyone down if they were offering me a drink. He filled the glass with rakı and passed it to me. "He gave all of them to you, didn't he?" I looked at him. "Fındık," he clarified. "I told everyone here, if he comes back with a lobster, grab it from him. They tried to block his path, but your Fındık's quick as a flash."

Had Fındık escaped from the sea? "Okay," I said, "I'll reserve one for you."

Halit's eyes lit up with the joy of a man whose appetite has been whetted. "Well, come on then, what was it like being in the papers? Rescuing fourteen people from the sea in the pitch darkness, in the middle of a storm."

Should I have pointed out that ten of the refugees had drowned, and that there could have been fifteen survivors? And of course, that scream: *Binti, binti . . .*

The rakı was excellent and I was a coward. I decided not to point any of those things out to him. That deathlike happiness spread inside me starting with my ears. I closed my eyes. When the alcohol had made it down to the tips of my toes, I told the other half of the truth as well. "Those poor people, they owe everything to Fındık."

"Don't make me laugh." I bowed my head. He had raised his hand and I thought he was going to tap me on the shoulder. "Fındık couldn't even drag a baby onto a boat."

Because he wouldn't have believed me, I didn't tell him that when we got to where the motorboat carrying the refugees had sunk, Fındık upped and flung himself into the sea, and one by one *he* found and brought everyone I hauled onto the boat from the depths of the dark water. I'd finished my rakı. I reached out my glass. "Well, you certainly know how to drink," he said as he gave me a refill.

"Yes, I do," I said. "Practice makes perfect."

First he smiled, then he laughed and asked, "They caught the man who was in cahoots with the captain, didn't they?" I nodded. "And I hear they threatened you not to testify." Without waiting for a reply, he steered the conversation back to Fındık. "Do you know, exactly thirty-five years ago that miserable, poison-suckled dwarf cursed us—me, my dad and my brother—the three of us." He was gesturing toward Akdağlar, which was in darkness. "It was August 1968, in the middle of the summer, after the floods that had lasted a whole fortnight. We'd walked twenty miles on our way back home. At the entrance to the village of Ambarseki, he blocked our path and yelled, 'Thee 'as it, thee 'as it!' He was stamping the ground like he'd gone mad, and throwing stones at my big brother. The strange thing was we knew he liked my brother, and he'd even written us down in the Register."

So our friendship, which I never could work out how and why it began, had started even before we met, in the Register kept by a delphinid family. I raised my glass. "To all fugitives . . ." I said, ". . . on land or sea."

Halit thought for a moment, then nodded. His eyes grew sorrowful. "My dad died the next week. My brother . . ."

I knew his older brother. He was a writer, thought important in certain circles. He lived in the next cove, in Bodrum, in an old stone house. They said he was ill. If Handan was to be believed, the only reason he'd come here was to die. I didn't remember hearing about his father. I took a big gulp from my glass. The growing sorrow in my burly friend's eyes was becoming more intense. Someone else who didn't like Fındık. We remained seated for about five minutes, practically without saying a word. I didn't feel like relinquishing the rakı still in my glass, so I took it with me as I stood up. He wasn't going to bring his sorrow down to his lips and confess. "Come by when you finish eating, and get your lobster," I said.

He didn't tell me to sit back down. We shook hands and parted. I finished my rakı when I took a break at the top of the slope. The wind had finally decided to blow the cool breath of the sea inland. I bumped into the reception supervisor in front of the Turkuvaz. He had taken his first step in the hotel business three years ago, working alongside Sami. I didn't like him. Still, when he offered me a beer, we stood talking for a few minutes. He said there was a woman phoning all the hotels and guesthouses in Karaburun asking after an officer called Emin Yıldız. Because our phone had been cut off, they hadn't been able to contact us. Ignoring the inquiring look in his eye, I said, "We haven't got anyone of that name staying with us."

When I got back to the hotel, I told Şükrü to put one of the lobsters aside for Halit Bey. Then, I took a beer and went out to the terrace. Sami was engrossed in a spirited conversation at the table of the girls who'd arrived late that afternoon. There was something strange about him. He'd changed; he seemed a different person. At first I thought it was the effect of the girls' beauty, but then I suddenly realized why he seemed so strange: he was smiling. That was what had changed him. On my way to Emin, I angrily veered over to where the three of them sat. The bastard, after having a long face for years—now he'd suddenly begun to smile.

My approach was noticed by Rana, who was feeding the cats at her feet. "Oh, look who's coming, it's Pavarotti."

I headed straight for Sami. "Do I know you from somewhere?" Let's see, how long would he be able to retain his metamorphosed face? "It *is* Sami, isn't it?" His face, which only a beautiful woman or abundant wealth could light up from the inside like that, suddenly froze. Bloody fake! He couldn't manage to stay the same. I brought my lips close enough to touch his ear. "One: don't you dare try moping around with a long face again. If you don't look at me with a smile, like you're looking at them now, I'll break your crutches: that's two."

Çiğdem, whose conversation I'd interrupted, came to the aid of the two-faced bastard. "Won't you take a seat?"

"I've got something to do," I said. I was looking at Sami. "Come on then, smile!"

Instead of smiling, he said, "Erica called. One of the old people in the group was taken ill. She's going to stay in the hospital this evening." His gaze was spinning the sorrow in his eyes like a thin thread. That's when I understood: the unhappiness in his face wasn't a reflection of his inner state, it was a reflection of me. "Have you eaten anything?"

When I saw the half-eaten lobsters left over on the girls' plates, I got even more annoyed. "Didn't your mother ever tell you it's sinful to leave food on the plate?"

Rana said, "Ooh, Pavarotti's tipsy." She turned to Çiğdem, looking for approval of what she'd just said.

"Wrong," I said, showing her the beer I had in my hand. "I've still got two more bottles to go before I get drunk, and four more before I pass out."

"I think you'll start singing marches soon."

As soon as I heard the word march, I left the three of them and went over to Emin. He had a questioning look in his eye. "No marches tonight," I said. "It's a beer break."

He invited me to sit with him. "Now that's what I call happiness."

Across from us, the lights of Foça marked out the east bank of the channel against the darkness of the night, as though a luminous marker pen had been taken to it. I sat there for a while. The silence was inquisitive. I thought about myself: that deep unhappiness inside me that I couldn't grasp, that I couldn't swallow, that spread to others too. Then I remembered that night. I was sitting here, looking straight at Delikli Burun. I had refused a beer . . .

I opened my beer five years later.

April 1998:

My neighbor appears at night. On the terrace, staring at Tuzla, behind Delikli Burun, smoking a cigarette. The air still has a late afternoon coolness from the rain; around me there's a limpid silence. The noises from the hillsides are spread out on the ground like butterflies with damp wings . . . First she waits, then she approaches with silent steps that belie her weight. "Good evening."

A shiver runs down my spine. It isn't her rising and emerging from within the dim silence, it's her smell: like a freshly picked flower. Like narcissus at the new year, or oleaster buds in May.

"You're early," I say, without taking my eyes off Tuzla on the other side of the channel. "You left your nest seven and a half hours ago."

She laughs. "Maybe eight," she says. I shake my head. "But how could you know that? You're not even wearing a watch."

And so I explain the peninsula's second secret, after the dolphin: "After a while, you lose your innate conception of time here. You measure it with light and shadows."

She laughs again. "What about in the evening, when there's no sun, what do you do then?" Before I can reply, she asks, "So tell me then, what time is it now?"

Her voice is hectoring like the voice of a child who's found a new game to try out. I can feel that I'll love her voice more with time. Looking at the reddening light over Tuzla, I say, "A few minutes to ten."

Silence! She must be looking at her watch. "Three minutes to," she says after that. "How did you know?"

"The moon will rise soon," I say.

The scratch of a match burns the night and the silence. "I can see it doesn't rise if you're not looking at it."

Why don't you look at me? That's what she means. I turn toward her. Her face stands out in the darkness, somehow illuminated. She's wearing trousers. She must have been feeling cold. "I promised Fındık," I say. "I'm looking for evidence."

She doesn't understand, so I explain: Fındık doesn't believe humans have set foot on the moon, and he won't believe it until he sees astronauts there with his own eyes. That's why every full moon, like wolves, we turn our eyes toward that burnished salver to try and find a shadow that looks like a human being . . .

She laughs again; actually, she's always laughing. All she does is have a break from laughing from time to time. "So he swims on dry land but doesn't believe in men who can fly!"

"He doesn't believe in billions either," I say. "If you tell him there are three billion people living on the earth, he'll say you're mad."

"So say million instead."

"He thinks a million is a thousand," I say.

"He's funny."

"When he gets angry, he can lay waste to everything. About thirty years ago, he once got so angry that he sent rains here like a mythical flood: the grapes and tobacco drying in the sun were abandoned, the winds uprooted the olive trees, the waves swallowed up the skiffs and motorboats . . ."

We laugh together this time. I turn away from her face and look over to Delikli Burun again. She waits there without speaking until the moon rises. Then, after a deep sigh, she stubs out her cigarette, and comes over to me. Everything smells of flowers: the night, the silence, the gentle sea, Delikli Burun, my fingers, even the moon. We don't speak. Both of us are searching for a shadow or trace that will convince Fındık. "It's so red," she says. "The astronauts cooking there must be done by now."

I'm on the verge of being drunk. "It'll get whiter as it rises." She turns as if to ask me something. "I know the moon well," I explain. "All its ins and outs. I never miss a full moon."

Ten minutes later, a sharp whistling noise slices knife-like into the hillside and the magical smell. I scrunch up my eyes. On top of Delikli Burun, lit up by the full moon, a shadow gets to its feet. The search is over. As Fındık, a quarter of a mile farther along, returns to his nest clinging tightly to his lack of belief, I place my fingers beneath my tongue and whistle back. Şafak covers her ears with her hands. "Hey, what was that for? Are you trying to make me go deaf?"

I point to Akdağlar and say, "I learned how to do it from a shepherd on the plateau."

She smiles again, then offers me some biscuits she's taken out from her bag. She hasn't eaten because she overslept. She says she's vegetarian. I go to the kitchen and fetch some cheese. As she's nibbling on the little sandwiches she's made by putting the cheese in between the biscuits, without me asking or showing any curiosity she tells me she was born in Bursa but she's lived in Istanbul since she was four. She's twenty-five. "We're Bosnian," she says, almost proud of it. She wanted to be a vet like her mother and father, but she couldn't get in to university to study it. That's why she's working in media. At the moment, she's working as a researcher for her sister's documentary film company, she says. And that's how she fell in love with seals: as soon as she set eyes on that unbelievably cute seal, which she later named after herself, one morning when she was in Foça for a documentary.

When she finishes the biscuits and lights her second cigarette, she says she actually wants to go to Africa. She's applied to the Red Cross. At one point she thought of going to Sarajevo too, while the war was still going on. But first because of school, then because her mother was against it, it never happened. "War's horrid," she says.

"It must be," I say, as though I've never seen a war before.

Suddenly she leans over to my ear, leaving a heavenly fragrance in her wake. She's going to tell me her secret now. "The ocean, that's where I really want to go." I close my eyes. My head sways from side to side as if I'm in a little boat. She takes the plunge: "You remember something?"

Lots of things: the ocean; the giant waves, born in front of the winds that unfurl from Antarctica; the Conrad novels I read with a dictionary on the deck of a rusty pile of junk that rocked like a cradle, Lord Jim, Kurtz, Marlow; the Portuguese man whose face I smashed in; Sami turning green as he kept looking up at the sky trying not to throw up; the little half-black, half-Chinese prostitute in Lagos I somehow couldn't get inside and fuck; what a shitty load iron ore is . . . I shake my head and say, "I don't remember anything."

Now we're face-to-face, or rather eye-to-eye. "Do you know what I said to myself when I first saw you?" She shakes her head, realizing that I don't know. "He's not the type you can have a conversation with; he always listens."

The best thing to do is to agree with her, so I agree with her and smile. "You're the one who's talking," I say.

"Yes," she nods, and doesn't say anything else until she's finished her cigarette. "This is a strange place: a dolphin man, a lunar magician, a time that has lost its innate meaning . . ."

"True," I say.

"You're from Karaburun, aren't you?"

"No," I say. "I actually came here to write." She looks at me questioningly. I reveal my biggest secret: "A novel."

"I love novels," she says immediately. "What's it going to be about? Please tell me!"

"A bit of love, a bit of adventure and, of course, death."

A long silence comes between us. She's watching the moon; I'm breathing in the smell of life wafting over from the young woman next to me. "How can we comprehend death, in your opinion?" she suddenly asks.

How? "I guess only by dying," I say, stealing İhsan Hoca's expression.

She talks about death. Without interrupting her smile: "Maybe we can comprehend it by dying, but in that case we can't talk about it. I mean, if a writer can't put into words something whose mysteries he's uncovered, wouldn't that be a waste of effort?"

"I guess that's why writers always leave death to their lovers," I say.

"I see, compared to death everything's meaningless, even death itself . . ." She puts a friendly hand on my shoulder. "So tell me, do you have a lover?" I shake my head. "In that case, concentrate on falling in love with someone."

"It would only be a literary delusion to think I'd love someone," I say.

This time she bursts out laughing. "Make sure you don't try to find a lover while I'm with you," she says. "Or I'll tell her it's only a delusion."

"Okay," I say. "If I do become deluded and fall in love, you can say that."

She looks at her watch. "I have to phone someone," she explains. "Can I call from here?"

She's got a boyfriend! The thought blasts my face like a jet of cold water. "The direct line in reception," I say.

She gets up. "Are you doing anything tomorrow? Come with me. I need a guide who can tell what direction he's going. North[5] if nothing else." Before I can tell her I'm busy, she continues: "It's not going

---

[5]   A pun on Kuzey's name

to rain."

"No, it's not," I say. "I promise."

First the moon, and now the rain . . . She looks at me, unconvinced, and then asks: "How about a beer?"

"I'm not allowed beer," I say.

July 2003:

Five years later, sipping on the beer I turned down that day, I muttered, "It's not my fault," as if the bastard who begrudged me his smile was sitting across from me. But it wasn't Sami sitting across from me, it was Emin. I should warn him that the shadow on his handsome face had turned into a permanent stain . . . What was he talking about? I think it was happiness.

"Happiness is as far from me as the youth I'll never have back again," I said.

"When you were young, were you happy?"

I didn't like that question, and I said as much. "Ask me something else."

"I imagine happiness doesn't depend on your age, but on what happens to you," he said, without really thinking.

"And what has happened to you?" *He* didn't like *that* question; he didn't reply.

"Apparently there's a woman phoning all the hotels, asking after you," I said. "The guys at the Turkuvaz told me. I said you weren't staying with us." We didn't say anything for a while. As my beer was coming to an end, I felt the breeze that comes before the waves. After a hot week, the wind was finally picking up. I stretched my arm out toward the breeze and mumbled, "Cooler weather! Good news, for the grapes and olives."

Then I opened my other arm. I wanted to embrace the wind as I would take a lover in my arms: naked. Should I take my T-shirt off? I suddenly remembered I wasn't alone and changed my mind. Emin, as if he knew what I was thinking, asked, "Where were you shot?" His face had darkened even more.

"In Laleli," I said. "Do you know Laleli?"

He nodded his head. "The marks on your back are cigarette burns, aren't they?" I didn't tell him they were. I think because he was looking at me like someone who had tortured people. "You must have made someone very angry. They burned you really badly."

"True," I said. "You know the worst thing about it? While the fuckers were branding me, instead of screaming, I felt hungry the whole time; I wanted meat. That's why I don't eat grilled or fried meat anymore. Only boiled." He might have been about to say something, but as Rana's laughter got louder behind us, he decided against it. "Those two girls! They're paying a fortune, but they didn't even touch half of their lobsters. God's taking the piss out of us. He's saying, 'Hey, I'm sending the most expensive seafood, that peerless white meat you go hunting after but can't find anywhere, to the stomachs of mangy stray cats, so there.'"

"He might be saying something else," Emin said.

"Well at most He's saying that the rich are idiots who have no taste."

"You don't like rich people, do you?"

"Like in the march," I said. "I'm still a communist." We were silent again. The wind was eagerly approaching the land; after midnight it would skydive onto the hills. I looked at the time. It was almost eleven. I finished what was left of my beer. "Let's say you were going to hide on the slopes of Değirmen Dağı . . ." Emin looked at me as if he knew what was about to come. "Where would you choose?"

He stared straight into my eyes a while longer. Then decisively, "The southeast slope," he said. "There's a juniper tree in the middle of the bushes to the right of the slope that goes down to Bodrum." The tree that had been bent double by the strong winds! I bowed my head. "Take a straight line due south, toward the plain: there's an old stone sheep fold from the days of the Greeks next to the dry well a hundred and fifty feet below; it's been covered over with bushes. I don't think anyone could find someone hiding there . . ." He took a cigarette and lit it; when he offered me the packet, I refused. "You've been threatened, have you?" I said nothing, giving the impression that I had been. "I'll help you if you want."

"There's no need," I said. "Thank you."

"No, thank *you*," he countered.

Then he cleared his throat. I took a good look at him. We were similar: the fact we were alive was just by chance.

I went through to the kitchen without Sami seeing me. Şükrü had tidied up, leaving the beer on the counter as usual. The bag he prepared every evening was next to the trash bin. I took the bag, shoved the cans into my trouser pockets and went past the pepper tree out to the tarred road again. This time I walked in the other direction. The wind still hadn't dropped; it was whistling through the bushes on the hills. I met the blond girl, Çiğdem, fifty yards farther along at the bend in the road that turned back to Bodrum. Or, to be more precise, I met her eyes because nothing else of her face was visible. She was in white; her blond hair had taken on the color of her dress and disappeared along with her face. She was standing there as if waiting for someone. She thought I wouldn't see her, so when there were still a few steps left to go, she raised her voice and said, "Good evening again."

I said a half-hearted good evening, and carried on walking past her.

"Can I walk with you?"

She started following me without waiting for my reply. After ten paces, I stopped. Her face was beginning to take on some color; slowly she started to appear. "If I were you, I wouldn't want to be alone with a man like me at this hour of the night." I took out the can in my left pocket. "Look, alcohol! You see? I'll be drunk soon . . ."

"Are you trying to tell me you're dangerous and you molest women?"

I was trying to tell her I wanted to be alone . . . Instead of that, "How old are you?" I asked.

"Twenty-five."

"And I imagine there've been people who've told you you're beautiful."

In an undecided voice that didn't betray how well she did remember, she bowed her head. "I think so."

"And looking at your car, at you ordering lobster, you must be rich too."

"So?" she asked.

"So what's a young, beautiful and rich girl like you doing here with a man who's going to be off his face soon?"

She didn't reply. In her eyes, which she restrained—deep, lifeless and gleaming like distant stars—there was that emptiness I'd encountered in Sami's: sorrow, maybe. When I started to feel her pitying me, I looked away. When she realized I was going to walk off, she went for it. "A bit of curiosity, a bit of business . . . Yes, that's why I'm here. I want to take a look around."

"This late?"

"Why don't you try being friendly?"

"I am," I said. "Can't you see I'm warning you not to get too close?"

Then I continued walking, avoiding her eyes, which I decided turn whomever she's with into a beggar. I never asked that stubborn God, who for some reason never throws snake eyes, for a long and happy life; what I wanted was a little wind and solitude. The wind was on its way, but solitude!

After 1970, as the number of summer houses on the hillsides increased, even the old dusty path that joined the two coves had been surfaced, bit by bit; random streetlights—some of them made of concrete, some of them made of iron that had long since gone rusty—were erected on both sides of the winding asphalt road that had appeared. I walked, following the gentle slope of the strange road, like a snake warning off its enemy with its various colors, which the lifeless light emanating from the lamps—very few of which were lit—at the top of the poles could not illuminate. That familiar fog which told me I'd soon be passing out was spreading downward from my head. Five minutes later, I leaned against the wire fence surrounding the military zone. Çiğdem, thirty or forty feet behind, continued following me closely enough for me to be able to hear her footsteps.

I planned to relax a little on the old bench that had withstood years of winds and harsh winters and was bolted down where the road met the plateau on the south face of Değirmen Dağı, and drink one of the beers before going into the scrub.

I lit my cigarette; Çiğdem reached me before I'd opened the beer: first her footsteps, then her shadow, and finally herself. When I looked up, I gave a start. Her eyes were like her mouth; they swallowed everything. That's probably why I moved over. She sat down next to me. "I won't disturb you."

There was a gentle, compassionate concern in her voice. I turned to the side. I didn't want her eyes or her compassion. Across the water, a large passenger ship decked out with multi-colored lights had changed course from Foça toward Büyük Ada to escape the gulf and put out to sea as quickly as possible. To the right, the music rising up from the disco in Bodrum was mingling with the howling of the accelerating wind. I opened the can of beer.

"If I'm not there, the moon doesn't rise," I said, as soon as I had taken the first mouthful. "If I don't stare out to Tuzla, it doesn't appear."

She wasn't interested in the moon. "Why are you always crying?"

So much for her promise! I'd been a complete idiot. I kept forgetting that the rich couldn't be trusted. "You're disturbing me," I said.

"Tell me, what's the reason for your tears?"

"Catarrh," I said. "The doctors say I've got chronic catarrh."

"Catarrh?"

I nodded, and I said it again: "Catarrh." But I didn't say the catarrh of sorrow. "There's no cure." I took a long swig of the beer. "Slobber, snot and lots of tears . . . That's it."

She said, "I understand." I swigged on my beer and watched the ship. The fog was clinging to my eyelids. "Why do you do this to yourself?" Since my life only consisted of drinking, what else could she possibly think I did? "Why do you drink so much?" she continued, as though she had read my thoughts. "As if you hate being alive."

I finished my beer at a leisurely pace, and then I summarized the life she thought I hated. "Mine's a simple life. I drink, pass out, come around, eat something, then drink and pass out again. Then it's time to come around once more . . . And there's a lot of things that are lame in my life."

"Apart from Sami Bey?" I didn't say there was a dog too. "Does drinking let you forget?"

Drinking doesn't make you forget the pain; it only makes it bearable. And that's all drinkers expect, and all they hope for from drink. Besides, who'd abandon their blessed pain in its entirety? But I had no intention of revealing the secrets of a drunkard to a girl who'd forgotten her promise of three minutes ago and was still disturbing me. So I said, "That's right. It makes you forget everything."

She'd gotten very close; what would I do if she tried to wipe away my tears with her hand? "You must have lost your hope." Her voice tinkled with that pity you feel at the end of prayers when you surrender yourself to God.

Had I lost my hope? We were probably both overrating life. "Living doesn't teach me anything anymore. That's all it is," I said.

"Then that's the reason you drink."

I closed my eyes. I was thinking. Alcohol: the mysterious river that bore those who weren't able to be masters of their destiny to the heaven of nothingness. And drunkenness: to dream without images! Then I laughed. Does anyone know a more pleasurable way of patiently finishing a life that has fallen on stony ground? But I didn't say that. "What do you want from me?" I muttered. "Or are you from the temperance league?"

"No, I'm not, but I'm interested in you."

Not only did she not know how to eat lobster, but she had her head in the clouds too. She had to come back down to earth! "I'm completely empty inside, young lady," I told her. "Nothing spurts from my loins anymore. The thought that I'll have a lover isn't literary anymore, it's a tragic delusion . . ."

I'm warning you, I was going to continue, but Çiğdem put her finger to my lips and silenced me. "You should be ashamed of yourself!" She was blushing.

"Ashamed? The good thing about drinking is that it saves you from unnecessary things like that . . ."

"Why did you get angry with Sami Bey?"

"I was annoyed," I said. "At him just smiling like that."

"Does happiness enrage you?"

"Why should something I don't believe in enrage me?"

I was wasting time; my drunkenness would wear off without me quite having passed out. And the things in the bag had started to smell. I wiped away the drops at the edge of my mouth without caring if they were tears or snot. Çiğdem was stubborn. And she asked her umpteenth question: "So you think there's no such thing as happiness?"

"No, there isn't," I said, spitefully. "And anyone who says there is fails to notice that what they think is happiness is really just an unhappiness they consent to."

She didn't speak for a while, presumably because she understood she was unhappy. Throughout the silence, I looked at the sky. There were only a few glimmers in the darkness that hung over the island. I guess God was drunk too tonight: he'd forgotten to light most of his stars.

"I don't know if you realize it, but you make people feel more stupid than they really are . . . you make them feel like they're always suffering."

"The problem's not in me, it's in us being human," I said. "In actual fact, there isn't really anything different in any of us."

"I don't understand."

"Humans are just a species condemned to relive their old pains over and over again."

She had things she wanted to say, but I got up from the bench and headed toward a tree before she could say them. Time was running out. If I was going to finish the job, I had to do so before the fog dispersed. Without falling over I managed to walk up to the leafless, dried-out juniper that had chosen to remain alone, far from the other trees. I couldn't keep my eyes open in the strengthening wind. I hugged the tree. That was when I realized it wasn't the winds that had bent its trunk; it was a question mark God had appended to the world.

Cursing, I opened my eyes. I didn't want any more questions, just a good roll of the dice . . . That's what I wanted. Just then Çiğdem called out from behind me: "Where are you going?"

I was going to say, *To find a lame dog,* but my voice didn't come out. And four or five steps later I slipped. Before my eyes closed, I managed to fling the bag I was carrying away from me. As it fell to the ground, it disintegrated in mid-air; the bones scattered about.

Why is a twenty-five-year-old rich girl, who at this hour ought to be dancing in a disco in Çeşme, interested in me? This was the last thing that went through my mind. Then the fog covered everything. *Spot,* I tried to say, but couldn't.

Sami Çetin, August 10, 2004:

"Embarking on a journey to the source of words and finding their primitive states . . . if it can be called a hobby, that's mine. For example, astronaut: *astro* means 'star' in Greek, and *nautes* means 'sailor.' In other words, a star sailor. Another example? The Turkish word *zifir* meaning 'pitch black' comes from the word Zephyros, like in the Odyssey—in other words *karayel*, zephyr, the west wind. Zephyros is the dark country in the west; the karayel blows straight from the Cimmerians . . . Our hotel being called Karayel has got nothing to do with its position. If they'd asked me when they were choosing a name, I'd have said Poyraz—Boreas—because if you've been paying attention, the facade of the hotel looks out to the northeast . . .

"I should say though, this tape recorder on the table, this type of conversation, do you know what it reminds me of? It's as if I've been arrested again and I'm making a statement. And you're not a writer, you're a prosecutor. Anyway . . .

"Crosswords got me into the habit of hunting down words and discovering their secrets. In 1979, when I was in the hospital for three months, practically without being able to move—that's when I started doing crosswords regularly.

"Kuzey says they're a meaningless hobby if you haven't been able to solve your own life. I met him in Germany, through the Party; they sent him from Berlin to Heidelberg so I could keep an eye on him. He'd stood out among the militants based in Turkey, and managed to escape from a trap the police had set for him. Then he came to Germany, giving the slip to two teams in hot pursuit that had sworn to kill him . . .

"I fled abroad before March 12th,[6] in 1970, once two of my prison

---

6   I.e., the military coup in Turkey on March 12, 1971

sentences had been upheld on appeal. I was in charge of publishing the Party magazine. Kuzey came to Germany after the coup. The beginning of 1973, I think . . . The comrades in Istanbul were worried about him getting caught, and the central executive told him to leave the country. First he went to Palestine, and he came to Germany from there.

"We were to disappear for a while; we weren't to be seen in public. That's what they told me. I said to me laddo, 'Let's find you a job,' but instead of answering, he just laughed. There was a reason for his laughter; it turns out he knew what he was doing. Back then I didn't know he had the luck of the devil. Five days . . . that was all he needed to trick me. And I had a girlfriend at the time, too . . .

"First we went to Amsterdam together, and from there we made our getaway in a cargo ship and sailed the seas for eleven months. We were part of the crew . . . No, I didn't like being a sailor at all. If you ask me, it's the worst, the most terrible job in the world. Kuzey loved it. 'In the final analysis, every activist is an adventurer . . .' Maybe because he made himself believe that tripe. He believed that if you went out to sea, sooner or later you'd become a writer: I think that's the real reason he had for making that challenging journey . . .

"Before he went underground, before the coup in other words, Kuzey studied literature at university . . . He tried writing once or twice, but I can't even remember one story he ever finished, or if he did, I didn't see it. If you ask me, his interest in publishing a magazine comes from this barrenness too: he wants to be close to literature in some shape or form . . . And there he was, supposedly going to write a novel he called *The Disenchanted*. And it was this novel he never managed to start that was behind his decision to settle somewhere off the beaten track like Karaburun after he'd lived in Istanbul all those years. But if you asked him, well, he'd say he came here after a woman. And in fact, when the third magazine went bust too, he did come to Karaburun with the woman he was with then. That was in 1995. They took over the Karayel Hotel as soon as they got here. But less than a year later, the woman walked out, saddling me laddo with debts . . . He used to drink then too . . . He got treatment in 1996 when Salim put his foot down. Salim is his elder brother, his only brother. They're always arguing. Between you and me, I don't like him either. He's turned out to be a right-wing nutcase . . . Kuzey gave up alcohol at the end of his treatment. Right until . . .

"After the general amnesty in 1974, we came back to Turkey together in November or December 1975. They'd thrown us out of the party while we were still in Germany . . . Me getting shot? That was later. In 1979, on April 19th, at ten to five in the afternoon, they emptied almost a whole clip at me. We'd just left the labor union building in Laleli, and we were walking down the street. Unbeknownst to us, the fascists had set a trap and were waiting for us. If you get caught in crossfire, you don't stand a chance. Kuzey was luckier than me: he was shot through the arm. I fell at the first bullet—it ricocheted off my spine, and I was gone. The street was banking like a boat that's taken on water. And just as one of the fascist thugs was about to shoot me in the head, Kuzey flung himself on top of him and knocked him to the ground. Then he took his gun and shot two of the bastards in the leg as well. Everything seemed fuzzy, behind a curtain of red fog. So in a way, I owe him my life . . .

"Why in a way? I don't know. Maybe . . . Anyway, let's change the subject. We've been friends for thirty-two years. And we haven't been apart except for a short period. Until 1979, I looked out for him; when my legs ended up like this, he took over being nanny, and when he started drinking again, it was my turn again . . .

"We both got married. Kuzey did as soon as he came back. He

was married to a rather well-off poetry lover for about a year. Vildan was three or four years older than Kuzey, but after a while, when his money ran out, she walked out on him. But she did seem to love him. She was mollycoddled though: she liked her creature comforts and living in the manner to which she'd become accustomed. She just couldn't seem to adapt herself to us no matter how much she wanted to. She thought poverty was a lifestyle choice. Like living under water . . . Kuzey went after her, but she'd disappeared. Her father kept saying he'd disown her. I guess in the end he won the war. We heard he'd sent her abroad. After that, Kuzey accepted the divorce. Then the inevitable happened to the magazine they'd published together. That was me laddo's first magazine to go under. It was called *Kuzey* too . . . No, not out of vanity; Vildan, she put a lot of pressure on him to name the magazine after himself. And the word 'kuzey'—'north'—evoked socialism too, in a way . . . Neither of us liked Stalin, but we always thought of ourselves as communists . . .

"In 1981, Kuzey was arrested again, after September 12th.[7] He spent thirteen months inside. He suffered a lot. Me? They didn't take me in because of the 'logistical difficulties involved in the torture of someone whose legs do not function.' That's what Kuzey used to say. In 1985, I married a brave, good woman called Nermin. It was obvious from the very beginning that it wasn't going to work. But still, it lasted longer than I thought it would. I eventually told Nermin I didn't want her anymore and we separated. It was me who wanted to split up. Why? Are you trying to embarrass me? Very well then, here's why: I couldn't stand her lying next to me at night with her eyes open showing me affection, all the while trying not to think about other men. If I hadn't left her, she would never have slept with anyone else. Someone as honest—maybe I should say as *stupid*—as she was, was

---

[7] I.e., the military coup in Turkey on September 12, 1980

too much for me . . . We divorced after ten years, and in 1996 I came
to be with Kuzey. Or rather, we met in Istanbul. He'd finished his
treatment, and we went back to Karaburun together . . . And there
you have it: that, in a nutshell, is the story of me and Kuzey that you
were asking about.

"Here's what he scribbled on the back of a photo we had taken
together: 'This itinerant is yours truly, Kuzey.' The photo's twenty
years old, but he always kept his youth; his face never submitted to
the ravages of time. 'Friends make us feel like we're good people . . .'
That's what he wrote for me . . . It's interesting, he'd introduce me
as 'my friend,' while I'd say 'my mate' . . . What's the difference, you
ask? I don't know. Maybe there isn't one. He used to come up with
interesting sayings about life. 'When we're young, we think life makes
us happy. But really it's just wearing us down.' That's a note he added
to the same photo years later . . .

"He was brave. I've no doubt about that. I saw it with my own
eyes a few times. I know I'm not wrong. Because you can't pretend
to be brave . . . They say your arms get stronger if you're paralyzed.
Just like how losing a limb develops the one that compensates for it, a
life away from women might have developed my imagination. That's
what Kuzey used to say. Do you know, Tolstoy suffered a lot in his
final years because he realized it was impossible to love humanity? I
guess that's what Tarkovsky was saying in Solaris. Even if he didn't
like people, Kuzey always believed in humanity . . . Who can bear
journeys, long journeys? And there he was, back on the road after all
those years. I remember how excited he got one time when he was
reading in the paper about a man who was getting ready to go to the
pole alone. He turned to me, trembling, and said, 'This might seem
nonsensical or meaningless to you. But if some arthropod living in
the sea, like that man going to the pole, hadn't become obsessed with

a dangerous adventure and come out onto land I don't know how many hundreds of millions of years ago, there wouldn't have been any life on land. Isn't it strange that we owe our existence to the bravery and curiosity of a small insect-like thing?'

"Yes, everyone would say that. Impassioned . . . His cheerfulness masks his madness. And in him there's only a hairsbreadth between cheerfulness and madness, that's why . . . Maybe if I'd been in his shoes, I'd have turned to the bottle as well. I was full of pain; he was full of sorrow. You only need anger to grind down pain. But he was powerless. There's no cure for sorrow. Once it gets hold of you, sooner or later it'll rot you . . .

"We didn't feel any kind of obligation to each other because obligations stand in the way of true friendship. He's my comrade and my true friend . . .

"Fındık? You must have heard the story too: His great- great- great- great-grandfather, or maybe it was five greats, was by all accounts a big, burly fisherman. He was fed up of a dolphin that kept stealing from his net, so one day he said, 'If I catch that bloody dolphin, I'll fuck it, so help me God,' and the story goes that the very next day, he found the dolphin lying on the sand at his feet, tangled in the net. He was apparently a religious man, and if we are to believe to the rumors, because he'd said 'so help me God,' he consummated his union with the dolphin that very morning. And according to some, it was after this coupling that the race of Fındık's appeared: a strange, short, hairless species that can also live under the sea . . . But they say the dolphin that Fındık's ancestor got intimate with was the daughter of the sultan of the dolphins. And when old Fındık refused to marry her, she cursed all of his male descendants so they'd find no refuge on land, and all his female descendants so they'd not marry and would remain spinsters . . . Yes, it's a nice tale with folkloric features, but for some reason Kuzey took everything about that freak of nature seriously. He really believed Fındık could dive to the depths, that he could stay under water for a long time, that he could see everything under the sea and find whatever he wanted. That's supposedly how he caught the fish, the lobsters . . . Oh yes, and he was the guardian of a secret treasure. The story goes that years ago, someone was going to steal that treasure, so Fındık pummeled the peninsula with a storm day after day for a whole fortnight; the wind and the rain were so violent that in the end the thief brought back what he'd stolen . . .

"Spot? That's the dog's name . . ."

"A woman in love is without blame . . ."

Ah, if only I could be as noble as I am when I write! But while living, I am a wretch. Even though no one says it out loud, I know: my regret is hollow and has no creative essence. It is temporary too, like the virtue of virginity . . .

To be ready to accept everything that will happen to you, as if lying on the altar stone . . . is this not a woman in love? I tell you: a woman in love is without blame. I am to blame. I have gone beyond the goal of my life. I have attempted to love. Why, though, would a man like me, a man who takes pleasure in his self-destruction, love a woman?

Perhaps it is no crime: perhaps loving is a salve that our brains produce by chance, a fire born of a sudden, heart-searing spark; perhaps it consists of the desire to capture the other by disseminating our self to them—instead of reuniting our self with them. Definitions, definitions, definitions . . . All definitions make me sick. I confess: the reason is simple; behind my goal lay hidden, not a noble shudder, but a selfish hope: the hope of escaping from myself! That is why I ventured to love her; that is why I let her love me. What a fool I was! Instead of striding directly to my pain, I tried to turn around when I was halfway there. But the path of fate is always one way.

Questions, I hear the questions that tear through the lace curtain of my drunkenness to reach my ear. And their answers. The one that makes me feel sickest of all is the one that starts off with, "To love is to re-create yourself." And listen to this: "Love is the endeavor to exalt our lives, and to challenge our destinies . . ." That one is even more disgusting. And, moreover, a lie. Oh fortunate ones who have not yet fallen in love, it is only in its beginning that love challenges death. Its continuation! Its continuation is no passionate resistance, it is a surrender to habit. I knew that . . .

Oh sober ones who have not tasted drunkenness, be sure not to fall in love! When you do, the harshest punishment that God can give will be waiting for you: *agonia perpetua*. I, for my part, have had my fill of agony: I dream of dying as soon as I can so that I may worm my way out of my shame. But God perceives my desire to escape from my body as a rebellion against His royal power. Is not our body a coffin of flesh in which our soul is buried alive? I seek not to deny Your existence; I seek to fling off my coffin . . .

Let no one speak to me about the truth! It would be wasted breath. Be it the truth of life or the truth of dreams, I keep my distance from every kind of truth: truth is for God and science. What I need are lies. Lies in which we hide the hope to come, the dream of happiness . . . And here you are: the real reason for love: the need for lies, the compulsion to believe that we are alive. That is why I fell in love. And she? Because, as she said laughing, of "the physical attractiveness of a man whose back is covered in scars from war wounds and hot sex?"

Whatever I do, nothing shall change anymore. I know: pain drives you mad eventually. It is just a matter of time. I shall patiently await that moment, drinking. Dear God, let me create my death, let me give birth to my destruction . . .

CHAPTER II

A tragic crime is a crime that no one can be blamed for.
And for this reason it has no suitable judge . . .
—Max Scheler[8]

---

[8]   Scheler, quoted in Kuçuradi, *The Tragic in Max Scheler and Nietzsche*

July 2003:

Will today be the day I pass through death's bright portal? If, out of spite, God changes His mind and agrees to keep throwing snake eyes, then maybe. Why doesn't He load the dice anyway? A little act of generosity like that is what I expect from Him. No one should think I'm ungrateful. The reason I'm impatient with Him is that he's hand in glove with Fındık and always delaying the meeting . . . I've grasped how meaningless it is to lead a life squeezed between passing out and coming to when you've got nothing that calls you to go beyond the sorrow; that's all. But His patience is endless. It's foolish for me to expect a God—content with the solitude He's condemned Himself to—to understand. I'm aware of that. It's God who expects to be understood, not His creation, and I should just accept this sacred truth, which belittles us humans even more . . .

These are the foggy thoughts that spread through my brain like poisonous gases billowing up from a swamp . . . A foggy consciousness or a shiny one? I've tried them both and it doesn't change a thing. After sleeping in Azrael's bed every night in the hope of meeting him, don't I always return with the same questions?

What's that on my face? A good question . . . I'm trying to turn the cool, indecisive touches into a picture. A finger, fingers! A cool hand must be roaming at my temples. I'm quivering with hope. Azrael? In vain! The thought that God will lend an ear to my call is a foolish hope, an innocent delusion, typical of the destitute; gods need victims. I'm powerless; I have nothing to offer apart from myself. A worthless offering . . .

New questions to dilute my solitude waft up from the swamp: does God never cheat, not at all? "He's talking in his sleep," said a voice, as I was wondering whether or not God would load the dice.

I opened my eyes a crack and returned from a serene world where being alive had lost its clarity to a troublesome one where my existence would start taking on definite contours. In front of me, with a pained look on his face, was the man stealing Azrael's role, the man coming between me and my death: Sami.

"He's waking up." I would have said I was sobering up, but the long-faced, stubborn mule turned and continued: "I told you he was as tough as old boots."

The person he was praising my toughness to was Çiğdem, who stood next to him. A demon and an angel in league with each other! If I'd been able to laugh, I would have. But laughing with the girls was his job. "Laugh, you thieving bastard," I said.

Sami moved gingerly, as if he was afraid his long face would fall and break. He was still talking to Çiğdem: "He's got a sharp tongue. So there can't be anything wrong with him."

Just like every morning for the past three years, I sat up slowly and got ready to watch the most frequent scene from our intertwined lives: he'll try to balance himself on his crutches, and as soon as he does, he'll plunge his raging, vengeful looks into my breast, because he walked in front that sunny afternoon in Laleli. And I'll close my eyes so as not to see his looks saying that I'd have been the one on crutches if we'd changed places . . . Then he'll list away toward the door like an unbalanced boat on a rough sea . . .

When the door closed, I turned to the uninvited angel. Çiğdem was perched at the edge of my bed. The ceiling fan was motionless. It was cooler today! So was her voice. "Come on, get up and have a shower. I need to talk to you."

She had something white like a hanky in her hand. Was she the one who'd touched my cheeks? "What do you want from me?" I asked.

"Nothing," she said. "I just want to talk for a moment."

I tried to sit up. My neck and back were aching. "What happened last night?"

She stood up. She was wearing shorts. In a quick rundown, she told me: "You fell over. I tried to get to you, but the bushes . . . Anyway, Emin Bey was somewhere nearby; he came to help. I came back and got the car and we brought you back here together . . ." I checked what I was wearing. They'd changed my clothes. I lay my head back again, scanning the room out of the corner of my eye. My trousers were on the chair to the side. I gestured to Çiğdem for her to hand them to me. "If you're looking for the beer, Sami Bey took it," she said. "And the ones under the bed." Bastard. Not only was he stealing my death, but he was stealing my drinks too. "What were you doing out there? Were you supposed to be meeting someone?" I was going to meet an unfaithful, cat-like dog. "If it was Erica, she'd gone to Izmir. The patient took a turn for the worse . . ." So Sami had mentioned Erica as well. Laughter had made him indiscreet. "She must mean a lot to you?"

What importance did Erica have? "Everyone should have someone in life they can bid farewell to," I said.

She thought for a moment. Then she said, "What about Sami?"

I shook my head. "I can't bid him farewell; wherever I go, he always tries to come with me . . ."

Çiğdem, laughing instead of Sami, left the room. I lay without moving for about ten minutes. The cicadas were silent. Why?

I stood up and went into the bathroom. My face was clean. Evidently, I'd managed to turn to the side when I fell. I went into the shower; there were a few scratches on my legs and shoulder. After the marks the torturers, fascists and women had left, now it was the bushes' turn. I laughed out loud. This must be what getting old is!

Neither Sami nor Çiğdem were on the terrace. The wind had come to stay. The garden was empty too; the Germans—like locusts—had swarmed off somewhere else. I didn't touch the breakfast tray beneath the bougainvillea. First, I needed the beer I hadn't been able to drink last night! I knew that Sami would have taken the keys, but I tried my luck anyway. The cupboard in the kitchen was locked. I waited a little, but no one came to open it. I could feel a trembling welling up from deep inside me. I went out into the back garden. Mücella's two sons, who did cleaning in the daytime and helped to serve food in the evening, were joking around while cleaning the car park. The blue BMW wasn't in its place. Just then I heard İhsan Hoca. He was with Emin underneath the pepper tree. There was a closed backgammon set on the table between them. Laughter, loaded with dice, the rattle of pieces and, of course, the poison of philosophy! Now I understood why the cicadas were keeping mum.

I walked toward them. "Is the Lord of the Compass, like Odysseus, seeking his country?"

I sat down on an empty chair. "Beer's what I'm seeking," I said to İhsan Hoca. "If a sailor's country is the sea, a drunkard's is drink."

The hoca, forgetting that his false teeth might fall out, gave a laugh like a dry cough. Emin was silent, pissed off. I could see his point. If someone like me were to come up to me, I'd be pissed off too. "Is everything okay?" asked İhsan.

"Everything?"

"I was born, I did a few things, then I died . . . That's how little everything is . . ."

"I don't seem to be able to die," I said. "My problem is that I can't seem to put a full stop after those 'few things.'"

İhsan burst out laughing again. "There's nothing strange about that. Man is a spiritual process that isn't in charge of his own destiny.

That's what me and Jung say." And they weren't too far off the mark either. Did Jung drink? The trembling was getting closer . . . "That's why people lose their hope in God and turn to the devil . . ."

I had to find something to drink. When I saw how exuberant İhsan was, I carried on the game of asking questions to quell the trembling. "So, you think that's why Goethe made a pact with the devil, to be in charge of his own destiny?"

"Precisely. And there's proof: Faust. Goethe understood how important the devil is for our destiny. The only people who take God seriously are those who care what posterity will say about their creativity and their existence: artists and philosophers."

"I guess he's right," I said, turning to Emin.

İhsan had turned to him as well. His eyes were glistening with the pleasure his words had given him—as if his male member were his tongue.

"What do we see nowadays when we look around? Signs that God has been routed, decisively defeated in the world that He Himself created. Half of his creation is dying of starvation; the well-fed half has destroyed one third of the animal species He created; His most noble work, the human race, is slaughtering one another; the strongest of His people, the Americans, keep breaking the record for killing the most children in one go, first in Afghanistan, then in Iraq . . ."

"You're the expert . . . what do you think we should do?"

Before answering Emin, İhsan paused. He was careful, like a wise man reluctant to disappoint his disciples. Then he explained, muttering the conclusions he'd reached: "We must make God human, and we must be explorers. Because to be more human, we need new virtues . . . Each person should be an explorer of his self."

None of us said anything. I for my part had no intention of being an explorer of anything, let alone of my self. The desire for alcohol, that's what I was, every inch of me, from head to foot. I turned to Emin. His face was pitch dark beneath the shadow pouring down onto us from the tree. He wasn't going to set off exploring either. He ought to know by now that whenever he set out on journeys like that, he ended up getting into trouble.

I stood up before İhsan Hoca got onto his project to turn this remote peninsula into a center of philosophy, like in the Ionian era. Emin remained transfixed. İhsan reached out his hand. No matter how important what he said, he didn't seem like a man whose fall would make a lot noise. What about me? Fear of the tremors interrupted me: my hands or my legs, which one would go first? What if I went for a swim!

On my way around to the front, I checked the kitchen again. The cupboard was still locked. When I gave the door a good kick, Şükrü, who was peeling aubergines at the time, gave a start, decided to pretend he hadn't seen me, and carried on with what he was doing without looking up. That made me even angrier. I yelled, "What if a German was asking for a beer just now!"

He looked at me for a moment, then went back to the aubergines. He'd decided to ignore my anger. "Come on, boss . . . Don't you know, you should shut up about the Germans, they don't drink that much . . ." He was tossing the aubergines one by one into the large pan on the cooker, as though counting them. "In between times, you're the only one who drinks beer here."

What sort of a boss was I! I couldn't even have a beer in my own hotel. This time I really swore. "Did Halit Bey come for his lobster?"

Şükrü shook his head. "He sent his chauffeur."

I went out from the kitchen to the front terrace. The wind was dying a death in the middle of the channel; an intrepid sailboat whizzed down from Foça, paying scant regard to the dead waves it left in its wake. I perched myself somewhere. I think my feet were shaking. Just then I heard the cicadas; they'd begun to sing again in chorus. Not long after that, Emin appeared at the corner of the building. He'd turned to go inside to his room, but when he saw me trembling, he hesitated for a moment and came over. I pointed to the plastic chair. He pulled it out, straightened its cushion, which had slipped to one side, put it against the wall and sat down. "Were you following last me night?"

He didn't reply at first, but then: "You could say that."

"Thanks for your help," I said.

"Now we're even," he said immediately. "Like I said, if you want . . ."

I didn't; I raised my hand and interrupted him. "Suddenly I'm surrounded by guardian angels. First you, then that girl . . ."

"You gave her quite a fright," said Emin. "She thought you were dead."

Dead! I laughed. "You and me both know how difficult it is for someone to die, don't we, mate?"

He looked away. We were both thinking about the same thing: torture. We both had similar scenes in front of our eyes. He turned to the sea as if he didn't want to look any longer at the picture indelibly etched into our memories, and muttered, "I've seen people who die easily too."

Captive and interrogator! He was right—it all depended which side you were looking from.

"Do you really want to help me?" He cautiously sized me up then nodded. "Find me some drink then." The spasms in my feet had finally caught his attention. "Soon the ants will be crawling up to my hands." He wasn't sure what to do. "Was there anyone around when I fell down last night?"

He thought for a moment and said, "No." Not even a dog? He couldn't read my thoughts, so he didn't reply. "I hear they fired at your room in the middle of the night. Two nights in a row. Didn't they?" If I'd been able to shrug my shoulders, I would have. "It was at the end of April," he said, as though he wanted to remind me.

"Maybe they did," I said. "I didn't hear it. As you know, I'm passed out by that hour." Who'd been talking? "Was it Sami?" He shook his head. "Şükrü?"

"İhsan Hoca," he said, after a pause. He wasn't going to hide the other half of the secret either: "The hoca says you're a good man."

"The only thing that's important for a good man at this moment in time is drink." I raised my hands. "They're next. Ten minutes at most. The ants are halfway there, you see. And my ears have started ringing. And when they start ringing, it means things are bad . . ."

He stood up and went inside. He returned with a metal hip flask in his hand. The amnesiac joy of drunkenness broke my heart in two. "Vodka," he said. "Will that do?"

I got a Coke from the fridge in the lobby and upended his hip flask into it. The first sip seared my palate and flowed straight down to the ants wandering around in my feet. I drew out the second sip until they were all drowned. Then I took a deep breath. The rust, like a membrane covering my mouth, my windpipe, my stomach, will dissolve; I'll return to a state of fluid happiness . . . Soaking up the only happiness I can handle, I scratched my face. My cheeks were wet. Again? And there wasn't even a girl in sight. "The first sip always makes my catarrh worse for some reason," I said.

Emin didn't say I was crying. Maybe because he saw Şuayip coming in through the garden gate. We waited for the rake-thin man, who was wearing a dark suit in the middle of summer, to get closer. Without taking my eyes off the man who managed to be a gentleman whatever the weather, "Sometimes God gets it wrong," I said to Emin. "Instead of giving the hotel to me, He should have given it to him."

I took a third sip. "Good morning, sir," said Şuayip.

Separately, we both greeted the man who went past bowing respectfully. When he was out of earshot, "He's running away from his wife," I said.

Emin shuffled uneasily in his chair. Just then it occurred to me that the woman who was after him on the phone could be his wife. I'd been ungrateful. The man had found me something to drink, and there I went making him feel awkward. "I need to get ready," he said. The shadow on his face had darkened his voice as well. "I'll probably be off this afternoon."

In that case, I'd have to go easy on the vodka . . . Something was thrust into my back. I didn't turn around. I knew what it was: the fear of spending the whole morning sober. It was carving me up. "Have you got another bottle?" I asked.

He shook his head and went away, taking his hip flask. He hadn't shaken my hand. When will that bastard Sami turn up? That was the question standing between me and the fourth sip. And Spot: is he still alive?

While Mücella's sons were lazily doing the sweeping—the cicadas were still singing—I closed my eyes and leaned back. Five, maybe ten minutes, until the shakes returned . . . When a few ants got as far as my knees, I opened my eyes a crack and reached for the bottle. This time it was Rana standing there. She was wearing a green bikini and had a shiny transparent cloth wrapped around her waist. She was like a man: I bet she tried getting into your bed before getting into your heart. She opened conversation; I chose the vodka and Coke. "Good morning, Mr. Pavarotti, how are you?"

She may have been brainless, but she was very alluring: an Aphrodite cast in bronze. A woman like that could easily grace any arm. "Greetings, slave," I said.

"Slave?" She was surprised, but laughed all the same. "Whose slave am I supposed to be then?"

"Beauty's," I replied. "A beauty like yours often enslaves."

She shrieked with laughter once she'd understood. The cicadas fell silent again. The two boys had stopped what they were doing so they could watch a woman they could only dream about. "Well, well, so our receptionist knows how to give compliments too?"

I took another sip from the bottle. "Not really," I said, "If I'd been able to write, I'd have used it in my novel."

"A drunken writer who sings marches . . ."

I shook the bottle. "That's right," I said.

She pulled the chair Emin had got up from shortly before into the sun and sat across from me. I was right, she succumbed to her beauty: even to having it mentioned. "Aren't you going to order me a coffee then?" she said.

"Okay," I said, "and why don't you order me a beer?"

"Have you got any more compliments up your sleeve?"

I nodded my head. "But don't forget, a bottle of beer's worth two compliments at the most." When she raised her hands, I called over to Mücella, "A coffee for me, and a beer for the lady."

Mücella looked at me doubtfully, but Rana repeated what I'd said. Five minutes later the can of beer was in my pocket, and the voluntary slave was sipping her coffee. The first discovery of the day: Mücella had the key to the drinks cabinet. Rana told me the second one: they had friends coming tomorrow. She was smiling. "Çiğdem doesn't know anything about it. We're going to surprise her."

Then she settled down to tell the whole story. She and Çiğdem had been neighbors since their childhood; because they both basically grew up without a mother, they allied themselves against the other children at primary school; they were going to set up a human resources company together in the autumn when they got back from holiday . . . I pretended to listen and kept on drinking. It was enough to make you laugh: I couldn't manage to die, but I could find a drink. God was equipping me with unnecessary skills.

It wasn't that I completely ignored Rana the whole time. She continued talking without depriving Mücella's two sons of the sight of her generously displayed body, as if she wanted to seduce them. She claimed to be a psychologist. Çiğdem, she said, had studied business administration and gotten her master's in America. Because her mother often went to Paris, Çiğdem lived with her grandfather, a rather well-to-do textiles magnate, and her grandmother . . .

After a while—the alcohol must have sharpened my mind—the clues she was dropping about the third discovery of the day began to appear on the horizon one by one. The woman sitting across from me wasn't talking about herself, she was talking about Çiğdem. Was it love? Jealousy? If I were a betting man, I'd have put my money on jealousy. Maybe, as happens in long-term friendships, her personality had dissolved in the personality of the stronger one, leaving only her beauty behind.

I can't say that Sami didn't come to mind as I was thinking about this. Out of me and Sami, whose personality had prevailed over the other's? As I was looking for an answer to this question, I heard Rana say, "Now it's your turn, Mr. Writer."

"I haven't started writing yet," I said, leaving Sami to one side.

"One beer equals two compliments. That's what you said, isn't it? So come on then, give me another."

"Women who are truly beautiful don't seek proof of their beauty."

She repeated the sentence to herself until she understood: "But you're being a spoilsport," she said finally.

I asked the important question: "Why did you come here?"

Was she going to let the conversation stray away from her beauty onto something else? "Honestly, I don't know either," she said, after a short silence. "We set off from Istanbul, supposedly to go to Çeşme. Everyone was expecting us there." When she reached her empty coffee cup out to the boys, who were watching her out of the corner of their eyes, they both rushed forward together. The shorter one was more nimble. "And Cenk's there too." Without me asking, she told me who Cenk was. "He adores Çiğdem. And if you ask me, madam isn't indifferent to him either." Then she suddenly went quiet. She was looking at me with guilty eyes that knew they were invading my privacy. "Have you been crying?"

"Allergies," I said.

She wasn't as obnoxious as she tried to be. If we spoke a few more times, I could even get to like her. We had a bit more banter, steering clear of her beauty. When she realized she couldn't bring the conversation around to the subject she was interested in, she went off down the path toward the sea. As soon as I was alone, I took four or five sips of the Coke. Then, sparrow-like, I picked at what was on the breakfast tray—bread, white cheese and a few olives—and sent what was left back to the kitchen with the lads.

After I'd finished the beer as well, the fugitives appeared. Çiğdem got out of the car first, and after that, with her help, Sami. They must have had a good laugh together along the way; I could tell from Sami's upward-curling lips. Çiğdem left him where he was, and came straight to me. "Get ready, we're taking some things with us and going for a drive."

She was standing where Şafak had stood, and saying the things

Şafak had said. But five years and thousands of bottles of alcohol separated them.

"Drink," I said. "I'm not taking a single step if I don't have any beer."

Then Sami came. The smile on his lips had ceded to one of the orders he often tossed about. "You need a shave. Go and have one."

April 1998:

"Are you all set to go?" She's standing across from me beneath the bougainvillea. She's still as young as she was yesterday, still smiling and I can still smell her. "There's no rain."

"If I make a promise, I keep it," I say.

"But first, your exam question," she says. "What time is it?"

I look for the shadows. The shadow of the pole topped with the weather vane Şükrü made hasn't moved from the wall of the building to the terrace yet. "It's after eight, but it's not nine yet," I say.

She spreads her hands to both sides. She must have looked at her watch before coming. "But there's a whole sixty minutes between eight and nine," she says.

I tell her the first truth I learned when I arrived on this peninsula. "There's nothing here that's so urgent that it needs to be specified down to the last minute."

"Oh, I see, yours is a life with a slow tempo, stripped of its details . . ."

"It's not so much the tempo . . . I guess we don't really worry about life itself," I say.

The moisture left over from yesterday's rain will focus the sun's rays onto us like a lens and burn us the whole day. A few birds are singing behind us. The open sea to the north and the channel are both calm. What interrupts the calm is the soldiers on the hill with their march. "Shall we take some things with us?"

I go to the kitchen and throw a few things into a bag, ignoring Sami's long face. He doesn't ask where I'm going. Or why. Anyway, even if he did, I don't have any answer to give. Maybe it's the desire to gaze at her, the flower-scented girl standing outside beneath the bougainvillea. Gazing at her is like glancing out of the window: it's remembering the existence of a world we've become alienated from, that we turned our backs on a very long time ago, or . . . Do I miss the past? That's a dangerous question. I leave, trying not to make eye contact with him.

"Which way?" Şafak asks as she gets into the car.

"Follow me," I say.

"So, north then," she says.

"North," I say.

We set off to the north, toward Yeniliman. We intend to go down to the Denizgiren plain, below Küçükbahçe, and meet with the Aegean, taking the narrow tarred road that follows the coastline along a route that goes straight through the scarps of Akdağlar, which plunge down to the sea, up to the west side of the peninsula, which looks out to Chios. Then we'll leave the sea and wind behind, and zigzag inland along the western slopes of Akdağlar until we get to the pine-covered plateau where they say there are bears and wolves. The rest of our trip will be returning to where we started, reaching the channel side after a journey downhill . . . A journey first to the north, then to the west for a while, after that to the south and after that to the east. An angular letter O . . .

She nods as if she can visualize the route I've mapped out, and says, "Okay." But there's only one fish farm on this route. "So be it," she murmurs. "This is a journey of discovery."

When she mentions leaving the research trip in the gulf until tomorrow, I shudder. That means one more day . . . The joy I feel diffuses pleasure and shame throughout my body. I start telling her how, thousands of years ago, the Genoese thought of joining Büyük Ada with the mainland to make the largest harbor in the ancient world, but that this dream sank beneath the waves that the northwest wind swept before it, and that the jetty which was destroyed even before it was completed looks like a giant dead snake collapsed at the bottom of the sea, and that the scattered rocks have become a fishery today . . .

She's looking in front of her. To the right of Mytilene, I point out the deep gulf where she'd be able to see Mount Ida if it weren't for the mist that looks like cigarette smoke.

We pass Yeniliman, and ten minutes after starting to climb to the hills, we take a break outside the old abandoned Greek village to the left of the road and smoke the first cigarette of the day. A windless morning. "This area gets battered by winds from the north in the winter and from the sea in the summer," I say. "That's why the village is tucked away."

Just then she lets out a short, loud whoop. "Look over there!"

I look over. At the entrance to the village, there's a purple water-fall flowing from the top of a wide stone wall next to a house that leans against the hillside. It's a tableau created by the gorse. The hills behind are dotted with Cezanne's yellow: even the most charmless shrub of all the scrub is in bloom—the *kirekli* plant that no living creature eats, that no insects land on.

I watch her walking off toward the wall. In front of me runs a foal, giddy with happiness. I'm feeling giddy too: it must be because of the sexual attraction emanating from the expanding and contracting, tensing and relaxing muscles of her body in motion. She disappears behind the wall. I put out my cigarette and walk to the village, taking the car keys with me.

I find her in the inner courtyard, bordered on three sides by old stone walls. The ground is covered in daisies as high as your thighs. In every direction clumps of poppies, and maroon marigolds. She's standing on a carpet woven from flowers. Our eyes meet. She mutters, as if in a trance, "This is like heaven."

And you're like an angel . . . is what I should say, but I make do with saying, "This is the village of Haseki."

In front of me is a woman who's forgotten the seals, and who's been enchanted by the sensual awakening that nature imparts. A bit later, when we set off for the summit, we'll be able to see Mytilene and Chios together from the same point. What will she do then? "I'm a hundred and ten percent sure heaven must be like this," she goes on. "How beautiful!"

"Maybe because there's no people," I say.

She thinks for a moment; then she says, "You mean, there's no people in heaven?"

I nod. "Heaven is what doesn't exist," I say. "Heaven must be a mirage dreamed up by God . . . the oasis seen by poor souls in the desert."

"So you think we'll all end up in hell then?" She's sitting at the foot of the wall, beneath the waterfall of flowers pouring down from above. I don't know. "Come on!" she says. "God must be more generous than you."

"The sunset's amazing here," I say. "And that's the only thing that's got anything to do with God's generosity."

"And this pour soul?" Her hands are on her breast; she's pointing to herself, as she always does when she's laughing. Should I apologize? But then she continues in an excited voice: "The sunrise might be dull compared to the sunset, but we remember it in personal names like Tan, Doğan and, of course, Şafak. Can you think of any names related to the sunset?" I can't. "What I think of is that the sunset evokes death." She's striking the stone lightly with her hand; I sit down next to her. "So tell me," she says, "what are you doing here, at the very tip of this peninsula?"

"You know what I'm doing," I say. "I look for astronauts on the moon, and . . ."

As I don't continue, she prompts, "And?"

"If we can find a gun, one day Fındık and I will go and invade Mytilene."

She laughs. I shouldn't leave her to laugh alone. Now we're laughing together. Hers is short and abrupt, though mine is silent. "Aren't you going to tell me about yourself?"

Should I? What if I hold her left hand? But I don't. Even though her little finger's only a couple of inches away from me.

"Mine's a simple tale like a sailor's story," I say. Her glances have me in a spin. "I came here after a woman, then . . . Then when she dumped me, I couldn't be bothered going back. I guess this is a harbor sheltering those who don't go out to sea and aren't travelers . . . I guess I found it easy to be a deckhand on dry land . . ."

She takes out another cigarette. I take one too. "You've dreamed of sailing the high seas and of going to Africa too, haven't you?"

I shrink back and say, "There was once a man who made his dreams come true; he was a traveler who sailed the high seas and set foot in Africa. He travelled down the Congo, like Kurtz . . ."

"The Congo," she says.

Her eyes are closed. If I let her, she'll go there. After we light our cigarettes, I tell her about the River Congo. "In the local language it means the river that swallows all rivers; the artery that comes out of Africa's heart of darkness . . ."

She opens her eyes. "I think you're that traveler," she says.

I'm not going to confess. "I learned about the oceans and about Africa from novels," I say.

"Who's Kurtz?" she asks.

Kurtz, Lord Jim, Learoyd . . . they're all the same person. "A real traveler," I say.

She thinks for a moment. "I remember a writer mentioning a type of man called 'a real man.' He must be one of those."

"Men are crap," I retort. "Real ones and fake ones. They spend all their time squabbling, either with their fathers or with God."

"That's so true!" And as soon as she's said it, she laughs. "And even you were teasing God just now." She carefully stubs out her half-smoked cigarette on a stone. "Whoever said that must have been an honest man."

"It was a lesbian, actually," I say. "In Germany . . . one of Sami's friends."

When I mention Sami, she pauses. People are curious about stories about cripples. So was she. "Has he always been like that?"

"If he hadn't listened to me, he wouldn't have ended up like that," I say. "Nineteen years ago, on an April day like this, I dragged him away from his work to go somewhere with me. We went outside; ten paces later, he was shot in the waist. Fascists . . ."

We're looking at each other, motionless. Her eyes are speaking. *It's not your fault*, they say. I'll reply with my eyes; I'll say, *If only I hadn't insisted.* She interrupts me. "And this is the best place for you to look out for him . . . is that it?"

She's observant and she's got strong intuition. "That's right," I say. "This is the best place."

She reaches out the hand I'd been thinking of holding, and touches me on the temple. Her hand is cool. Is she feeling sorry for Sami or for me? What's the difference—she feels sorry for us. How long has it been since someone felt sorry for us? I try to remember.

A car goes past . . .

July 2003:

We were driving along an empty road. We hadn't encountered anyone since turning inland at Yeniliman and leaving the sea behind us,
neither person, nor car; life and motion had blended into the gray
color of nature and disappeared. We'd seen a few horses sheltering in
the shadows beneath the trees on the left and right, but all around us
were signs suggesting that we were entering another kind of world.
The green scrubland and fields covered with olive groves had suddenly transformed into valleys surrounded by volcanic rocks coated
with plants dyed yellow by the salty winds, and shear slopes . . .
Before we got to the hills, as we were going over the long bridge in
the middle of the final piece of flat ground, "Charmless places," said
Çiğdem. "They really give me the creeps."

What if we'd driven through at night? "We're on top of the
stream of hell," I said. "And when we've gone up the hill, we'll see
Kanlıkaya."

I wasn't looking at her; I wasn't looking at anything, actually. As
the view I'd learned by heart was flowing past outside, I was drinking
my sixth, maybe seventh, beer of the day, enjoying the coolness inside
the car. Çiğdem was still uneasy: "Such strange names!"

"They date back to Şeyh Bedrettin's uprising," I said, as if it was
common knowledge who Şeyh Bedrettin was. "Have you ever heard
of him before?"

She waited a moment; then, crawling out from under her silence,
she said "No" in an embarrassed voice.

"He died a long time ago," I said. "His father was the *qadi* of
Simavna."

"Simavna?"

"It used to be a district of Edirne," I continued. "Now it's part of

Greece. Six hundred years ago Şeyh Bedrettin's followers mobilized the poor and rose up against the Ottomans. So the Sultan sent his armies against them to suppress the rebellion, which was in the Izmir area. Bedrettin's supporters retreated this far, fleeing Beyazıd Paşa's soldiers . . ."

She'd be able to piece together what happened next for herself. I took a sip of my beer. "So this . . ." she said, and stopped without finishing off her sentence.

She wasn't going to get the blood that had been spilled all around us on her hands. "The last rebels were slaughtered here," I said. "The most loyal ones. There's no escape if you're loyal . . ."

Then I shut up and turned to my beer. I still had three cans to go. The BMW took the slope running.

"Did you know, Constantine apparently means something like 'loyal' . . . But Aphrodite comes from *aphros*, meaning 'foam.' Sami told me. And Odysseus supposedly means 'ascetic' . . ."

Windbag. "If you ask me, he's making it up," I said. "It's all nonsense. Crosswords have clouded his mind."

"You do realize how important you are to him, don't you?"

That's just hot air too. "If only he loved me," I said. "Then I'd bid him farewell instead of Erica."

"Don't be unfair to him." Her voice believed that I was. "He admires you; only two hours ago he was telling me how brave you are."

"So he admires my bravery, does he?" She nodded quickly, as if that would make it more convincing. Did she know that bravery is only smoke and mirrors, and is only the business of cowards? "Often bravery is just the ability to conceal our cowardice."

She turned toward me, so I raised the beer I was about to down, and saluted her with it.

"If there is something you're concealing, I'm sure it's not your cowardice." She was shaking her head. Like all rich people, she was stubborn. "I believe your friend."

"The crux of the matter is that if you're susceptible to self-destruction, you don't have to be afraid of other people. Because the only person who'll harm you is yourself." The car went through a dip in the road. We were going to get to the top quicker than I'd bargained for. The top! "Stop the car," I said, hastily. She was going to ask why, then changed her mind. She pulled over on the right. "A bit farther up," I said.

When the car stopped, I opened the door. "Where are you going?"

I pointed to the village off to the side. "I won't be gone ten minutes."

"I'm coming too."

"I'm going to be sick," I said. "I'm sure you don't want to watch . . ."

I took a can from the bag, and got out of the car. The wind, which had run from the sea, five hundred feet below, all the way up to the mountaintop, wasn't out of breath; it was shaking out the dried bushes that extended along the edges of the road like a horse's mane. I left the asphalt, which had melted in the heat and had its surfacing of stone chips sticking out, and went into the empty courtyard that was like a coffin with an open lid between stone walls. A strange coolness reigned. The noise, the wind, the dust and its smell, the ghosts of Börklüce Mustafa and Torlak Kemal's loyal followers, wealth, facts—everything was left outside. There was only me, my drunkenness and Çiğdem in the courtyard.

I waited for a moment without moving. Dried gorse, like an old curtain full of holes, hung down from the wall in the middle. The floral carpet that had been on the ground was gone; a fine layer of dust covered the floor. A plump lizard chasing a grasshopper scurried away into the chinks in the stone wall as soon as it noticed me. I was in a cemetery, a cemetery of memories, a cemetery where I somehow couldn't be buried, a cemetery that rebuffed me . . .

I waited without praying, and tried to hear the voices at the foot of the wall—one of them belonged to a woman in pain, the other to a tired man who couldn't be bothered to look out of the window. Nothing. The past was deaf, distant and mute. I opened the beer and sat down on the stone that the tender, cool hand had pointed to years before. For half the can all I thought was, *This is the snake eyes that God has never managed to roll.* I'd found my grave and my coffin, I'd gotten my shroud, but unfortunately I was the creature of a stubborn God. I drank half of what was left in the can. And Fındık? Do fish have their own gods?

Just when I was thinking of trading in my God for a new one, I heard the voice I'd been straining to hear. It was like that cool hand coming out from where it was hidden inside the silence; it was stroking my temples; it was raising the cover of the past. It no longer felt sorry for Sami and me. It felt sorry for itself, I guess, judging from what it said.

Remembering the end of life . . . it was saying. *It stops me from being content with my little happinesses. What I'm looking for is something greater, much grander than happiness . . .* Without the slightest hint of fear, I went right up to the window and replied, "Love. That must be what we're looking for . . ."

"Please don't cry . . ."

I opened my eyes a crack. The whisper didn't belong to the woman I missed. In front of me was someone else, someone who didn't smell of flowers. "Shut up," I said angrily to the whisper. "We're talking about love."

The whisper whispered again. It was surprised: "With who? There's no one here."

"Shut up," I said again. "'What is love?' That's what she's asking."

"What is love?" repeated the whisper.

"'Our heart's most exquisite fluttering . . .' That's what she said. Here? No, that evening, on the terrace, after our long trip. While I was trying to coax the astronaut-swallowing moon from out of its hiding place. It was after ten . . . 'That most exquisite fluttering . . .' What was I thinking? I had no idea; I'd never been in love. And I told her. Then, 'Love is born out of screams of loneliness . . .' she said. At first I thought she was talking about herself, then I realized she wasn't; she was talking about me. She wasn't lonely, you see. There was someone she used to call in the evenings . . ."

"Who are you talking about?"

I looked up. Çiğdem! Yes, I had wanted to talk to a twenty-five-year-old woman, but she wasn't the one I'd summoned. I should have realized because she didn't smell of flowers. I finished the beer. Why had she brought me here? "Why did we come here?" I asked.

"Don't you remember? When you got in the car, you said, 'Follow me, to the north.'" Then she repeated her question: "Who is she?"

"Let's go back," I said. "To the south."

She perched herself next to me although I hadn't told her to sit down. *There's no room for you; this a single coffin . . .* That's what I should have said. I couldn't. "What happened next?" she asked.

What happened? I told her: "We talked about love until the moon went down. But I'd have wanted to tell her about the oceans. I'm very plausible when I talk about traveling. But she said, 'All men are plausible when they talk about love,' and asked me to continue . . ."

The hungry lizard had reappeared on the sunny side of the wall. Should I take him to the path where the grasshoppers with a death wish dance? I looked up. There was a bird of prey circling up above. "Have you ever been married?"

I turned to her. It hadn't even been twenty-four hours since she arrived, but she'd acquired a ferocious curiosity. "What do you want from me?" I asked.

"You're asking me that for the second time?" Her voice had a note of impatience again. The actual problem was her wealth, her wealth that made her believe she was entitled to everything. "I told you. I'm interested in you," she continued.

I would have laughed at that. In fact, I did. "In a man like me?"

"Have you never felt you were worth anything?"

That was a good question. "Once," I said. "The night I thought I could write." Our eyes met. And I told her the rest. "But the next morning I woke up and I wasn't worth a dime . . ." She was going to console me, but I preempted her: "Why are you interested in me?"

She shrugged her shoulders. "Let's say, it's not just you, it's the whole area too."

"That's even more ridiculous," I said. "What is there on this forgotten peninsula that could possibly be of any interest to you?"

"The vineyards . . ." I leaned back. "In San Francisco I spent a whole year taking winemaking courses. I might buy some land here."

"Alcohol . . . That's the only thing we can have in common." There were two cans of beer waiting for me in the car, which was a calming thought. I closed my eyes. I still had to buy a bottle of gin before going back to the hotel. "Let's go back," I said.

When she was curious about something, her eyes would avoid the glances of whomever she was with; they'd turn inward toward her nose. I hadn't noticed it before. "Did you love her a lot?"

Every woman who wants to hear your confession is dangerous . . . said a voice. I ignored the warning. "If I hadn't loved her, I would have died." Then I told her the other, the dramatic half of my confession as well. "But now I'm dying and loving at the same time."

I didn't say anything else. She got up first. She reached out her hand and I took it. I postponed my burial to a later date, left my coffin to the lizard, and walked with her. Her grip on my hand was like a lover: at times passionate, at times fragile, ready to be withdrawn at any moment. When we got into the car, "To the south?" she asked.

"To town," I answered.

We drove through the secret graves of Şeyh Bedrettin's followers on the way back. As the silence continued, she asked, "Are you asleep?"

"I'm thinking," I said.

"About that woman?"

"About that bastard in the scrub who's turned into a ghost."

"Sami?"

She didn't know I had more than one ghost. "No, a dog that's run away from me," I said. She was surprised. She didn't say anything for a moment.

"Why did it run away? What did you do to it?"

It was for its own good, what I did to it. "I threw stones at him," I said.

"What?"

"He shouldn't trust people. He needed to learn so he wouldn't get poisoned."

"Was that what you were hoping to find last night?" I nodded. "But you were trying to feed it."

"That was just bait," I said. "If he'd come, I'd have thrown stones at him again." She shook her head. "You know, there are many different ways of protecting dogs: they say that in Iraq the Americans give their dogs body armor . . . That makes me laugh."

I chuckled to myself for a while. Çiğdem handed me a tissue at one point. Did she think I was crying? Maybe I was. I stopped laughing—or crying—after ten minutes. We didn't say anything until we got into town. We parked in the small square in front of the bust of Atatürk. Everywhere was deserted. I sat her down in the sea-view cafe at the entrance to the old town, and popped into the super-market across the road. The drinks were at the back. A bottle of gin! Then, giving ear to the experienced drunk's voice inside me, I took two bottles from the shelf and charged them to the hotel. When I got back to the cafe, Çiğdem had moved over to the corner that gets the sea breeze, and was drinking tea. I thought about telling her whose place she was sitting in, but then I changed my mind. I got a beer from the snack bar and sat down opposite her. She pointed at the plastic bag in my hand. I said it was alcohol and pointed to her big cloth bag. "Can you put it in there?"

"Sami?" I nodded. She put the bottles in her bag. I lit a cigarette. There were no boats in the channel. I started sipping the beer. "I was never allowed to eat it when I was a child," she said when I was half-way through. She was pointing at the ice cream cabinet a little farther along. "So I used to hate her."

"Her?"

"My mother," she said. Her face had taken on a strange form. "I prefer to say 'her.' She gave birth to me, but she was never my mother."

"Mine died," I said. "A few years ago. She was a teacher."

"Mine's very much alive," she said. "Spending money like water." She didn't look away. "What about your father?" I asked.

"He died last year." Her voice trailed off. She really loves her father! "Ostensibly of a heart attack, but if you ask me, it was because of her."

"Mine died by himself, when I was still a child . . ." I paused for a moment as though I was about to hear the coughs that used to keep me and Salim awake when they filtered into the narrow room where we slept. "He had a weak chest. In 1944 he was arrested and got a chill; he never recovered."

After we'd exchanged our dead, we didn't say anything for a while. Actually, I was well aware of how paradoxical it seemed: my mother and father had managed to die easily, so where had I gotten my stubborn resistance to death from? Çiğdem drank her tea, thinking of the ice cream she couldn't eat; I sipped on my beer. An inquisitive twenty-five-year-old girl with a BMW, who reeked of wealth, who had learned how to make wine in San Francisco . . . I shook my head. Even if she *was* sitting in the place *she* had sat in five years ago, the person across from me wasn't the twenty-five-year-old girl I missed.

"What's wrong?" Çiğdem asked. She'd finished her tea, and had seen me shake my head.

"Nothing," I said. "I was just reminding God of a few things."

She didn't smile. There was an impressive statue across from me. The freshness of her cool, limpid beauty seemed impervious to the heat. Then she suddenly spoke: "You know, I was jealous of her. Of that woman who wanted something much larger, much grander than happiness . . . but I've spent my whole life building thick, high walls around me to protect myself."

I looked at the girl who'd just realized she'd spent her whole life building herself a prison. Who was the jailer? If I'd asked, she'd most probably have said her mother, and I'd have had to tell her it was herself. So I didn't ask. After all, she was carrying my alcohol.

April 1998:

We're on the terrace. In front of me is a woman who awakens such happiness as can only be found in dreams; nearer, though, is my fate, which will turn to dust like a butterfly's wing. We're looking at each other without speaking, from within a guilty silence pregnant with everything. A short while ago, we scooped the full moon from out of its well: it has faded the color of the sky and dyed the gray Akdağlar purple, making them stand out against their background, and turning them into a silhouette without depth, like a picture painted by a child. We're alone. Sami! He must be in exile somewhere in the darkness where the moonlight can't reach. In the hole in which he imprisons himself whenever someone comes between us.

We're both surprised: when, how did we get entangled in this lithe, rippling silence that's like a velvet shawl? Although I've less faith than Learoyd, who closed the door screaming "Out with God," I'm on the verge of believing once more in the God I abandoned when I was thirteen. Everything—like after a storm that suddenly appears in the middle of the day and then disappears as quickly as it came—is in utter disarray. Is it the sensual spring that appeared in front of us at every step of our journey today, each time with different colors, on the hillsides we came to, on every hill we climbed, in the valleys we felt the desire to disappear inside—is this what has aroused her so? A voice whispers: *She's young!* Which body blessed with the birthing instinct can remain unmoved by nature's magnificent awakening? What about me? What is it that's playing havoc with me, goading me with a painful urge to create that's just like the desire to write? I look at the face that has been awakened by nature. It's a stupid question. Especially when the answer's so clear and right in front of me. Chance and necessity! No, neither speech nor silence is appropriate for this life-defining answer. Ours is just chance; there's no necessity for us. Still, I'm scared to death of a woman I've known for all of thirty hours.

The compelling silence is broken by Fındık whistling. I don't whistle back. Şafak rolls her eyes—eyes which I thought I'd always look at when I first saw her. I should tell her why I'm afraid: I should tell her that sooner or later women always leave me. But she's deaf. With the hunger to create that flows from nature to her body, she looks at me, promising everything. I've got no chance: what on earth can you tell someone who's yet to be schooled by pain?

From Delikli Burun Fındık whistles again. This time it has a cheerful timbre of disbelief. He must be telling me he hasn't been able to find any astronauts. I hear the noise a third time and I give a start. Şafak stands up. That's when I realize it wasn't whistling; it was the telephone in reception. In the distance, something jumps into the sea. Fındık must have decided to return to his nest.

I endure the silence with the unshooting stars that are fixed in place. The horizon's on the other side; here there's an emptiness jammed between the nearby hills and mountains. I'm watching the sky through the bottom of a narrow-mouthed glass. That's why I linger at the Great Bear, who's leaning against Değirmen Dağı. When I turn around, she's taking a cigarette from the packet and lighting it. She wants to explain, but for some reason says nothing . . . She wishes the telephone hadn't rung at all. "You have a lover," I say.

"My boyfriend," she corrects me. After that, "My fiancé, I mean." And then, as if she's blowing something out, she releases a long breath. "Uff, is there really no beer here?" She didn't say lover . . . I find myself shivering with a foolish, inappropriate joy. "Are you in the temperance league, darling?"

"Six months ago I was treated for alcoholism."

She's surprised, but not with her eyes or her face. With her hand: the cigarette that's unraveling smoke into the night remains hanging in the air. She must be thinking whether or not she should ask. She doesn't. "Come on, tell me something," she says.

Something! "What about the stars?"

"Fantastic," she says.

What should I begin with? "If we were at that high point now, as the sun is setting, where we watched Chios and Mytilene, I could have shown you Orion the Hunter escaping from the scorpion." She has a childlike curiosity and looks intently in the direction I'm pointing to until I continue. "Orion was a very skilful hunter from ancient Greece. He got so confident that he began saying that no animal could kill him. Finally, Hera got sick of hearing him boast, and sent a scorpion to kill him. Orion crushed the scorpion with his stick, but at the last moment the scorpion managed to sting him, and soon after, both of them died. But the Pleiades cried so much over Orion's death that, to escape their wailing, Zeus eventually placed the scorpion and Orion in the sky, but in such a way that when one's rising, the other's setting."

"So that's why Orion the Hunter runs away from the Scorpion every night." She puts her cigarette on the ground. "What else?"

"Homer often mentions Orion in the Odyssey." This time I point to Izmir. "We're not very far from where he watched the sky 2,700 years ago." Her eyes! Shall I continue? "Erich Maria Remarque, in a love letter to Marlene Dietrich, described Orion as the Virgin Mary's brooch."

"And you?" she asks. "How would you have described it?"

"A signpost. That's what I'd have said. If you follow his belt, you'll find Sirius, the brightest star in the sky."

She picks up the cigarette from where she's left it and waits a moment. At the end of the silence there are no stars, only facts. "We're thinking of getting married in November."

We descend from the sky to the earth. I know she's warning herself, not me. "Congratulations in advance," I say.

The voice that reaches my ear doesn't sound like mine. It's an awful, serrated rasping. The only indication that it belongs to me is the tearing in my throat. Soon my mouth will be full of blood.

The whisper on her lips interrupts my thoughts: "Remembering the end of life . . . It stops me from being content with my little happinesses. What I'm looking for is something greater, much grander than happiness . . ." she says.

The hairs on the back of my neck are standing on end. Because the resonance in her voice makes what she's saying seem more real. "Love," I say. "That must be what you're looking for."

"What is love?" I don't know. I've never been in love, not like in a fairy-tale romance anyway. As if she knows this, she gives the answer herself in an ever-thickening voice that draws everything in. "Our heart's most exquisite fluttering?" I'm shaking; the blood in my mouth is sloshing around. She's not sure either. "Often love is born out of screams of loneliness," she says.

She might not be head over heels, but at least she has someone she loves. I'm the one screaming screams of loneliness. "What's he like?" I ask.

"Good," she says. "He's a good person . . ."

As she says this, she looks at me as if I'm worthy enough to learn her secrets. And me? Even if I look, I'm blind. In front of me is a woman twenty years younger than me, on the threshold of marriage, and I'm talking to her about love and the stars. I need to find an opportunity to spit out the blood that's filling my mouth. "I've become used to being on my own," I say. "Loneliness saves you the bother of being a good person or a bad person."

She laughs. I don't; I'm in a lamentable state, that's why. Maybe it's not love I miss, but women. Why don't I seduce one of the healthy German women in the neighboring cove?

"I've had a few relationships before," she says abruptly. She doesn't have to explain anything. But as if she feels the need to, "I couldn't make a success of any of them," she continues. "I think it was my fault. I can't connect with anyone. But he's different; I don't get bored with him . . ." Then she changes the subject. "Hey, tell me about the novel you're going to write."

"It'll have the stars and the sea in it," I say. "And Sami too, of course. Maybe I'll throw in a German woman as well."

"German? What's wrong with Turkish women?"

I tell her what's wrong with them. "They leave me."

She puts her cigarette to her lips. It's gone out; she doesn't notice. "I'm going tomorrow," she says. "And I can look at the farms on the way by myself."

"You see?" I say.

This time I'm laughing. I'm past caring now about the blood spilling out of my mouth. She reaches out a hand and touches me on the temple. It's a friendly, even apologetic, touch. But her words are provocative. "Maybe I should have dyed my hair blond."

What if I kiss her! No, she's going tomorrow; it'd be wrong. She isn't one of those women you can kiss just once, only for one night.

Just then we hear a faint sound rising from the base of the pepper tree. Something's crying. Şafak gets up. When she comes back, she's nursing a little dog. A pup. It must be one of the puppies left behind by the female that was run over yesterday on the road below.

"My God, look at him," she says. "He was so cold and afraid." Except for the spot on his forehead, he's practically snow white.

"What should we call him?"

We're not just adopting a dog; we're planning out a shared future too. We both know this. Trembling, I say, "Spot," as if I'm kissing her.

"All right," she says, avoiding my eyes. "Spot it is . . . You'll take good care of him, won't you?"

"I will," I say. "I promise. Until my dying breath. And I keep my promises, you know that."

Any other time, what we were saying would have made us both laugh. But we're not laughing. Our destinies are being tacked together. Is this exaltation what we're looking for? Is it what's greater, much grander than happiness?

Then we start petting the puppy, who's yelping with joy. But we're not actually caressing him: we're embracing each other, touching each other. From time to time our fingers meet. And I'll enjoy touching her too . . . As we continue living out a forbidden lovemaking on the little body, he starts to cry. We look at each other: we're giving birth to the moment. Or are we giving birth to love?

We give Spot some milk we find in the kitchen; then Şafak goes to her room, taking him with her. I'm all alone in the middle of the night. I spit out the blood in my mouth and light a cigarette. Tonight, for the first time in months, I don't feel like drinking. As the moon passes behind the top of Değirmen Dağı, Sami returns from his exile. He has a long face, as ever. Before starting to speak, he waits for me to finish my cigarette. I get in first. "We've got a dog now."

"What are your intentions?" he asks.

"I'm going to look after it," I say. "He's called Spot."

"You know I'm not talking about the dog," he says. I'm not going to pay any attention to him, no matter what he's talking about. "The word 'tragedy' comes from the ancient Greek for "goat songs,'"[9] he

---

[9]   In Turkish culture, goats are associated with stubbornness.

says this time.

I interrupt him: "I'm not stubborn. Anyway, she's leaving tomorrow. And besides, there's nothing tragic about a man liking a woman."

"Not even if there's a considerable age difference between them?"

Bastard! The word rings in my ears. No, I shouldn't be unfair to him. He can't sleep with women anymore; the fiery dart of lust has been extinguished, and that makes him right. Still, I put up a fight: "Picasso, Wagner . . . they all chose women much younger than themselves . . ."

"You're not a painter or a composer . . ."

"Fine, Sade's Justine was twelve, Nabokov's Lolita thirteen and a half, and Shakespeare's Juliet fourteen. Şafak's old enough to be their mothers." He doesn't find that funny. Shall I tell him the real reason? I mutter: "I want her so I can bathe in the fountain of youth that brings immortality."

"So, you're in search of immortality?" he asks.

"Yes," I say. "I've got no intention of dying."

"Wasn't she leaving tomorrow?" he reminds me.

"Not tomorrow, not the day after: I'm not going to die. As long as the dawn[10] breaks over Foça each morning, I'll not die . . ."

---

[10] I.e., Şafak

"The only thing that makes tomorrow bearable is that it comes with the possibility I might die," I said. "Apart from that, it has no meaning."

Sami didn't make eye contact. Maybe he hadn't heard what I said, maybe he had; he couldn't take his eyes off the straight razor moving up and down along my throat. Like him I said nothing. We spent a while listening to that tantalizing noise of the sharp blade scraping against my skin, a noise that brought death closer and made it more concrete. It was surprising: how did someone who had difficulty keeping his balance even while standing up manage to lean on a single crutch—wandering around as well—and shave someone else sitting on a chair? What if the crutch slipped? I shuddered with hope. How blind I'd been! The hand I needed was beside me, right on my throat, and I'd been looking to God's maladroit hand that never seemed to roll snake eyes. I'd just been stupid: death was as straightforward and as close as giving the crutch a little kick. I looked at Sami's face. A bit of courage . . . That was what we both needed. To work! I sat up slightly. When Sami felt me shift, he pressed my shoulders back with his arms as if he'd sussed me out. "Don't move."

His arms were as hard and strong as ox horns; very well, but was he as stubborn as God? I continued to push my luck. "Don't you ever feel like cutting my throat?"

The hand that was heading back to my throat hung in the air. Indecision? No, he was going to admit it. "Yes." Could I make him believe I was just leaning toward the mirror? "I told you not to move. Why didn't you get shaved while you were in town instead of buying booze?"

I shook my head and denied everything, as I always do. "I didn't buy anything even remotely intoxicating. Didn't you search the room?"

"You'll have squirreled it away somewhere."

So he had looked. "I didn't get shaved because I didn't want to keep your new best friend waiting. Anyway, you're the one complaining about my stubble."

He had a valid for reason not liking it. "When it gets straggly, it's like a sponge dipped in alcohol." He'd finished on my throat, and left the razor blade in the bowl of hot water. We both looked at my face in the mirror. He'd wasted his time: we didn't like the unfamiliar face that had appeared. As if he'd found an excuse, "I guess it's not your stubble, it's your face I can't stand," he grumbled. I pointed at the cigarette. "Wait a moment . . ." While I was waiting, he started talking again: "Anyway, Çiğdem isn't my new best friend. I treat her well because for one, she spends good money, and two, she says she wants to do some things around here . . ." Liar! He knew more than that; he knew the third, even the fourth reason as well. "Has she spoken to you?"

I tried to find his eyes in the mirror. They weren't in his face; they'd slipped away to the razor blade in the bowl. I trembled with hope. Was the killer inside him awakening? He looked up. No, there was just a fraud in front of me. A liar who had no intention of revealing what they were hiding. "We talked about our parents," I said. "Was there anything in particular we were supposed to be talking about?"

"No, no. If only we had a few more customers like them, then we wouldn't be in this sorry state. Yesterday they had lobster, and this evening I hear they're having guests. I sent Fındık word about the fish."

So that was why he was shaving me: we had guests coming this evening. "We went under a long time ago," I said. "There's no way back anymore."

"You never know."

I reached out for the cigarette. I had to find Çiğdem as soon as possible and think of a way to hide the alcohol. But then there was that question I was burning to ask: "I always thought you didn't like young women, especially not twenty-five-year-old ones. You even used to call one of them an ecowarrior, or have you forgotten? So what's happened this time?"

He handed me the towel and started gathering up the shaving kit. "I never said I didn't like Şafak," he said. "Be fair."

I laughed. If Şafak had heard, she'd have laughed too; even Spot would have laughed if he could understand. "You know, the God we don't believe in has given us a harsh punishment." Because I knew he wouldn't ask, I explained: "He condemned us to each other."

"I agree." His voice was friendly. "I only meant to say you weren't right for each other." In fact, having a razor blade in his hand suited him. His strokes were masterful. "She was like a delicate butterfly, and you were like an elephant, my friend."

"Sometimes elephants go after butterflies . . . to find a watering hole."

"But only during a drought."

Don't all our lives swelter along in a drought? I didn't say that. "When Fındık comes, I want to have a word with him," I said instead. Sami didn't say whether or not he'd let me know when he came. And I said, "You can go now. I might get some sleep."

He was going to say something, but the noises coming up from the back garden meant that the Germans were back from the sea. And the rest of his dithering was spirited away by the sound of knocking on the door. I turned and called out to my savior: "Come in!"

It was Çiğdem. She was beautiful, she was elegant and, thank God, she had her bag with her. We waited until Sami had disappeared down the corridor. Once the sound of his crutches on the stone floor became inaudible, I took the bottles she handed me, stuffed one of them under the pillow, and put the other on the bedside table. She was looking out the window with a long face, as if preoccupied.

"You're getting more and more like Sami," I said. She looked at her feet. I pointed to her long face in the mirror.

"Rana and I had a fight," she said. It turned out she was one of those people who gets angry with everyone whenever she gets angry at all. Another time I might have asked why, but the gin was waiting for me in the bottle. "She invited someone over here without telling me, someone I really don't want to see."

I took the first three or four gulps without pausing. With the consistency of molten lead, the gin slowly percolated down through my veins. A sharp heat and that shudder that comes after: soon everything would take its place in that magical world of meaninglessness. Ah, not to have to put up with anybody! I smiled. "Don't take any notice."

"He's always hanging around . . . he's always following me. So much attention . . . Is it love, do you think?" I took a few more swigs from the bottle. The net curtains were soon to come down all around me. She asked again, "Is it love?"

"It's love," I said.

She stood there as if I'd just slapped her. "Why?"

"Love is an emotion whose essence is in its manifestation, that's why," I said.

"No, he wants . . ."

She stopped in mid-sentence as if the man who was after her wanted something so terrible that it couldn't be uttered. "Some men start loving from the body, not the soul," I coaxed. "You need to accept it's a conscious starting point, a more certain one even."

"No, it's only sexuality in disguise."

"Don't look down on sexuality," I said. "An attempt at resisting having to go through the trivial details of life: that's what I think sexuality was invented for."

She was as timid as a virgin who had never slept with anyone. She looked at me square in the face and left. Finally, I was alone with my gin. The net curtains were cascading down from the ceiling. Blood-red net curtains . . .

* * *

Centuries later I woke up to an earthquake, bathed in sweat, on the verge of a shaking fit. There was a woman screaming; my head felt like it was going to explode. Every part of my body ached. I opened my eyes a crack. One of Mücella's sons—the younger one, I think— had taken hold of my shoulder and was shaking me. When he saw I could sit up, he took a step back as if he were face-to-face with someone who'd been raised from the dead, and stammered: "F-Fın-dık's here . . ."

He must have been afraid of Fındık too, just like his mother was. Or maybe he had noticed my eyes. After he'd run off, I shoved my head under the tap without looking in the mirror, and drank a large amount of gin from the bottle on the bedside table. Time to meet the sea creature! I was ready to fool him.

Fındık was out back. Far from the Germans' table, but with a view of the pepper tree. It was a mild night. There was no wind, but the heat had dispersed. If I'd looked up, I would have been able to see the Great Bear. I didn't. I was tipsy, that's why. Fındık didn't turn around until I'd gotten very close. "Are you thinking of burning down the knocking shop, then?"

That's when he turned to me. I was surprised for a moment; I'd forgotten how fish laugh. He smelled of seaweed. "Even'n . . ."

I sat on the wall; we were at the same height, ready to talk about the same things. "You were off quickly yesterday evening," I said. He carried on laughing. "Did you dive where I told you to?"

"'As thee vound one?"

Did you dive? Have you found one? We played that game for a long time. First I'd ask, then he would. "No one's going to bring a Kalashnikov to this peninsula," I said.

"Vuck all vrom Deaf Ahmet and 'is vriends," he said. "Useless twat. Just like 'is vather . . . That zwoldier, the captain, ask 'im."

The stubborn sea creature! "First, dive where I told you to. Take a look around there."

When he reached out his hand, I gave him the packet of cigarettes. He took two as usual. "Does thee know 'ow many vathoms it be there?"

He was boasting. When the conversation reached this point, I spread out my arms to both sides in exaggeration, as I always did. "Come on . . . no matter how deep it is, you'll get to the bottom."

He put one of the cigarettes behind his ear, and I waited for him to light the other. He was shaking his head. "No pwoint, it be nowhere . . . I's looked everywhere. There be nowhere I 'asn't dived, all the way to Mordoğan."

"This is the last time. I'm sure it's there," I said. "The place where the road from Eğlenhoca goes straight down to the sea."

"Thee zaid that last time too . . . Zaid it did be below Boyabağ. 'Twasn't."

The collective laughter from the Germans came between us like a large wave. I was driven backward; he didn't move a muscle. Anyway, he was used to rough seas. "Thee's been drink'n again. Look, thee be a-reel'n."

We didn't say anything for a moment. He puffed on his cigarette; I watched the lights of Foça. When he'd finished his cigarette, I made him the offer he'd been expecting: "If you dive there, I'll talk to Captain Emin. I promise."

He stood up without saying if he'd dive or not. He would. Although he tried to hide it, he was a generous delphinid who liked to play. Each time he'd let me deceive him. "'As they gwone?'"

The astronauts! It was time to say good-bye. "They've gone," I said. "The next full moon I'll show you."

He spun his hand next to his head. "'I's wridden thee down in the Register . . .'"

Then he got up and left. Not swimming this time, but walking briskly. No one could call him old. As he disappeared into the darkness, I realized the secret of his youth: he never spoke about death.

Time for the next thing! I went back hoping to have another drink. Sami and Çiğdem were waiting for me at the entrance of the terrace. A double obstacle between me and my drink! Had they seen me talking to Fındık? I went right up to them. Çiğdem spoke first: "W-what hap-pened? Why . . ."

I could tell from her stammering. She was going to ask why I was crying. "I was laughing," I said quickly. "Fındık always finds something funny to say."

"Come on, wash your face and come back. I want you to join us for dinner. Sit next to me."

I turned to Sami. He still had a long face, but for some reason he was nodding his head as if to encourage me. Dinner! I could turn it into an equation that was to my advantage. Dinner equals a table plus drink! "All right," I said, and turning to Çiğdem, "I'll sit wherever you want me to. Even on your lap."

They didn't laugh, and I stopped talking. Sami went off toward the terrace. Çiğdem waited next to me, as if she thought I was going to run away, until I'd washed my face. Then we went together to the front terrace. She'd applied her makeup with care. Did she want to seem attractive to the ill-intentioned young man who was after her?

I noticed him as soon as I turned the corner, from that repulsive smell of wealth. He was hefty, rather pretentious, in his thirties, and well dressed. I was face-to-face with someone whose personality was formed by the objects he owned, wore or carried on him. It seemed strange to me that he was wearing a jacket. But it wasn't his clothes, or his broad shoulders, or his glances that betrayed the shameless greed with which he devoured life that was interesting: his eyelids sagged down toward the corners of his eyes, turning them into two triangular holes. The trickster God had placed a sign saying he was dangerous right in the middle of his face. A hunter who gave himself away right from the start.

First I looked at the drinks, then at the people at the table. Apart from triangle eyes, Rana and Sami, there was also a young woman and a man at the table. "Cenk, Yücel and Sinem," someone pointed them out. Cenk was the ill-intentioned suitor; his was the only name I had to remember. Rana was looking attractive again, especially her breasts, most of which she had left exposed. And it looked like she was enjoying the proceedings the most. I was expecting her to call me Pavarotti. She didn't. As Çiğdem was sitting me next to her, she introduced me as her friend; she held my arm. I wasn't sure if it was because she was afraid, or because she wanted to provoke the hunter. When I sat down, instead of looking for an answer to this question, I started looking for a glass. Sami pushed a plate in front of me. I hurriedly bolted down a few things to keep him from grumbling so I'd be able to drink in peace. During the first glass, I listened in on what they were talking about. Rana and the newcomers kept talking about expensive objects. After a while, I gave up listening. They came from a world where price, not value, was important; they were speaking in shallow, feeble sentences that harbored no thoughts. I didn't actually know what I was doing there. It was strange, Sami letting me sit at the table with me being so close to losing my head and passing out.

They were speaking and I was drinking, trying not to attract attention to myself. You could say I was in good spirits. I wasn't looking at anyone; I didn't take my eyes off my glass, which was often empty. I thought about Fındık at one point. Was he going to dive like he'd promised? And if he was, then when? Did dolphins sleep? If they did, then how much? All sorts of questions like these, some I'd asked him before, some I hadn't, came to mind. And at one point I heard voices. First Spot's barking, and then that woman's shrill screams mingled with the barking. And then that silence that crumpled and rustled like paper. When I looked up, I found everyone at the table looking at me. "I guess you didn't hear what I asked," someone was saying.

It was the ill-intentioned hunter. It'd be wrong to say I wasn't surprised because his voice, in contrast to his appearance, was soft, melodic even. But there was a threatening glimmer in his triangle eyes. What had I ever done to provoke him? "No, I didn't," I said, not mentioning the voices I had heard.

"I was asking you what you do apart from running a hotel. I mean, what line of work are you in?"

That was an easy question. "I drink regularly," I said. "That's my real job." Soon my head would be spinning. Maybe I'd see those lace curtains again. The hunter, like a gladiator preparing to deliver the final blow, circled and eyed the whole table before asking his next question: "And what made you go into that profession?"

Some of them sniggered, but as far as I was concerned it was a stupid question. "Is it really so important? Every drunkard has a reason, valid or not," I said.

"So you're a drunkard?"

As if he wanted to warn her about the man she'd sat next to her, he directed his barbed glances at the empress.

"Well done!" I reached for the glass and turned to Rana. "And in my spare time I sing marches. Isn't that so?"

Rana gave a sharp, cautionary laugh. Çiğdem looked worried for some reason. But we were having fun, and we were drinking. I still hadn't told them I was a receptionist in a brothel. Suddenly, as if throwing down a challenge, Rana turned to the hunter. "Actually, Kuzey is a writer."

I turned to Sami. Bastard! So he'd told them that too? Or had I told them . . . Of course, I couldn't remember. The woman whose voice I'd been trying to suppress since yesterday kept screaming, and she was making me confused.

"Oh! Really? I didn't realize we were sitting at the same table as someone special. How many books have you written?" I showed him with my hand. "None?" I nodded. Now it was triangle eyes' turn to laugh. "So that's why I haven't read you."

"A good writer doesn't want to be read, he wants to be memorized, like Nietzsche, who wrote in his own blood." I said, nicking İhsan Hoca's expression. Sami shifted in his seat. He was beginning to get annoyed too. "But it's not because I'm anemic that I don't write."

"So why don't you then?"

"Unlike Rimbaud or Baudelaire, who had monsters for mothers, mine was a good woman."

"So you need a bad mother to be a writer?"

It was the other girl who said that; she had triangle eyes too. Maybe the alcohol had relaxed the muscles in her eyelids. Or maybe

I was completely off my head. Was she his sister? As the silence drew on, the girl leaned forward, as if she wanted to remind me of her question.

"That's what they say," I offered helplessly. "But if you ask me, I'd say it wasn't so important. Because writers aren't born from the wombs of their mothers, but from the tips of their pens."

"Hmph . . ." snorted the girl. "Anyway, who's your favorite writer?"

"One that doesn't have a mother," I said. Everyone was looking intrigued now, even the boy whose name I'd forgotten. "The most famous creator." I emptied my glass down my throat. Çiğdem was still holding my arm even though she knew it made the hunter angry. "God," I said finally.

"God?" It was Rana asking. I nodded. She was surprised. "Fine, but why on earth should God be a writer?"

"I guess He's got a lot to say. Besides, he knows people well. And as luck would have it, he's a bestseller, the inventor of popular culture. The Torah, the Bible, the Qur'an . . . Can you think of another writer whose books sell as well as His do?"

No one laughed. They must have been scared off by the Writer God. Taking advantage of the surprise, I refilled my glass. The ill-intentioned suitor said, "He's crazy," once I was halfway through the glass.

"I told you so."

I didn't turn to Rana the snitch. I was looking at the hunter, who in the end had decided to break out of his cocoon of politeness. His impertinence, bolstered by his physical strength, must have made him giddy. That's what it would have done to me if I'd been as strong as him. I grinned. He gritted his teeth. He must have wanted to smash my face in. Maybe he was going to. As he opened his lips, I preempted both him and the woman who'd been screaming inside my head for the past few minutes. "Anyway, what do you do?"

He didn't reply immediately. First he scrutinized the girl sitting next to him, then the young man who wasn't taking part in the conversation, and finally Rana, with an expression alerting them to listen to what he was going to say. Like all self-centered people, he needed an audience. The disdain, peculiar to rich fools, that was on his lips had emerged from its hiding place, and come out into the open. He stank of wealth now. If I could have been quick enough, I'd have sworn at him. But everything had slowed down. The man said, "I'm in the private sector."

The private sector! I guess I knew what that meant. "Does that mean you work with your father and earn his money?"

A silence pregnant with lots of things filled the air. Rana, who was having the most fun of all of us, acted as midwife. She answered the question I'd asked triangle eyes, smiling as if her own beauty was being described: "Cenk's vice president in the family business his father set up."

And another blow to the daddy's boy hunter came from Çiğdem. "But his real job is collecting expensive cars."

"Singly or in pairs?" I asked. There was a word that I somehow couldn't get off the tip of my tongue. But I continued with the cars. "I suppose you don't get them all the same color, do you?"

This time everyone laughed. But even amid the laughter, I could hear the woman's screams. My head was spinning. I looked at Çiğdem. She was determined to put the hunter in his place. "One stormy night last winter, behind Büyük Ada over there, Kuzey saved fourteen drowning refugees. He's a hero. Whoever you ask will . . ."

So! She too had heard the woman who'd been hiding somewhere behind my ear for months? *It could have been fifteen people.* That's what I was going to say. But I met the woman's imploring, begging gaze.

Just as I was going to say I didn't know, I found myself repeating the screams of the woman returning to the boat: "Binti, binti . . ." I had to go after her.

It wasn't Fındık holding my arm and preventing me from jumping, it was Çiğdem. I looked around in surprise. We weren't on the sea—we were on the terrace. Then I think hugged Çiğdem. My tongue was bleeding, but finally I was free of that barbed word.

Çiğdem Boran, August 3, 2004:

"Then he hugged me and started crying. It was strange, very strange. In several different ways. I was in shock . . . Think about it, there's a grown man crying in your arms . . . that was a shock in itself, but what was really surprising was that I was touching someone. It must have been years since I'd hugged someone. His tears were falling onto my arms, my legs; there was blood seeping from his mouth, and on top of all that, he was sobbing, 'Binti, binti . . .' For a moment we all stood there frozen. The only one who moved, the only one who was alive, was Kuzey. Then Sami tried to get up from where he was sitting. He was embarrassed; I stopped him. I had my hand on Kuzey's head. I was trying to calm him down . . . At first I thought he was saying 'please' in German. When we put him to bed, Sami told me what he'd been saying. It turns out it was 'binti,' which I learned means 'my daughter' in Arabic. Here's how the story ends: apparently, the night he saved the refugees, the last Iraqi they took out from the water was a woman, a mother in her thirties. Once she was on the boat, she took a look around; then, she started wailing, 'my daughter, my daughter' for a few seconds and looked at Kuzey before throwing herself back into the dark, stormy sea once more . . .

"Sami said that Kuzey blamed himself for not jumping into the sea after her. It was actually Fındık who stopped him. So you see, that was the kind of man Kuzey Erkil—who was crying in my arms that night—was. It's surprising, isn't it, how his desire to blame himself was out of all proportion? It's impossible that anyone who didn't know the victim well could be more upset than Kuzey was . . . I'll say it again: if you didn't actually know him, it would be very difficult to believe someone like him could exist. And it was difficult to understand him. The next day, he said that being known as a hero made him laugh, and that his life consisted of a long, drawn-out apology. He was always apologizing to people . . . That's it! This is what he said: 'I'm sorry . . .' And that must be why he went out to sea that night in the storm . . . Why was he always apologizing? Neither he nor Sami gave me a clear answer to that question. 'Disbelief in our species: if we were human, we could have found many reasons to apologize to others . . .' His words. The real reason though, I think, is something to do with a secret event, with a death, in his past. He caused someone's death . . . No, actually, he probably killed some-one . . . It was difficult to believe, or rather, I didn't want to believe it. What would you have done if it had been you? But when Mücella said she'd heard Kuzey talking in his sleep . . . I asked Handan too. She didn't want to say either; she looked away.

"After putting him to bed, I came back to the terrace and threw them all out, Rana included. When Sami joined me, his eyes were puffy. The poor thing, he was feeling everyone's pain. I didn't look at his face at all that night because I didn't want to embarrass him. No, I didn't cry. I was full of anger . . . Sami told me about Şafak and Spot. He thinks Kuzey's memory is to blame; he was complaining that his closest friend—actually he said his comrade—couldn't forget the past. 'A life that we haven't been able to decant into memories! That's the heaviest burden to carry,' he was saying, and I had no place, not even on the peripheries of that life. Their world was so far from me that I didn't actually want to have any place in it. It wasn't that world I wanted, it was the actors in that world, and especially Kuzey . . .

"I learned of Kuzey's existence for the first time the autumn before. October 2002. About nine or ten months before going to Karaburun to find him, in other words. It was after I'd come back from San Francisco, I think. My grandmother told me the story the evening we buried my grandfather; I realized she was trying to protect my mother—drunk at the time and snoozing in bed. Our family's wealth goes back to Karamanlı İsmail Efendi. That is, to my grandfather's father. My mother's an only child like me. Yes, you could say I have de facto control of the companies today . . . My mother? She spends most of her time either abroad or passed out in bed. She's never been able to focus her attention on anything; it's only directed at herself . . . I haven't spent a lot of time with her. I mean, we didn't live together. For the last ten years she and my father were separated. I was generally with him. Two years ago, at my grandfather's insistence, they tried to make a go of things one last time . . . It was dramatic because it resulted in my father's death. A heart attack. Poor man, he spent years working with my grandfather; he was his right-hand man, so much so that people used to think he was my grandfather's son, not his son-in-law. Besides, he only married my mother because of pressure from my grandfather. Karamanlı Hasan Bey must have thought he could use the young, handsome, up-and-coming engineer he had at his disposal to keep his feckless daughter reined in . . . It was my father who made it possible for the company to shift from textiles, to ready-to-wear, to a recognized brand. He's the one who brought the business to where it is today. He spent his whole life chasing the empty dream of winning his wife's love, of making her fall in love with him. Even though he deserved someone so much better, he wasted his life on a woman who didn't appreciate him. But how handsome he was! How can people be so blind?

"Yes, when people asked me, I generally used to say I was unhappy. But it wasn't until I got to know Kuzey that I realized my unhappiness was so shallow you couldn't even drown in it . . .

"Of course you can ask . . . Was I in love with my father? That's a very silly question. What makes you ask?

"I saw Kuzey's back that evening. His wounds and those deep

scars . . . The next day, when he noticed I was looking at it as he was going into the sea, he said, 'I've summarized my life, and recorded it on my back.' Because his life was boring, he said, this was the easiest way—he didn't have to waste time explaining things. It was a scary sight and it set your imagination going . . . when you looked at his back, you could see that the man before you belonged to different kind of life—one that was foreign to you. And you know what was strange? For someone like that to turn into someone who needed protecting in bed . . . No, quite the opposite, it made him more attractive, in my opinion. In some men, weakness can be attractive. A strong man possesses you; but a weak man, *you* possess *him*. I understood that that night, in the wee small hours when I went down to his room to check on him. No, of course not. I had no intention of sleeping with him or anything like that. Even if I had, it wouldn't have been possible anyway. There was a well-built woman sleeping next to him. Sami said it was Erica. She left early the next morning. If I'd seen her, I'd have asked her if Kuzey was talking in his sleep . . .

"He told me I was a narcissist. Do you know why narcissists fall in love with themselves? 'So the suffering of life can't touch them . . . When your existence comes into contact with life, if pain is produced instead of pleasure, then it's a defective narcissism . . .' That's why he had to drink. So pleasure could be produced instead of pain. But still, I can't think of him as one of those dissolute men who loves women two-by-two, you know—one of those men who becomes carnivorous in middle age and keeps hunting for new flesh. It might be cruel to say so, but pain and sorrow suited him. In August, he used to sit on that bare hillock on Küçük Ada for such a long time that you could watch his shadow draw a broad arc around him, like the hands of a clock. I'll never forget his sorrow . . .

"Ah yes, I wonder what you'll make of this definition: 'A nomad is

someone who can't spend summer and winter in the same place . . .'
I think he was talking about himself. How can someone who's lived in
the same place for years feel like a nomad? Only if the seasons change
in his head. Of course, I thought very highly of him. Ever since that
strange night I discovered and read what he'd written. When I spoke
with him about Şafak, he told me, 'Love is the troubled adolescence
of our soul.' Do you remember, that's what I told you the first day
we met as well. I never saw him looking as young again as he did at
that moment. Could he have fallen in love again? No! 'If you're seeking belief, it means you're without belief. And if you're seeking love,
it means you'll never fall in love . . . Because if you've been in love,
you'd never attempt it again . . .' Do you think someone who said
these things would ever have fallen in love again?

"I've never been interested in politics. But I tried to understand
him. 'A vast darkness dripped onto our lives . . .' That's what Sami
said. We were on the terrace, and Kuzey was two hundred yards
away, motionless on top of the island looking out toward Mordoğan.
When had this darkness descended onto their lives? When he started
to think he'd lost his *raison d'être*? When he realized that the revolution he'd fought for in the deserts would never happen? 'Only the
build-up to war is romantic. When people can still be divided up into
women and men. After that, gender goes. They all turn into people
who've fought or who've experienced war . . .' We spoke about war.
Out of all we spoke about, that's what sticks in my mind the most.
And I asked how he could fight, if he was afraid. It was as if he didn't
know: 'The more danger there is, the more courage there is too, I
guess,' he once muttered. 'No one can face death for you. Courage is
the steadfastness we show when that time comes . . .' Have you ever
met anyone who defined courage like that?

"If you're asking me how I would describe him, I'd say he was like the horizon. You could see him, you could watch him, you could even fall under his spell, but you couldn't get close to him, you couldn't be with him . . .

"Do I express myself any differently? Perhaps. It'll be from talking about Kuzey, from repeating the things he said."

From the diary of an itinerant drunkard, page 41:

"Dawn[11] is immortal, dawn is immortal . . ."
—Ruben Dario, "Swans"[12]

". . . And a black swan said: 'Night announces day.' / And a white one said: 'Dawn is immortal, dawn is immortal!'" I loved her in the morning, I loved her at noon, but most of all I loved her in the evening. I loved her yesterday, I love her today, I shall love her even more tomorrow—if I have a tomorrow. We were not like waters that converged; we were like waters that mixed together. To whoever said our meeting was chance, I would say, I would scream it was necessity . . . right until God poked His nose into our business . . . After that, I chewed up and swallowed my screams; I silenced them. She was the golden cloud on the horizon. And me? A drunkard, a drunk who puts his faith in the direction,[13] not the road . . . Who said drunkenness is a loss of honor and memory? If the lakes were made of alcohol, and if I drank all of them, I would still be ready for the big reunion. I have a date with a sparkling shadow waiting for me between the white rose branches. I can see, feel everything: somewhere in the distance, trumpets that only the two of us can hear will be playing. Even if they are not in season, the scent of the narcissi shall intoxicate us. I shall sniff her out; in one hand roses, in the other, laurel leaves . . . When I find her, I shall sever myself from myself, and mingle with her nothingness . . . The sun will sink into the water like a drop of blood from God's wound falling into the sea . . .

A sinister sky hangs over my head. I am ready, for everything . . .

---

[11] A reference to Şafak

[12] "Cisnes"

[13] A reference to Kuzey, perhaps

So, who is going to judge God?

"... And a black swan said: 'Night announces day.' / And a white one said: 'Dawn is immortal, dawn is immortal!'"

CHAPTER III

One always walks toward young women in the same way;
with the same hope, with the same anxiety; with the same need
for eternity . . .

—Jorge Semprún, *La Montagne Blanche*

July 2003:

Will I die today? When will God show me some mercy and let me migrate to those golden coasts where no ship passes, where no bird flies? I'm in a hurry because I've given my word about the big reunion. It's nonsense—once you've set sail for the darkness inside your soul—to wait, come what may, for old age so you can die. Why shouldn't we die when our bodies are young? If the idea is to prepare a suitable cover for death, it's a meaningless waste of effort . . . What is death if not unadulterated and absolute sleep? If I'd been an animal, I'd have wanted to be an eagle. And not because I wanted to fly. Have you ever seen an old eagle? Like I say, I'm in a hurry . . .

"Get up!" It was Sami again, it was morning again, and I was sobering up again. The noise got past the eagle soaring at the tips of my eyelashes, and re-echoed at the end of the labyrinth. "The chairman's on his way." I opened my eyes. The chairman? "The chairman of the local council," said Sami.

Outside, the cicadas were singing in a frenzy. Noon! Why noon? "Is he staying for lunch?" I grumbled.

Sami nodded. He was alone, and he looked tired, as if he'd been on his feet a long time. "He did make a point of saying on the phone that he really missed our aubergine salad."

"Bingo," I said. "Aubergine puree makes a good carrier for poison."

He didn't laugh. So I took the opportunity to address that difficult question I ask myself every morning when I awake: can I get up? I haphazardly examined my body. I could move my feet, but there was a thick film in my throat, and I couldn't swallow. And there was an insidious pain trying to burrow its way into the back of my neck.

"Let me do the talking," said Sami. "It wouldn't be very clever to rub him the wrong way at the moment. We owe more than eight hundred million lira in unpaid water bills. He could have us cut off tomorrow if he wanted."

I was willing to forego water. "Let him see what poisoning a dog really means. If anything happens to Spot, I'm going to hang that bastard by the balls from Hisarcık Kayası. That is if he has any balls . . ."

Sami was looking at me as if he thought I really would hang him. That made me feel better. "He'll more than likely tell us to keep our distance from Handan and the association."

"And he should keep his distance from dogs," I said. If I had a couple of sips, maybe I'd be able to get up. Sami had nothing to do with the question or the answer. He avoided my eyes when I tried to look at him. "Did I make a fool of myself again?" He nodded. "Who did I hurt this time? Çiğdem?"

It wasn't Çiğdem, I could tell from his eyes: his glance had lost its intensity. He reached out his hand and stroked my hair. So it was even more serious. "You," he said after a long time. "Actually, it's always yourself you hurt."

Empty rhetoric! I can't hurt myself because I don't have an existence: I'm a nothing. But to get him to take his hand away, "Don't worry, I'm thick-skinned," I said. "Anyway, you can go now . . . I'm going to get up."

He still had a sheepish look in his eye. He knew I'd start drinking as soon as he left the room, and he'd probably found the gin as he was putting me to bed last night. He didn't object, as if it would hurt me more if he took the bottle away from me. If it would make it easier for me to find drink, I wouldn't mind getting hurt every day, actually.

"Erica came very late," he said. "She dropped in to say good-bye. She said she was going back to Germany with the man who fell ill . . ." As if revealing a secret, he added in a low voice, "She stayed until morning."

I put my hands up. "Nothing happened," I said.

He gave a faint smile for the first time that day. But it wasn't because I was admitting I was impotent. "Things are looking up. We've just taken a reservation for one week. Two people, full board. A couple from Ankara. They said they might stay longer if they like it here."

He had a naive optimism. This time, I didn't say it was too late. Weren't we believers in the future? For a moment I thought about asking him if he'd seen Fındık, but that would only draw out the conversation, so I didn't bother. As the silence continued, he turned and went. As soon as he was gone, I took the gin out from underneath the pillow, and poured it down my throat. The fireball slid down my gullet and into my stomach. I gulped; when I could tell that the film in my throat was torn, I suppressed the pain in the back of my neck and stood up. I slowly made my way to the bathroom—without staggering—and got in the shower. I hadn't seen Spot for three days now . . . My heart sank. After standing there for five minutes without moving, without thinking about anything, I turned off the water. As soon as the noise of the water stopped, the racket from outside filled the room, just like cold replacing heat. It was as Fındık had said: the pepper tree had turned into an open-air brothel. Hundreds of insects repeating a lustful chorus.

I approached the hand-washing basin. Was it the face of someone who'd been hurt or was it a nomad's face in the mirror? I didn't know, but it was a desperate face: a face that was desperate to know if Spot was dead or not, if Fındık had dived or not. I put the bottle back underneath the pillow and straightened out the bedclothes. There was a rose in the vase on the bedside table. Erica's signature. A woman polite enough to thank a man who couldn't make love to her when she lay next to him . . . I'd never been able to give her what she deserved.

Just as I was about to walk out the door, I went back and had a bit more gin. The bottle had gotten a lot lighter; that was bad news. I stretched. I'd turned out to be in thrall to a God who was withholding death from me.

As soon as I set foot on the terrace, Mücella intercepted me. The tray she'd been carrying was on the bench in reception, and she was looking sullen as if she'd been waiting for a long time. "Çiğdem Hanım is beneath the pergola," she said.

"Have you seen Fındık?"

From the way she recoiled, shaking her head, you'd think I'd mentioned the devil. Then we walked, me in front, Mücella carrying the tray behind me. Çiğdem was drinking coffee beneath the dark shadow that fell to the ground like a stain. She was alone. When she saw me approach, she stood up and kissed me on the cheek like that was what she did every morning. She'd become my friend without telling me; I was surprised. The shadow of the pole had descended down the wall and receded to the base. "Good afternoon," I said.

"Well done, it's ten past twelve . . ." She was looking at her wrist. "Will you have your breakfast with me?" Without replying, I sat down across from her. I was going to have a bit of fruit and cheese and bread anyway. The grapes were sour and the watermelon was too sweet, so I turned to the bread. Three minutes later, when I signaled to Mücella for her to take the tray away, Çiğdem intervened. "You haven't eaten a thing."

I'd eaten enough for me to have a cigarette. She didn't want one. I could feel that an awkward silence—for both of us—was going to settle between us. "Your friends don't seem to be around," I said.

"They've gone," she said immediately. "And Rana went with them."

She didn't say anything else. And I didn't ask. The harshness in her voice revealed how they'd left. When the silence, in contrast to the shrinking shadows, started lengthening, I said, "You don't go in the sea very much."

"I was waiting for you," she said. "I thought we could go for a little boat trip around the islands." Ignoring the silence, I didn't say if I'd take her or not. There was something strange about her, something I couldn't quite put my finger on. "There, you're going back into your shell again."

"The chairman of the local council will be here soon . . ." And I told her what I planned to do. "I'm probably going to poison him." She gave a sharp laugh; the cicadas shut up for a moment as if they'd had water sprinkled on them. Without bringing up the whole thing about hanging him from Hisarcık Kayası, "Or maybe I'll just rough him up," I added when she said nothing.

"Is he pressuring you?"

"We owe money to anything that moves, to every official body," I said. "The taxman, the local council . . ."

She gave me a look that seemed to say she'd never borrowed money in her life, and had never been chased away by debtors. Just as I was about to crack a joke, she suddenly turned serious. She tensed her lips like a bow whenever she became serious.

"I think the time has finally come." Before I could ask what it was time for, she continued in a voice that warned me to accept what she was going to say without arguing: "I spoke with Sami yesterday: I want to take over a half share in the Karayel Hotel. In return for that, I'll put up the necessary working capital for the coming period, and I'll pay off all your debts. The taxman, the market, the staff— you won't have a single penny of debt. Oh, and the local council of course."

Half the hotel! I knew I ought to say something, but to do that,

I first had to pick my jaw up from the floor. Finally, half-heartedly, I said, "You're talking about at least seventy billion. You do realize that, don't you?"

"It could be as much as eighty-five, even ninety," she said.

Her tone of voice had changed; it had turned into the self-assured, commanding tone of wealth. I tried to close my mouth again. It was no use. My jaw kept dangling downward, like someone was hanging from it. In the end, I had to prop it closed with my hand. I was thinking. Actually, I didn't really need to think that much, for the conclusion I was going to reach was clear: what she was saying was meaningless, and I should forget about it.

"Why on earth would you do something like that? Wait four months, and buy the whole hotel from the taxman for half that money." I could have continued, but without beating around the bush got into what was truly annoying me. "Besides, Sami doesn't have the title deeds for the Karayel, I do."

"I know. And there's no need for you to get angry. I spoke to him first to find out how I should make you the offer, how I should approach you."

So it was the hotel she'd been after all along? "First winemaking courses, then looking at land for a vineyard . . . Excuses a fool like me would believe . . ." After grumbling a bit, I started thinking again. So why? Why would someone like Çiğdem think of spending so much money on someone she'd only known for a grand total of three days? "Are you a fairy godmother? Or are we sitting on top of a gold mine we don't know about?"

"I'm not a fairy godmother and there's no gold beneath the hotel . . ."

She was about to reveal who or what she was, but just then Sami and the chairman turned up. As soon as I saw Sami with that man who sweated continually whatever the weather, my stomach clenched itself like a fist. It had been three years since he was elected, and I hadn't liked him since day one. While thinking, he'd screw his face up in pain; while speaking, he'd strain as if he was giving birth. Which explained why he produced a maximum of one idea per year.

I looked first at Çiğdem, then at Sami, and then I stood up. I didn't look at the chairman at all. I had a terrible stomach; if I stayed, I'd be sick. "The hotel's yours," I said to Sami. "Sell it, blow it up, do whatever you want with it."

I was wasting time. What business did a man who was trying to die have with them? And I wasn't even curious. Not about anything: not Çiğdem's strange interest, not Sami scheming behind my back, not what the fool who'd come to finish off our aubergine salads wanted . . . I left the three of them alone with the fate of the hotel and went to the kitchen. The cupboard was open. I took three beers. Spot! I wondered about him, and, of course, about when I would die.

I walked toward Bodrum, and disregarding the midday heat, walked around for a bit in the scrubland I'd almost flown into the night before. In this heat, there were no living creatures in the bushes apart from a confused snake looking for a field mouse and two frogs trying to mate. In the end I went out to the road, sat down on a bench and opened a beer. Foça was directly opposite, shimmering—half of it had been erased—behind the heat rising into the air. I kept my head in the sun, on the off chance my brain would evaporate and my body would merge with the nothingness inside me. The end of pain! There was a question somewhere in my mind, but I couldn't get it to crystallize. I closed my eyes . . .

I didn't open them again until a hand touched me on the shoulder. Just as a shepherd can distinguish one sheep from among a thousand in the flock, I recognized whose hand it was immediately. It wasn't her voice that gave her away, it was her smell: "You'll roast!" Handan! "I looked out from the house and said to myself, who this madman sitting under the sun."

I was mad, but I was submissive. I took the bag with the beer, and got up, holding the hand she proffered. The house she lived in with her nephew was on top of Delikli Burun. Hand in hand, we quickly—apart from a break of about ten seconds or so for me to finish my beer—walked along the narrow road toward the sea. As we got closer to the shore, the air got cooler. In a few minutes we were on her roofed balcony. Here the sea breeze was strong enough to blow the tablecloth off the plastic table in the middle and onto the ground. On the windowsills facing onto the balcony, there were flowerpots with cheery basil plants growing in them arranged side by side. And the freestanding binoculars Handan used like glasses to observe the surroundings all day long were at the right-hand side of the balcony. Was that how she'd seen me?

When she went inside to wash her face, I put the bag with the two beers underneath the wicker chair, picked up the tablecloth and spread it on the table. In Bodrum, two speedboats pulling water-skiers, one at the tip of the cape, the other close to the shore, were making diamond patterns in the cove.

Handan returned with a tray of fruit. I was going to say I didn't want any, but when I noticed from the way she was looking at it that she'd brought it for herself, I kept quiet. "So, what's new?"

I started with the first piece of news: "I'm getting rid of the hotel. There's a buyer, but I'm giving it to Sami. He can do what he wants with it." Handan sat down, flexing the wicker chair. She had her back to the breeze. She didn't seem surprised or concerned. Or . . . "Did you know about it?" I asked.

She nodded. "I bumped into Sami yesterday morning . . ."—and instead of calling the town, which couldn't have been more than fifty meters above sea level, "town," she called it "up top"—"up top, in the market. He told me about the project when he introduced the girl he had with him."

Project! I took a beer from underneath the chair. "You know, it turns out I never knew Sami at all."

She waited a moment before swallowing the watermelon in her mouth. She seemed oblivious to how angry I was. "So you don't know him?" I shook my head stubbornly. "Let me remind you then: first off, he's a very good person."

Why on earth was she getting agitated? "His goodness is just like badness," I said. "It's like a punch that floors you."

She shook her hand. "What you don't realize is that most friends don't drag you into their own lives; instead, they seep into your life, right to the furthest recesses. And that's why we know our friends so little when they're very close to us . . ." I looked at her. She must have thought a lot about friendship. "The beautiful one or the dominant one in a friendship generally doesn't really know the other one . . ."

As soon as she'd said beautiful, I understood: she was a Sami too. She offered me the tray; I shook my head. "Why do you think she wants to be a partner in a hotel that's doing so badly?"

Seeing she was swallowing it without having divided it up, she was going to eat all the watermelon on the tray. "Who knows?" she said. "Maybe she's taken a shine to you."

I laughed. "What? When she first clapped eyes on me?" I drank half of my beer, and I chuckled again. "Who actually believes in love at first sight?" She didn't say anything; she just looked at me. Into my eyes, right into their depths. I thought of telling her not to look at me like that, but she would anyway. I put my beer down on the ground. And I was shaking my head. "You're wrong," I said. "What happened between me and Şafak was different . . ."

I didn't say anything else. I waited for Handan to say it was different too. It was pointless. My cheeks were being finely cut with a razor blade dipped in salt. Handan reluctantly got up and went inside again. When she came back, she had a tissue in her hand. "Here."

As I was about to take the lavender-scented tissue she was offering me, I changed my mind. If I felt like crying, what was the point in stopping myself? I didn't, and next to the only woman I could cry in front of without feeling uncomfortable, I cried my eyes out for a while. We didn't embrace each other like we did that evening five years ago. We both made do with less: she with stroking my head, and me with her touch. She had only fallen in love in childhood; she was a woman who'd never grown up, and yet the curious respect she showed to those in love was humbling.

"I should have fallen in love with a woman like you," I said.

She shook her head. When the subject was love, she was as cruel as an evil goddess. So as soon as I began to speak in Şafak's words, her anger surfaced. "You never really fall in love. Because you're not possessive. But that's what you need most for love . . ."

Was she right? Perhaps. A man who was possessive, who'd do anything for love . . . If that was what was important for women, I wasn't like that. Drunk or sober. Who would have thought I'd be a man whose life story would be told in women? And what about her? Why had she never married? I hazarded a guess at the answer. A man can live happily with a woman he isn't in love with, but a woman can't. I cried a bit more, and then asked that question, the question I couldn't coax out when I was sitting on the bench: "If God commits murder, how can we ever judge him?"

"Don't talk such nonsense," she said. But she looked at me as if she knew I wasn't talking nonsense. Maybe she remembered admitting I was right that night as I rebelled in her breast. "God's not to blame. He only brought you together; the rest was up to you."

"And is that what he always does?" I asked. Handan shook her head. She was determined not to get involved in God's business. And I changed the subject. "That bastard chairman of the local council is at the hotel just now, but we won't stop supporting you. I'm going to talk to Sami . . . the association can meet at the hotel whenever it wants."

She looked at me indecisively for a moment. Then she gave the second surprising piece of news: "Thanks, but Çiğdem's going to make a donation to the association . . . so we can hire somewhere else if you want."

What could I say? "She's using her money to get her hooks into everyone," I said eventually. "Don't you see that?"

Her shoulders twitched slightly; even if she did could see it, she didn't seem to care. "I guess you're the one she wants to get her hooks into." I greedily downed the bottle of beer. Handan was determined to ignore my anger. She deftly changed the subject. "What were you doing in the scrub in this heat?"

Should I tell her? She was still gazing at me. If she hadn't been, I wouldn't have told her. "I was looking for Spot," I said. "He's hiding somewhere out there."

She reached for the final slice of watermelon. She was shaking her head. "I'm telling you, that dog you were throwing stones at the other day wasn't Spot."

She'd seen me through her binoculars. "It *was* Spot," I said. "Don't you think I'd recognize the dog that slept at my feet for three whole years?"

"It's been almost two years now since he ran away."

"He couldn't stand the smell of alcohol," I said. "I did treat him well. I didn't so much as flick him. I threw stones at him because . . ."

She put her fork down on the tray and stood up. "All right, that's enough . . . No one said you treated him badly."

She was right next to me, and she was pulling my head toward her stomach. Instead of telling her Spot was my witness, proof that I loved Şafak, I told her why I was crying: "I'd promised her . . . I'd look after Spot until he died . . ."

"You know what's wearing you out so much?" I turned my head from side to side, and it sank into her stomach like a corkscrew. "You're trying to seem worse than you are . . ."

I couldn't see her face, but if I had been able to, I was sure I'd have seen her looking at me as if to say, *What am I going to do with you?* She was right. And I didn't know what I was going to do with myself either. Someone who hasn't been able to come to a decision about himself, someone who's looking for his destiny! Wasn't that what tragedies were all about?

"You know, just as I'm telling myself you're nothing but a drunk, demented, good for nothing, and I'll have nothing more to do with you, you go and pull a rabbit out of your hat, and all of a sudden you're a knight in shining armor or a hero . . ." Her plump stomach was as soft as her breasts. Even though she'd been sweating, how did she manage to smell so much like a flower? "In actual fact you're really sensitive, to the point where it becomes unbearable . . ."

As she moved her body from side to side like a cradle, my head too went to the left, then to the right, then back again. "Actually, I'm a really crappy guy," I said. "I'm good at pulling the wool over people's eyes."

"It's not your manliness that's crappy, it's your goodness. You've got a naive, poignant goodness that shames and enrages whomever you're with because they're not as good as you are . . . We're all forced to love you! What on earth can anyone do apart from love you?"

I laughed; it might have been strange for me to laugh while I was crying, but I continued laughing. "Do you think God has condemned me to be good then? It must be the greatest punishment you can be given: always to have to suffer the consequences of being good. That's what Sami says—that I'm the one who proves him wrong."

She took a step back. She wanted to look at my face. Or maybe at my eyes. "You know what your problem is, don't you?" She knew. "You don't know how to age gracefully . . . God has actually punished you with eternal youth." Maybe she was right. "Is it possible to think of you as a father, sitting by yourself in a corner without interfering with anyone, without saving the world?" My eyes must have told her that it wasn't. "Are you still going to testify?" I nodded. "There are people who say it's a stupid thing to do. The bastards will get off one way or another."

"I've got a logical reason." I told her what it was: "Seeing I can't die, I may as well make myself useful."

I'd decided I was going to give the dirty bastard hell—whoever abandoned the sinking boat as I was looking into the eyes of the woman wailing "binti, binti . . ." I was going to avenge that little girl whose face I'd never seen, whose name I'd never known . . . I swore I would. I could have told her that, but I didn't.

Handan said, "Everyone says they're dangerous," as if she wanted to make me change my mind.

"Anyway, Fındık is going to testify too. I can't leave him on his own on dry land for long," I said. "He forgets how to walk."

She was going to laugh, but went back to the tray on the table without changing the expression on her face. "Aren't you afraid?"

"If everywhere's hell for you, why should you be afraid of death?" She stopped talking as if she had finally grasped why I was without fear. The sea breeze was stronger now, and like a sickle was lopping off the peaks of the waves that it swept along. Before long, the channel would be trimmed as white as snow. "Have you seen Fındık?" I asked. "Yesterday or today?"

"How am I going to see him?" I looked over to her binoculars. She threw up her hands. "I've never encountered him on those rocks. I just hear him whistling from time to time, and it's such an annoying noise!" True, she wouldn't be able to see him because Fındık was whistling from the bottom of the sea. "Spot, Fındık . . . You do realize you're dealing with ghosts?"

I finished my beer, and she finished what was left of the fruit on the tray. Neither of us attempted to speak. As I was getting up, I asked her if she had any beer. She said she had a bottle left over from last week. For a moment, I also thought of asking her if she had a drug to make you dream, but I decided not to.

Ten minutes later I jumped from Delikli Burun into the sea. Everything I owned was in a plastic bag that I'd tied shut and hung around my neck: two beers, half a packet of cigarettes, shorts and a T-shirt; the T-shirt was covered in stains.

And the water was as hot as the air. If I could get to Küçük Ada, I'd apologize to Şafak for not being able to take care of Spot, for leaving him to the mercy of a sweaty man who had nothing better to do than run after free food. At first I was swimming comfortably. Once I was about fifty meters out, the waves crashing into my face made breathing more and more difficult. When I felt the burning salt in the water going down into my lungs through my nose, it did occur to me that drowning might be a good idea. But the beers made me change my mind. It would have been stupid to die without drinking them. Besides, Handan must have been watching me through her binoculars.

May 1998:

I don't eat, I don't drink, and I don't sleep . . . I only wait. Every day I wait for Şafak, for her suddenly to appear: in the morning on top of Foça, then the whole day at the top of the dusty road that goes down from Değirmen Dağı to Burgazardı. Waiting, thirsting for a woman whose hand I haven't held, whom I haven't kissed, whom I haven't slept with. For twenty-three days, that's what I've been doing resolutely, like an act of worship: and this waiting contains the dream of a passionate pleasure that more and more approaches obsession . . .

Diving in the deep sandbank about thirty meters out to sea off Küçük Ada, and bringing up seashells and—if I'm lucky—pen shells for her, without knowing if she'll ever come or not, or if I'll ever see her again, is part of this dream too. Every afternoon for two weeks, I've been sneaking precious pieces of this unique treasure—which I'd been content to watch since I discovered it last year—past their guardian, a large octopus, and stowing them in the cupboard in my room. Sami watches my waiting, my sleeplessness, my desperation— and, I daresay, my treasure hunting—and thinks I'm a fool. I can tell, not from what he says, but from how he looks at me. Only Spot, who sleeps at the foot of my bed at night, a white handful of cotton wool that's always at my feet, looks on me with unconditional friendship.

I enter the water from the edge of the shallows. In front of the sea breeze, the cold current licking around the island toward Delikli Burun slowly cools down my body, which has been heating up for hours under the sun like a piece of metal. I feel the heat leaving and being shed from my heels as if it's a skin. A few strokes bring me to the top of the sandbank. I stop when I can see the entire front of the black rock reminiscent of an eagle getting ready to take flight on the summit of Değirmen Dağı. There's a ten-meter body of salt water between me and the treasure. It's a ten-second journey to the bottom that extends from a pure blueness, to a bottle green interrupted by lines of white light, and then to a colorless darkness.

I take a deep breath and pivot at my waist in a somersault. I'm going to breathe out the air in my lungs as I descend, just as Fındık taught me; I'm going to copy how a dolphin empties its lungs. The first few meters are easy. Diving into the depths is like listening to Sibelius: it reminds you of the heart-rending sorrow of departing from life. Now, turning my head downward and making my way toward the bottom, I can understand, I can grasp Sami—and that he often thinks of death. I'm diving, but inside I'm full of life like never before.

It's a mess down there: the grains of sand whipped up from the bottom by the storm that blew all night long before subsiding mid-morning are still suspended in the last five meters. It's impossible for me to see the treasure while the water's so cloudy; I change my mind about going down to the bottom, and I return. The pressure in my ears eases off. And silently I come up to the surface.

As soon as I take a breath, I look at the hotel. There's a small red car in front of it; I try to push my heart, which has risen to my mouth, back down to where it should be: it's her! It's eleven o'clock; dawn is breaking for the second time, in the middle of the day . . .

Ten minutes later I'm with her. I find her at the garden gate waiting for me with Spot, her bag in her hand, as if she knew which direction I would come from. She's lost weight . . . But her eyes are the old eyes I know and remember. "Here I am," she says, when I reach her.

It's a long sentence that summarizes everything. I respond with a sentence as long as hers: "Here you are."

What if I give her a hug! No, that would be admitting to the yearning I couldn't extinguish, not even at the bottom of the sea. I lean forward to take her bag. She opens her arms and hugs me. That's what youth must be: to yield honestly.

* * *

It's night: we're inside. Outside the northeast wind's running riot, furiously attacking the mainland. It roves about the windows and the roof tiles trailed by a whistling, now descending to a low pitch, now climbing to a high pitch . . . Sami's in his room, descending into his womanless hell. I'm alone with Şafak in the lobby—Spot's in the corner snoozing—and we say nothing at all as we eat what Mücella has hurriedly prepared: the silence has practically gained an existence and is like a third person joining our meal. Only Spot, with whimpers of happiness, breaks the silence—which is full of promise, which is pregnant with so many things, which is almost palpable. As I look at her, I tremble with the pleasure of the kiss I haven't yet stolen from her lips. She doesn't look away; she'll give more than she takes; she doesn't realize it, but that's how she's looking at me.

As soon as the meal is over, the same silence separates us. She goes up to her room and I go outside, around the back. I light a cigarette; my face, my hand, and then the cigarette in my fingers are getting wet. That's surprising. Because there are no clouds to be seen. The wind, like a sword slashing open the saturated night, must be discharging its moisture. I exhale the smoke, which leaves its nicotine on my tongue, in my throat. The northeast wind obstinately winnows the stars toward the southwest like so much chaff. I'm face-to-face with a foreign sky. The Little Bear isn't where it normally is. It must have been swept behind the mountains like a floundering ship . . .

As I look at the sky, I'm thinking: I'll love her, I'll be with her, I'll become one with her, years later I'll wake up with her female smell . . .

On the border of the deep shadows, getting wet as I smoke, one after the other, I line up dreams that would make Sami, if he could hear them, tell me I was getting old. Maybe he's right: I am dreaming. But isn't the threshold of old age when we need dreams the most?

"You'll get wet." I turn around. She's behind me, at the door, with Spot. She looks like an angel: a strange being from a distant heaven. "Come here," she says. I walk over and stand right in front of her. "What are we trying to resist? What are we trying to fight?"

It's not a question; it's a definite decision. She's spoken to herself upstairs and come to let me know the outcome. She won't resist! I should warn her! *You're willfully nestling in the bosom of disaster, aware of the consequences; it's like climbing to the crater of a volcano. That's what your coming here again means . . .* That's what I should say. But only a single phrase comes from my lips: "I don't know."

She reaches out a steady hand. Everything's so clear: she's not giving me her hand; she's giving me herself. My indecision doesn't last long. I walk after her, clinging to her hand, her, her existence and our future. Spot blesses our union with little yelps of joy. We go up the stairs, we enter her room, where the lamp on the wooden bedside table pushed flush with the bed radiates a cool dimness. Inside there's a hushed passion separating the two of us from the fabric of time. I can feel it. This time, I hug her. It's the most highly charged moment of my life; it contains everything: hope, hopelessness, desire, fear . . . Am I going to be able to handle it all?

Her skin is warm and balmy with the scent of flowers. Her hands aren't shaking, but her body's shimmering like a candle flame. She's shorter than me. I'm going to kiss her. I'm leaning forward: her face full of promises and pure lips. She's not going to hide anything from me . . . That thought makes me uneasy. Am I strong enough to get to know someone, a woman no less, as she really is?

Her breath dispels my indecision. Our lips come together, not like two mouths coming together, but like two hands coming together: groping for each other, holding each other tightly. I'm startled. In her eyes, her passion is set free, unbound like a pair of hands . . . It's a shame! Her whole life will be spent loving men who'll bring her sorrow . . . If nothing else, I should tell her that. Just as I open my mouth, "Wait," she says.

As I wait in silence, she gets undressed, without embarrassment, almost without taking her eyes off mine at all. She must have gotten undressed in front of me before, rehearsed it in her mind. From beneath the clothes she leaves on top of the bed, a surprise slowly appears: a curved, provocative body that's more feminine than I'd thought. This discovery spreads a sexual pleasure whose existence I'd long forgotten to my loins. She remains motionless, and I realize it's my turn. I'm embarrassed. At any another time, my embarrassment would make me laugh, but now my teeth are chattering. I must never have thought I'd get undressed in front of her.

When I take my T-shirt off, she touches my scars. Her fingers are full of curiosity, not pity. But she doesn't ask. We hug each other again; we're naked this time. In her body, which she doesn't withhold, which she offers generously, there are two seasons: her feet are cold, but her breasts are warm. We help each other into bed. We don't dally; we're impatient. We have to rid ourselves of the tension that's been ratcheting up for days. That's the only thing on my mind. Outside, the northeast wind is going crazy. I'm trying to kiss her and caress her; I'm hopeless. "Stop, let me," she says.

She does whatever is necessary. I watch her. Then that moment comes. I become the dart of lust and enter her. Before long, the pleasure that has been fermenting in my loins rises and gushes out.

I should be ashamed I couldn't wait for her. But I say nothing, withdrawing into a silence without shame. In spite of the noisy wind outside, we pull the soft silence that bulges in the coolness of the night over us like a blanket. Once it has covered her, she starts to cry. She doesn't have to explain anything; everything's obvious: it's not the body that's ashamed, it's the soul. I leave her to her tears of regret without touching her. So she can be washed, so she can be purified. It's her first encounter with sin—she's learning betrayal, and betrayal gives her pain.

A while later I ask: "Do you regret it?"

She shakes her head. "I'll never regret it. It's just . . ." She shouldn't have done it to him, her other—good—man. That must be what she wants to say. She's learning that honesty is a virtue you lose once you fall in love. "Coming here, being with you. That's all I've fantasized about for weeks; I haven't been able to think about anything else. Why do you think that is?"

Maybe I should say it's love, but I'm suspicious of passion. "Do you want a cigarette?"

She shakes her head. I light two cigarettes anyway and give her one of them. "Life's so strange. Two months ago I was so sure about my future. Everything was definite and planned out. But now . . ." She turns onto her side. "What do you think life is?"

"Chance and necessity," I say. "That's the most correct definition of life. I read it somewhere."

"So?" she says, pointing at our naked bodies leaning against each other. "Do you think this was a necessity?"

It is for me. Still, to say yes would be to decide in her place . . . I forget about life and necessity, and approach the heat she radiates. Her body is more real than anything else. She hands me her cigarette. I put it out together with mine in the ashtray at the side of the bed. She's going to hug me. I nestle, as if seeking sanctuary, between her open arms, which are about to envelop my existence. She's still crying. I drink the salty sorrow in her tears. She whispers, "I'll never regret it . . . I swear." But the birth pangs of the pain she's just felt will beat her like a hammer on an anvil. We both know that. "But he . . ."

I put my finger to her lips. "He's a good man, I know."

She sits up suddenly, pressing her naked breasts down onto my chest. There's a twinkle in her eyes, as if the stars that have escaped from the wind have taken refuge there. "What are those?"

It's the pen shells! "I brought them up for you," I say. "From Küçük Ada."

"Let's have sex there tomorrow," she says, in a provocative, sultry voice that has forgotten her regret. "What do you say? Next to that strange tree."

She's thought about that as well; she must have rehearsed the whole thing from start to finish. "Okay," I say.

Lust is the body's friend: it frees us from enslavement to the soul . . . Is escape from her soul what she wants? Those are my thoughts.

"So do you think I'm a literary delusion now?" She's laughing. "Do you remember saying that on the terrace?" I do. I should tell her that I love her. But as if she's sensed what I'm going to say, "Not yet," she says.

Then she moves away and lies on her back. She'd said what she was looking for was something greater, much grander than happiness. I wonder what she'll find. If I was brave enough, I'd say, *Come, sleep, my darling. May sleep, like a delicate butterfly, alight upon your eyes.*

As if she's heard me, she immediately falls asleep. Her presence is like a delicate hand on a pane of steamed-up glass: it wipes away memories, faces of other women. She's so beautiful I tremble with waves of undeserved happiness as I look at her. But this spiritual pleasure, this deep contentment I feel doesn't make me forget that I'm a thief. I've stolen nature's freshness. Ignoring my theft, I hold her and watch her until morning. The larks don't announce the sunrise; Spot does. I sit up. She's not as young as Juliet, but she's just as beautiful . . . We're going to have sex on Küçük Ada soon. She needs to wake up.

July 2003:

If it hadn't been for the noise of the motorboat, I would have kept Şafak in my arms. The barking noise it made reminded me of Spot's unhappy growling before he ran away. When it got closer and flowed in through my ears on top of that deceptive, forgotten happiness, I opened my eyes. The sea breeze had died down; the sun had declined toward Hisarcık Kayası. Everything was the same: it was like any other day without Şafak . . . When I sat up, the empty beer bottles on my chest rolled onto the ground. As I reached for the plastic bag, the boat was approaching the cove in front of the wild fig tree, the only plant on Küçük Ada.

Lighting my last cigarette, I watched the boat maneuvering. Çiğdem was steering; she was alone, wearing a blue bikini. It was clear from her mastery of the boat that she was used to the sea. I told her as much when she jumped into the water and swam over to me. "I practically grew up in a boat," she said.

I didn't ask how big the boats she grew up in were, or why she wanted to buy the hotel; I carried on smoking my cigarette there, on the small beach where, five years ago, Şafak had lain on her back in my arms. Çiğdem's presence annoyed me. Because she reminded me of Şafak: she became an attractive, different woman when she was naked. If I could have stopped my eyes, I wouldn't have looked at her. But until she spoke again, I watched her fleshy, lustful lips and her hips that curved with desire.

"I got rid of the chairman of the local council for you. He won't be bothering you anymore."

"So Sami's sold you the hotel. He didn't waste any time."

"If that's what's making you uncomfortable, let's pretend I never made you the offer. I'm willing to help and I don't expect anything from you in return." She was expecting me to ask why, but I didn't. She must have been thinking of coming and sitting down next to me. "And I've never thought of coming between you and Sami."

"Don't get all worked up for nothing," I said. "We're like the front and back of a head, me and that stubborn pig: even if we wanted to, we can't break away from each other."

She wrung out her thick hair like a piece of wet laundry. When she'd finished, she sat down next to me. Her left knee was almost touching my leg. "So you two are very close?"

"Yes," I said. "We're closer than close, but we look in opposite directions."

She didn't say anything until I'd finished my cigarette. I scraped out the stub on the rock that was between us. Pulling back her knees, she spoke: "You were sleeping, weren't you?"

I'd passed out. "I was making the most of God's generosity; he lifted his interdiction for the day." She was surprised; she waited without asking. "The interdiction on dreaming," I clarified. "Just now I dreamed for the first time in months."

"So it was terrible of me to wake you up." I didn't say it was. It would've been good if there was some beer, I thought. "What were you dreaming about?" Then, without waiting for an answer, she asked what she actually wanted to know. "Who were you dreaming about?" There weren't any cigarettes left either. "Was it that girl who dumped you?"

Sami! He must have sold out the past too, along with the hotel. "Girlfriends are created to dump or be dumped," I said. "How can we ever know who dumped who?"

The itch on my right leg was reaching a peak of intensity. I had to get back to the hotel as soon as I could . . . That was the thought in my brain blending in to the faded face that was getting fainter and fainter. Çiğdem kept looking away as soon as her eyes encountered my back. I laughed; we were both trying not to look: I at her hips, and she at my back.

"What's wrong?" she asked, pointing at my spreading mouth.

"Nothing," I said. "I've summarized my life, and recorded it on my back and arms. That way, I don't have to waste time explaining things."

"I saw your scars yesterday evening. When I was putting you to bed."

Then we talked about wars for a while. She asked the questions, and I answered. Honestly, she'd have been better off talking to Emin. Ten minutes later, I stood up. The distance between the sun and Hisarcık Kayası had become quite a lot narrower.

"Let's get back, it's almost six o'clock." She looked at her watch, and was about to reply but said nothing. Pointing to my leg, "The ants are coming out of their nest," I said.

"You were in love with her, weren't you?"

"The shakes will start in a bit too."

Her stubbornness was extreme. "What is love in your opinion?"

"The troubled adolescence of the soul . . ." Then I quickly added: "I need a drink immediately."

"Or our heart's most exquisite fluttering . . . That's what you said in that abandoned village."

"That's her definition, not mine . . ." I was parched. I gulped and repeated: "I want a drink."

She stared at me for a moment, like I was spoiling her fun. Then she stood up, walked decisively to the edge of the rock, and jumped into the sea. As she was swimming out to the boat, I shuddered with a premonition: she'd brought some beer with her . . .

The silence surrounding the island had scales like a snake's. It slithered along across all the sounds and noises. After three minutes, I'd already made it to the bottom of the first bottle. I stretched; I got caught up in the feeling of pleasure spreading through my blood vessels, newly flowing with blood, to my skin, and I looked at the almost naked body next to me that was more and more attractive. She didn't have a spear, but she looked like the goddess of the hunt. If I'd been going to choose a woman, it would definitely have been her. A white, untouched, pristine, mysterious body . . . When our eyes met, I smiled. I was going to be back to my old self. The ants were returning to their nest; the shakes that rippled through my muscles were evaporating. "I'm feeling good," I said.

"You could be feeling even better. A little time," said Çiğdem, emboldened by my smile. "Maybe that's what you need . . . Why don't you trust in the future?"

If your past is too rotten to be a bridge to your future, what meaning does time have, present or future . . . That would have been the best response, but instead I said, "I'm happy how I am. I'm waiting patiently." And I told her what I was waiting for. "For God to make up His mind."

I didn't mention what Fındık was going to dive for and find. She persisted, "You're even more alone than you think."

"When you're in love, you're as alone as you are in the face of death . . ." Who said that? Şafak? Maybe it was me who'd said it. I couldn't remember. "I don't remember," I said.

"What don't you remember?" I didn't reply, so she asked again: "Being alone?"

I opened the second bottle, and said, "Don't take any notice of me."

"I love you. I'm in love with you." Love! The word that has no immediate conceptual response bubbled through my ears into my head and flowed into the murkiness, like the other stagnant words that the voice can't carry: my loneliness, the silence—which was becoming stranger and stranger—ants, God . . . It was a long time later—only when our eyes met—that I realized what she'd said. I almost dropped the bottle. When I looked back at her eyes, which had become knives, I understood: she hadn't finished; the second blow was on its way. "And I'll never leave you."

There was a sexual desire, a masculine innuendo in the voice saying these things to me. But who was speaking? Was it Şafak or was it a mad woman? Finally I saw the reason behind the generous interest she'd been showering around like tips ever since she arrived. I saw her with her true colors displayed before me, but I couldn't look at them, or at her hips, which her blue bikini bottom didn't cover. I turned inward and inclined toward deliverance at the bottom of the bottle. Soon after I'd started on the beer—I hadn't even gotten halfway yet—she started to speak again, as if she'd decided I'd had enough to drink: "Aren't you going to say anything?"

This was all rather tiresome for someone who's waiting to die. I looked up helplessly. She was scrutinizing me with non-judgmental eyes. But these looks weren't helpful either—jarring glances overloaded with questions.

"I'm surprised." I looked blankly at the ground, at the cigarette butt I'd put out a bit earlier. That was the only thing that came to mind. "It's not possible," I said eventually. "You must have lost your mind. You've only known me for three days."

She launched in excitedly. I tried not to look at her swimsuit. "You're wrong; I know you well enough, believe me."

There was no doubt about it: she was stark raving mad. "In three days? No one falls in love in three days. It's impossible."

"But you did. You and Şafak." I was going to tell her that was different, but when I remembered how foolish that sounded, I said nothing. Besides, who was I to deny her a right that nature had accorded to every woman? "Love is wanting the impossible, isn't it?"

I'd once written something similar to that. But there was something unnatural about her sentence. Maybe I could have told her. "I don't write things like that anymore," I said.

"Look, if you want, you can publish another magazine. I'll help you . . ."

Magazine! The talkative bastard. "Did Sami tell you about that?" I asked.

"No," she said. "I've read every issue of *Kuzey.*" When she saw I was surprised, she hastily added, "I know a lot more about you than you think. I know about the notes for a novel you published too."

Her eyes, burning with a strange light, confirmed her fervid words. I was going to say, *You can't make literature happen with money, I've tried*, but I bit my tongue. "You don't have to do this . . . I mean, you don't have to give me money, thinking you love me . . . Besides, I'm not very good at bringing out magazines—I'm very good at bankrupting them."

"When I read you, do you know what I thought? No, thought isn't the right word . . . Felt, do you know what I felt?" How was I supposed to know? "That I'd been constantly deferring my existence . . . In the things I read, real life had voices that I'd not wanted to listen to until then. I was twenty-five years old, yet I hadn't been able to realize myself. But I had imagination, and I had plenty of dreams: I was going to study psychology, not management; I was going to work for a charity in Africa; I was going to go on a trip around the world; I was going to have creative hobbies . . ."

We both finished at the same moment: she finished listing her dreams, and I finished the beer. Twenty-five-year-old girls wanted to go either to Africa or to Sarajevo. I put the bottle on the ground. Her now unfamiliar eyes were on me.

"You'll be a partner in the hotel, we'll publish a magazine together and that's how you'll realize yourself, is that it?"

She said yes without hesitation. "It's a start if nothing else. For the first time in my life I'm going to do what I want to do, not what I have to do." I understood why her eyes had become unfamiliar. She'd ditched her generosity, and was looking at me as if she was a creditor. "Do you think I'm talking nonsense?"

I did, but I said, "You're too optimistic," and pointed to the empty bottle. "The only thing you'll be able to realize with me is drinking. Apart from that, everything else is nonsensical optimism."

"That attitude again . . . You've forgotten the future." She paused for a moment, giving me time to remember it again. "But it's actually the past you should forget. Haven't you suffered enough? She's . . ." She drew back and stopped talking when I raised my hand. "Oh my God, you were going to slap me."

Her words were loaded with her surprise, her disappointment. "I won't get used to it," I said spitefully. "I won't let my pain wear off."

"But she's gone. It's been five years."

"We'll meet again."

I was shouting. But the sound bounced off that snake coiled at the top of the island and sank into the sea. "Will you? When? Where?"

She didn't believe it either. I shrugged my shoulders. Even if I didn't know where or when it would be yet, *I* believed . . . Fındık! The embers of the burning rage rose to my throat like a groundswell. I opened my mouth: *Wizened dolphin, where are you?*

This time my voice didn't come out, I think because of the sobs that plagued me. I waited for a moment without knowing what I was going to do. Finally I chewed back the scream that was still on my tongue—the scream I couldn't let out and be rid of—and stood up. I needed something strong, something stronger than beer. Gin?

"Are you all right?"

"I want gin," I said.

We swam out to the motorboat together. She got on first and reached out her hand to help me clamber aboard, as I couldn't manage it by myself. I was surprised by the attractive warmth of her wet body. She started the motor with a single pull on the cord. I closed my eyes; as we got further from the island, I started to be able to hear again. Finally I was free from that coiled snake that scattered sounds into the distance.

Ten minutes later we were at the garden gate. The Germans, who were leaving, had gathered and were boarding the minibus in single file. I shook hands and said good-bye to one or two who looked familiar. Sami wasn't around for some reason. I asked Mücella, who was on the terrace kissing the women good-bye one by one, if she'd seen Fındık. She scowled as she always did when the old dolphin was mentioned. The third day! The bastard, he must have changed his mind about coming on land. We went straight to my room. My treasure hadn't been raided; the bottle was still where I'd hidden it.

Çiğdem's patience lasted for three sips. "'If we haven't learned how to love, then what we think is love is often no more than a cruel passion . . .' Do you remember that?" The only things I remembered were about Şafak, because all that was left of my memory after the alcohol-fueled fire was full of her. I shook my head. "You wrote it, it was among the notes you made for *The Disenchanted*."

"If you say so," I said.

"Was it to say that some of us don't know how to love?"

"I wrote other things as well," I said.

"'Whether it's a rowboat or a transatlantic liner: in the ocean, all ships are small . . .' From time to time, there's rubbish like that too." Rubbish, eh? You could hardly blame her for never having been caught in a storm on the ocean. She sat down beside me. She seemed even more naked on the bed. "You haven't answered my question." She was right; I hadn't. And I had no intention of doing so. I took two more swigs from the bottle. "And, to cut a long story short, that's the problem I suffer from . . ." She paused for a moment. "I don't know how to love."

"That doesn't count as a problem," I said.

She seemed not to have heard me. As soon as she started to move toward me, I pulled away with the bottle. She wanted to hold my hand. "Do you think it's possible to learn how to love? Or is it a skill you're born with?"

"Like I said," I replied hastily, "it's not that important. If you can manage it, don't hate yourself; that's what's important. Because . . ."

"Because our dreams are actually born from a single wish: that of loving ourselves . . . That's what you were going to say, wasn't it? You see, I remember that too. It's what the hero of *The Disenchanted* said to the woman he loved, but who didn't love him back."

She dwelled too much on everything: dreams, loving, realizing herself and sentences I'd written . . . When she leaned forward, I looked away. She'd given up trying to catch hold of my hand; now she was after my eyes. "Yes," I said. "If you turn your back on yourself, it means it's all over."

"And that's what you did, isn't it?"

I put the bottle down. She was good at hitting below the belt. "At least three times," I said. "But that's not why I drink."

"I'm sorry. I didn't mean to upset you." It was an empty apology. It didn't contain any pledge or promise not to do it again. I smiled as if I wasn't upset. But the gin had turned my lips into soggy bread; it dispersed my smile. Obeying the darkening sorrowful voice, I closed my eyes. "Sami said darkness had dripped onto your lives. When did that happen?"

I ignored what she was getting at, and said what I'd thought for years: "When we understood that the world no longer had any need for our rage . . . The world betrayed us; it turned its back on the revolution. Just like a person turning his back on himself."

As the silence drew on, I opened my eyes. She was beautiful and almost naked, but the revolution didn't interest her. But that dream had been the whole of our youth. "At least you realized yourself."

Realizing yourself! That again! What did she mean?

I understood what she meant two glasses later. Gin definitely made me smarter. I was going to laugh, but I didn't. The problem was that she was twenty-five. Before you turn thirty, you can't avoid being foolish.

"You're twenty-five years old and you've never . . ." Before I managed to say "been with," she bolted upright. Without giving her the opportunity to open her mouth, I added: "Don't turn it into a problem. Take a look at me: I'm over fifty, and I've slept with six women altogether. What's more, three of them were prostitutes . . ."

If she'd let me, I was going to say, *So you've still got time.* But she didn't. Her slap didn't hurt, but the bottle, as if struck by a jinn, flew from my hand to the floor. Then something even more surprising happened. She reached out and pulled my head toward her and tried to kiss me on the lips. She didn't stand a chance of course; she didn't know the drink had ground up my lips.

When she understood she was wasting her time, she backed off. Our eyes met: she looked at me, not like a woman who loves, but like one who expects to be loved. Then I understood that I was face-to-face with a new Çiğdem whom I didn't know. She wasn't one of those women who takes a handful of everything. She was one of those who lived love with passion . . . What's the difference? I couldn't think of an answer. The tears flowing down my cheeks into my mouth were choking me.

It was only then she became the old Çiğdem. And I didn't object to her wiping my tears away with her hand. "I love you and it's a real love. If only you could believe me."

I looked at the eager face in front of me. She was crying too. It was a non-believer's world. I hadn't believed in Şafak, and God didn't believe in me. Now it was her turn.

"How did it happen?" We're on Küçük Ada, in the shade of the fig tree. Şafak's in my arms, and Spot is running away from the waves that splash him as they strike the coast. "Come on, say something, answer me!"

I can't: it's a question that doesn't have an answer. Besides, who can know what'll happen between a man and a woman? She's staring straight into my eyes! It's useless, my darling, the answer isn't in my eyes either. Maybe love is as miraculous as the fig tree growing between the rocks on this waterless wasteland, on this island washed by salty winds. Without mentioning miracles, "I don't know," I say. "It's happened. That's what's important."

"But it can't last long." There's that regret again! It appears after sex and seizes her brain, her body, her thoughts. "Love comes to an end when we begin to think what happens next . . . Do you think that's true?"

Last night she said she'd have no regrets. "You're having regrets," I say.

Yes, it was obvious from her not saying she wasn't. "If only," she says. "If only we'd met a year ago."

If only! Two words she's stuffed with her regret and her desire to change her man, her life. But hers is a regret that has not yet matured: it's directed not at God, but at her destiny . . . She lies down; I kiss the butterfly wings that land on my lips. As if to console her, "If only," I say.

Those two words, like a prayer, calm us both down. Her cheek is on my cheek, like she wants to fit into the same shot. Who's going to take the photo? She speaks first: "That hill over there . . ." I leap from the tip of her finger to the other side of the cove, to behind

Kuyucak. Hisarcık Kayası . . . "It's so interesting, isn't it? Have you ever climbed it?" She becomes cheerful as quickly as she becomes sad. I nod. "Why don't we climb it? Do you think it's too steep?"

"There's a really flat plateau behind it," I say. "All the way to Chios."

"But it looks so inaccessible . . ."

"That depends on where you're looking from."

Her happiness is like a child's face: it changes immediately. "I don't want to think about anything now," she says, as if she's understood what I mean. "All I want is to get to know you . . ." I open my arms: she'll snuggle up. When her fingers start roaming over my body, she finishes what she was saying. "You know the stars, you don't even drink beer, but apart from that I don't know anything about you."

"You know that I've never been in love," I say.

She leans over and whispers in my ear. "You've never been in love like in a fairy-tale romance, that's what you said." Without pausing she asks, "Are you going to fall in love with me?"

It's a question designed to strip, and leave naked. "What do you think?" I say.

"You're not." She's so sure that I'm surprised. "But I'm going to fall in love with you."

The problem isn't falling in love or not falling in love; it's not knowing what to do with what you get. Love takes skill . . . anyone I've ever tried to fall in love with has always left me. I could tell her this, but that's all I know about love. "I'll love you," I say. "Come what may."

She shakes her head. "We're talking about *falling* in love. Not loving . . . Anyway, it'll be over soon. Maybe it'll all be easier . . ."

What does she see in me? "Why are you here?" I ask.

She smiles as if she knows the answer: "Maybe because you're not like the others, maybe because you've been to Africa, and maybe because you're going to write that novel."

"You know I haven't written anything for years," I say.

"So you never had a reason to write."

The look in her eyes says that now I do have a reason. I notice that her fingers roaming over my back have paused. She's examining the scars one by one. I have to tell her about them. I put her hand on my shoulder and start with the first one.

"I got that one in 1971, in Latakia, during training. Someone called Abu Mahmoud fired too low."

She's surprised. I'm expecting her to ask where Latakia is. She doesn't. "He was obviously a clumsy bastard."

"When he injured two more people after me, they gave him a checkup. Turns out he was short-sighted and astigmatic . . ."

When I laugh, she does too. "And what about these?"

Cigarette burns . . . "1981. One of the interrogators happened to be a chain-smoker," I say.

"Can't you be serious about anything?"

She changes her mind about laughing. I bring her hand to my lips and kiss her fingers. Her naked body intoxicates me. When she frees her hand, she points to my arm.

"April 19, 1979," I say. "The bullets were fired from the same gun that left Sami paralyzed."

Now it's time for the one on the back of my waist. "And this one?"

Without telling her the woman I hurt was a prostitute, "A Chinese lady left that scar with her nails in Lagos in 1972," I say.

She sits up. Her lips and her eyes are mocking me now. "A man whose back is covered in scars from war wounds and hot sex! Is that the secret of your physical attractiveness, sir?"

"You tell me," I say.

"You're very tall," she says. "And your back's broad. And if you don't want a fresh scar on that back of yours, get up—I'm hungry."

We'd had sex twice; I'm acting like I didn't notice she didn't come either time. "Okay," I say. "Would you like fish or lobster?"

She grimaces. "Just vegetables," she says. "It didn't take you long to forget." Yes, I forgot she's a vegetarian. We get up. "What did you do while I was away?" she asks.

Instead of telling her I missed her and waited for her, "I looked after Spot," I say.

She grabs my arm and says, "Well, I missed you."

I watched the moon too, on the nights it appeared. I could have at least told her that. Will falling in love make me honest? We're going toward the motorboat. Spot comes out from behind the rocks where he's been hiding and jumps onto Şafak's lap. "What about him, your fiancé . . . Have you told him where you are?"

She turns around. It was stupid of me to ask. Her face is utterly confused. In a sullen voice, "The seals . . ." she says. "Don't you remember, that *was* why I came here?"

"I'll tell Fındık then, and he can find one for you," I say.

"Can he really?"

Her voice is disappointed like a disbelieving child's. "A dolphin can even find a pin in the sea," I say.

Talking about dolphins cheers her up. "So if I ran away now and hid at the bottom of the sea, could he find me?"

We're both blissfully unaware of what she's talking about. "Yes," I say.

That night, we have sex for the third time. The attraction of our bodies is like the desire to reach the promised land: unavoidable. I lean over her; her eyes close like lace shutters; she's imprisoning herself in an involuntary darkness. She doesn't come this time either. What's the reason she doesn't, can't climb to the peak of pleasure? A guilty unconscious? A large part of the pleasure she feels is spiritual. I pause. If it's not sexual, what kind of attraction is there between us? She's after something, something she thinks she can find in me. But what do I have left in me?

Sami Çetin, August 10, 2004:

"Going by what he said, he was in love with an amazing woman, but Şafak wasn't like a woman, she was like a moth: a small, helpless, defenseless being, unaware of her fate, caught in the magic of the light . . . That summer, her excitement brought her back to Karaburun four, maybe five times, just like a moth—flying into the first light to appear after darkness falls. It was normally in the evening, as the sun was setting, that she'd suddenly turn up at the top of the slope in that small, funny car of hers. Kuzey would be waiting for her, and she'd throw herself into his arms; then—after staying a few days—she'd go back again . . . 'In the end, she'll get burned; she'll get roasted alive; that's a moth's fate . . .' That's what I used to think as I watched them. When it got too much for me and I had to say something, Kuzey turned his hunter's eyes from where he was staring and looked at me. His glance was flowing like a flood of light, and had the consistency of molten metal. I remember it well: it was late; we were on the terrace, waiting for a stubborn day to finish. Even though the sun had long since kindled the horizon and withdrawn behind the mountains, there were still lights in the west determined not to surrender to the darkness. And it must have been these strange lights that were reflected in his eyes, but I suddenly felt a chill. I could remember that glance, you see. It wasn't *him* who was looking at me. It was his *other*, imprisoned inside him, the one he stopped from appearing, his alter ego . . .

"The first time I met his alter ego was on the Indian Ocean. It was years ago, when we were on the high seas. That time he left a Portuguese sailor worse than dead . . . Stupid Raul, he was called Raul, had faith in the people with him and tried to get protection money from us. I wasn't like this in those days; I could stand up for myself. There was two of us, and five of them . . . And the second time I met his alter ego was on April 19, 1979. When Kuzey shot the people who'd opened fire at us and pointed their own gun at their heads . . .

"Oh, I'm sure of it. When I said Şafak's destiny was sooner or later to get burned up, even today I can swear that the thought of killing me passed through his mind . . . Even if the urge didn't last very long, even if it never took root, he did think about killing me . . . At times like that, his eyes narrow, his lips get thinner, and he turns into a knife wound.

"Still, I didn't keep silent; I continued. If he loved Şafak, he should break up with her for her own good. Why? It's nature. I believe in nature, and them being together was against the laws of the God I serve. If you're asking me why they couldn't just have fallen in love, let me put it like this: there is no love. It's just a trick our sexuality plays on us to engineer a union from which new generations can spring; it's a sexual impulse, in other words . . . That's why I thought at first that Kuzey was taking care of his long unsatisfied and starved body, that he was going after sensual pleasure. 'Don't worry, it'll fizzle out by itself,' I said to myself. Because when a man's been having sex with the same woman for a few months, what new pleasures do you think he can find in her? True . . . their relationship didn't fizzle out. And that was when the thing between the two of them . . . Yes, I realize that, I'm still saying 'thing.' Whatever that 'thing' that developed between them might have been, it must have been some 'thing' that was different from physical pleasures. Maybe anxiety about the future: first the revolution, then literature . . . After he'd lost his other dreams, couldn't he have wanted a new one to put in their place? Because Şafak was like a woman he could have dreamed . . . He said it himself. 'In the end she'll leave you,' I told him, 'and you'll get hurt.'

This time, instead of looking at me like that, he laughed; he'd sent his killer back inside him. 'I will,' he said, after a long pause. 'And who knows, maybe more than you think, more than I think even . . .' He was going to pat me on the shoulder like he used to, but he changed his mind. 'Don't forget, I'm like a dog; when I get hurt, I disappear off somewhere and lick my wounds . . .' He'd shut me up with my own words: it was me who told him he was like a dog. Anyway, there's no point in going on about it . . . you know what happened. His tongue and licking weren't enough, so he decided to cauterize his wounds with alcohol. If you ask me, the best woman for him . . . No, not Çiğdem—Erica. Çiğdem's difficult to understand. Her feelings were very confused. But it's all timing, isn't it? They both appeared after the watershed. The watershed! It turns out Şafak was the watershed for us all . . . At least we've learned *that* if nothing else, haven't we?

"Here's what I asked Kuzey once: 'Was the revolution just something Lenin dreamed up?' He didn't reply. My head was full of questions. 'So what about being a revolutionary? Did we want it, or did it just happen to us?' This time, he shook his head and coughed. When he'd decided on something, he'd cough and clear his throat as if he was going to give a speech. 'Skepticism is the easiest thing, my friend. So what if it's dreamed up or not? I'm all for dreaming.' Yes, he was a dreamer, in every period of his life. 'We thought the revolution was bigger than life.' That's what I said to him. He thought for a while, then, 'Wasn't it?' he said. His voice was trembling with a mystical belief. 'China?' he continued. I replied, 'The Chinese revolution was ultimately a peasant uprising; there's always been peasant uprisings in China.' So he continued, 'What about Castro?' 'Cuba's very small,' I replied. 'If it had been Czechoslovakia, I'd have believed it . . .'

"You know, our generation has the finest traitors. I'd say it's the generation that likes to suffer, the generation of masochists. It's as if we're obliged to take on all the pain of the world . . . As if the homeland wasn't enough, there's Vietnam, South America, Africa, and of course Palestine too . . . And it's this desire to escape from pain that's behind our tendency to suicide, our susceptibility to give up on our lives, in my opinion . . .

"When I'm asked what I do for a living, I say I'm in the business of gathering useless information . . . Did you know the number five is the first number obtained from odd and even numbers? We're not going to close the Karayel Hotel. No, we're going to expand it and develop it. That's what we've decided. Or actually, that's what Çiğdem's decided. I'm going to help her out.

"At the last moment did Kuzey want to escape from love? I'm not sure. Maybe he was a moth too, but we didn't notice. My poor friend, if it exists, love is like wealth: you have to have it first before you can escape it . . .

"Some of us have fear, and some of us courage. Courage was his lot. That's the side of him that seems strange, surprising to us. We should look at what's said about him through that optic, I think . . ."

İhsan Kıymaz, August 11, 2004:

"If everybody read just a little philosophy, if people knew the first thing about it, this planet would become heaven. Ah yes, if heaven was at our feet, would we believe in God? That's a different question . . . That's why God knows that those who are involved with philosophy are secretly digging a hole for themselves. I'll tell you who God is: an ideal that selfish people have designed for themselves. And I've got a problem with this designed ideal. I've never denied that I don't believe! I've heard, apparently they say I'm godless . . . That's the only true word that puppet of a chairman of the local council says about me . . . Greed and insatiability, that's where the problem comes from. Behind the chairman's greed is his gluttony, but in the gods' is their immortality. But never mind the chairman; the gods are truly unlucky beings. It's obvious why, isn't it? Even if they wanted to enrich themselves with philosophy, they have to settle for religion. And on top of that, they don't have any art either. At most they can be the subjects of art . . . And then there's His indifferent neutrality; that's what I can't stand about God. Why do I say that? Let's say because He didn't have mercy on Kuzey. Who do you think is going to show mercy to an adventurer who won't give sacred life any more meaning than it actually has?

"I'm here because I'm fed up with evil. That's my answer! And you can add to that the struggle of looking for the purity of goodness. Pure goodness! Let me give an example I saw in a film. In the temples at the top of the Himalayas, when the monks who live far from everyone leave their monasteries, they close their eyes and walk behind a child so as not to encounter evil. Temporary blindness for the purity of goodness. So you see, I'm talking about a jealously guarded purity . . . If we could make the God we've corrupted into a human, there won't be a problem anymore. We could put evil back in the box it came out of. How can we do that? We'll find out. Maybe we should rethink our definition of God. To escape our own obligation of pure goodness, we've put it wholly at God's doorstep. We've used God for our own ends . . . I'm going to organize a conference with broad participation about this. That's one of reasons why I'm here: to re-create Karaburun as a center of philosophy. Don't forget, the ground we're standing on at this moment was ancient Ionia . . . True, I live here now. Yes, yes, I've been living in that stone hut by the dahlias for six years. In that wonderful historical structure the chairman wants to tear down because it's 'derelict.' If it's derelict, it's derelict; what's it to him? Anyway, he won the election again, of course. What can I say? God loves and protects the ignorant. Even if they do say it's a sheep pen, I'm happy with where I live. No, if civilization means simplifying life, then I'm anti-civilization, sir. Because I'm all for making some things more difficult—just like Kierkegaard. If you're asking what I'd want to make more difficult, my answer is ready: my state of existence . . . I always tell people who don't find my words clear and meaningful: clarity holds no secrets. That's why I like a lack of clarity in people . . . My work aims at learning about my own death. And to do this without turning to God. So you see, there's another reason why I came here . . .

"Who can blame Kuzey for loving, for choosing a young woman? An orientation toward youth, beauty and vitality is an expression of the desire to live, is it not? Why do you think the best paintings were done in the middle Ages? Because in the Middle Ages the average life span was short; in other words, everyone was young . . . Time! Look, if there is a real God, He could be time. Because time has the power to change everything—the value and importance of people, of objects. For example, a colorful pot someone shat in three thousand years ago could easily be a museum's most valuable exhibit today . . .

"As time passed, Kuzey started having deep doubts about where Şafak was; it must have turned into an obsession. Doubt is a very, very important obsession. I have great respect for it. And it has rather strange children: murder, malady and, sometimes, knowledge . . .

"I vaguely remember Şafak. She was an attractive young woman. At that time I hadn't made friends with the youngsters yet; I was staying up there in the old hotel in the town center. It was thanks to Handan Hanım that I got to know them . . . Sami kept avoiding me in the first stages of our friendship. Like most people here, he thought I was crazy. Ha ha . . . And you can't really say he was wrong, can you? Anyway, I liked Kuzey right from the start. He'd started drinking again. I don't know if you've ever witnessed it, but his drunkenness is sublime. Alcohol must melt away the rust on the surface of his intelligence . . . Handan told me about the drama. Why do I say drama? All love stories that end in separation are dramas, that's why . . . My friend Kuzey! The Lord of the Compass, a true person . . . I didn't admire him, I liked him. Now, my thoughts about the generation of '68! In actual fact, I don't think he really cared very much about being from the generation of '68 or whatever. Besides, younger people care more about the generation of '68 than they do themselves. Me? How can you be indifferent about a generation like that, which was kneaded with a Dostoyevskian guilt, which has a raging consciousness? It's obvious they had a passionate, libidinal love of humanity . . . God gave them an unbearably heavy burden: a conscience. By the way, I should say that these characteristics of theirs sit very nicely with the project of making God human. Imagine humans have turned into beings made up of conscience, where all our virtues can grow . . . Although we can't be sure it's a conscious choice, we have to accept that they're trying to suffer on behalf of humanity. It might seem ridiculous to us, but for them the concept of humanity was a religion; it was a God they paid homage to. They desperately tried to make their mark on the world. Their efforts might have been naive, but they didn't give up. And that's what's important . . . Oh, I should add that they reminded me of beggars: they were begging for approval and admiration. What romanticism! In an age with no princesses, to try and be a knight in shining armor, to set about scaling imaginary towers . . . To summarize, we need to accept that they're the type of people who won't be buried, who won't end up six feet under. They don't belong to the earth; they belong to the sky. We can say many things about them, but never that they're boring . . .

"Where's Kuzey now? Who could know that . . . ? Yes, I've heard that too; they say Fındık is supposed to know. Suicide! He promised, first to Sami then Çiğdem, that he wouldn't do such a thing; both of them will have told you that. And isn't that why he spent his final months begging God to let him die? I think for someone like him life was never valuable enough to be glorified with suicide . . .

"No, I haven't read anything he's written. But he got what he wanted. A good writer doesn't want to be read, but like Nietzsche, to be memorized . . . Kuzey's masterpiece—that is to say, himself—will never be forgotten . . . what's written in blood is memorized. Creating immortal works of art and having sex with women. They're both rooted in the same insatiability: immortality; it's our truest and most powerful emotion. And that's why people write. Kuzey had no such desire for immortality. But if you ask me, the real reason is that he couldn't wear the mask of fakery. He never managed to be two-faced—not in his life, and not while writing. Because writing, in the final analysis, is fakery. Or if you prefer, you could call it going cap in hand to God . . .

"Yes, God again. Of course I don't believe, I told you! But God's a necessity. How can an artist be satisfied with only mortal approval? They accept the existence of God so their mastery, their permanence can be rubber-stamped, so they can become immortal. Be careful not to get them mixed up with those poor souls who submit to the temporal adoration of God . . .

"My views on art? Art is to transform the large nothingness, the nothing we call death, into something. Even if that explanation doesn't seem logical to you, that's how it is . . . They call me a charlatan? Maybe I am. But if I am a charlatan, then I'm a charlatan like Kafka, who wrote love letters to women even though he found sexual union abhorrent. I mention Kafka so you'll take what I'm saying seriously . . .

"Whores and children pay for the sins of cities; the sins of the world are paid for by philosophers. I stake a claim on the sins of this peninsula . . . That's right, I'm not a philosopher. But so what? The important thing is creative, courageous thinking. And there you are, Pure Goodness and Making God Human . . . Taking risks is the key. And there are examples from history. Take the Marquis de Sade: where do you think Sade's greatness lies? Not in him being a philosopher, nor in his literary creativity. His uniqueness lies in the courage he showed while writing. And that's what I do . . . What do I care if it breaks with tradition? Leave tradition out of it. Once traditions take the place of thought, it means we're up shit creek . . .

"What did women see in Kuzey? Şafak, Erica, Çiğdem . . . Oh, there's his ex-wife too by the way, so her, even Handan Hanım . . . They all fell in love with Kuzey for one reason or another. Yes, women do move in mysterious ways, but if you ask me, it's obvious. All of those women picked up the scent. As soon as they set eyes on him: the scent of a man who knows how to love a woman. A man whose love is permanent, not temporary, a man who doesn't know how to give up or forget . . . Once he loves, he'll love for eternity. That's Kuzey. He didn't give up on love . . . Çiğdem and Kuzey? I don't know, but love is sly. In its gestation period, it has many disguises: friendship, pity, trust, sometimes even enmity. Here's a secret for you! There are three things we can never escape from: our shadow, fear of death and love . . . So no one should be angry with Kuzey; why are they angry with him anyway? Because he wasn't the only victim of his fate?

"Yes, I had two daughters and one wife. No . . . not a car accident, they died in a fire, all three of them . . .

"You're difficult to understand as well. Why on earth did you decide to write this story?"

Çiğdem Boran, August 3, 2004:

"I didn't tell Kuzey I was the daughter of his ex-wife. And Sami only found out a long time later. Why did I hide it? I don't know. It would have made me less convincing. Maybe that's why . . .

"For years, my mother jealously kept the letters and poems Kuzey had written to her locked in a wooden box. Whenever she was unhappy, which was most of the time, she'd lock herself in her room to read them and cry in secret. We could never get through to her at times like that. Not me, not my father . . .

"It's all so funny! I didn't know who he was, but I started hating Kuzey when I was eight years old . . . The only thing that kept my mother from us was these letters written by an unknown hand. My father let that slip in a moment of sadness.

"Until last October . . . yes, until nine months ago, I hated him. Then . . . The night my grandfather died, my mother and I had a terrible fight. She got drunk in the middle of the night and shut herself up in her room; I stole the famous box from her when she passed out. I spent until noon the next day, without a break, reading what he'd written. Those provocative letters, those passionate poems . . . And that evening my grandmother told me about my mother's marriage to Kuzey . . .

"After my mother left him and went back to her father, Kuzey wrote a total of fifty-one letters to her over six months. Between February and July. Every time my mother passed out after that, I read each one over and over and over again. First in chronological order, then at random. Some of them were a piercing scream; some, the ones where he gave form to his pain, bore the traces of a larger work he was trying to construct. A total of one hundred and seventy-two handwritten pages . . . You were curious about it, so let me tell you. You see, those letters are why I fell in love with him—without having seen him. Of course, I should also mention the forty pages of notes for *The Disenchanted*. He put them down on paper as they occurred to him: descriptions, discoveries. But what's interesting is that he sent his most precious treasure to the woman who left him! What generosity . . .

"Everything he wrote was pervaded with regret and guilt. I could see that even from his first letter, and it struck me as odd. He was the one who'd been dumped, but he was feeling guilty as if he was the one who'd walked out. That's when I understood. I was holding the tears of a naive, fragile man between my fingers . . . And I can say that was the beginning of my strange journey, which from time to time was to surprise even me. When I realized I was being drawn toward him, I'd already come a long way. At first I was surprised; then I found it strange; after that, I chased after his mysterious, addictive sorrow and I reached him through his writing. The result? Here's the result: I fell in love with him without him even knowing I existed . . . I can't think of anything like it. For example, I didn't have any photographs of him. I imagined tens of faces, innumerable bodies for him. That's why his existence as a lover was always mental rather than physical. Later, even when I held him in my arms, that's how it was . . . Nothing I did with him happened or materialized by itself; I designed, set up, rehearsed, changed and re-formed everything myself over and over again. And that's why I wasn't surprised or upset at him recoiling in fear when I kissed him for the first time. You see, I anticipated he'd be surprised, afraid, or even that he'd reject me . . .

"Back in May, before you started writing this story, when we were coming to an agreement on your terrace, I promised you I'd be open about everything, I'd answer your questions, I'd give you all the information you needed. I remember that well. So, bearing my promise in mind, I can tell you this: behind my feelings for Kuzey, was there something like an urge to punish my mother, or to steal from her the only precious—or what she thought was precious—thing that she had, maybe an existence that she could have loved her whole life? I'm not in a position to answer with a yes or no. Maybe that urge was what started me on my journey, but make no mistake, before I was halfway through the letters, I'd already forgotten my mother and become smitten with the sorrowful screams of a man in love. If I'd wanted to take revenge on her, wouldn't the first thing I do be to tell her what had happened? She still doesn't know anything and we haven't seen each other for a whole thirteen months. No, only my grandmother knows anything about what's happened.

"If you still don't believe me, here's a bundle of proof for you. Take them! What are they? They're my replies to Kuzey's letters. They're what I wrote to him—without having seen him, without knowing him—as if I was the woman he was in love with, as if he'd written to me. No, he hasn't read any of them . . . Why would 'someone like me . . .' whatever being like me is, be with 'someone like him?' Loving isn't about being someone. It's about being yourself. And I was myself. What could be more attractive than the honest display of weakness from a man with a past full of adventures? And what if I say I learned a lot from him too? The first thing was pain . . . Until I read him, I—like everyone who's arrogant and self-centered—thought that anger was pain, and that getting angry was suffering. My journey with Kuzey taught me that someone who suffers is noble, more human. He was the one who ripped open and threw away the cocoon I was hiding my feelings in. Learning how to love? I learned how to love and I finished the job my mother couldn't. She wasn't brave enough to love him right to the end; she wasn't able to pass anything on from him to the future. I was. See, there's the living proof . . .

"How does anyone fall in love? You think it's a foolish question too, don't you? Can anyone explain simply and logically how love takes shape and comes to life? I don't think so. Look at Tolstoy. Did he explain how Anna Karenina and Vronsky fell in love with each other? Which magic words did Vronsky use to convince Anna Karenina of his love, or which provocative words did Anna use when she surrendered herself to Vronsky? In the hundreds of pages, there isn't even a single paragraph about that. It's all just glances and a few stock phrases. Here's the answer: Anna and Vronsky were ready to fall in love, and when the opportunity popped out in front of them, they yielded to their destinies. Just like me. Tolstoy, as well as Vronsky and Anna Karenina, knew from the first time they met that they'd fall in love. Like me. As soon as I'd read his letters, I realized I was going to fall in love with Kuzey. Falling in love is an opportunity, and when I encountered it, I didn't let it slip away . . .

"Lots of people say I made a big mistake being together with Kuzey. Maybe that's true, but believe me, it was the most correct mistake of my life . . .

"To understand my mother you'd have had to have seen my grandfather. Actually, he reigned over all our lives, mine included . . . They say when you can't be master over your own life, you covet other people's . . .

"Who sent me to you? Why's it so important for you to know? Fındık? My answer's neither yes or no. I promised not to tell."

From the diary of an itinerant drunkard, page 44:

Who can possibly be more lonely
than a person who has been abandoned by death?
—Kuzey Erkil

Oh bastard of Satan, oh stubborn body of mine, do not resist . . .
yield after all this time. Yield that I may go and pick the fruit of the
nothingness at the bounds of my consciousness, my ripened death.
Permit, oh stubborn body of mine, that I may quietly cover myself
with the cloak of death. Oh body of mine, look at me: my mouth,
my smile is a gaping wound. You know that only he who was not
made any promises is free. Know, oh body of mine, that I have not
promised anyone that I will live. Since my Şafak has stopped dawn-
ing, my desire to live is not strong enough to sustain me. Tell me,
tell me, body of mine, who can blame me for this? Oh blind body of
mine, you no longer have before you an epic hero who attacks you or
someone who has set out to discover the adventure of life. I am tired
and wounded. I have wounds but they are bloodless wounds. Oh deaf
body of mine, it is a waste of effort to carry someone who is afraid not
of death, but of life. Ask, oh body of mine, ask: is this him? Is this the
one who believes in the sacredness of pain, who knows the value of
pain? You say those who suffer are noble, but is he noble? Leave me,
oh body of mine, leave me that the piercing light of death may illuminate all colors. I am ready to do anything; release me, release me that
I may lie down inside the cocoon of my drunkenness like one entering
a coffin, and that I may await my tardy death as a free drunkard . . .
If I cannot die, let me at least scream: "Spirits of my drunkenness, of
my sweet light-headedness, of my unhappiness, where are you? Oh
painters of shameless images, appear, bring a little cheer to this abject

soul who cannot hold himself within the bounds of your infamy . . ."

If God is responsible, I curse Him; may my pain beat Him like a hammer on an anvil . . . Tell me, oh body of mine, since my life has turned into a poem of sorrow, what is the meaning of leading such a life?

CHAPTER IV

What else is life
but a—short or long-lasting—story of death?
—Kuzey Erkil

August 2003:

Will I die today? If God remembers that I'm lain out in my coffin waiting for his messenger, then perhaps. But I realize it's an empty hope, like yesterday's, and the day before, and the day before that. There are rules. Even about dying. Why does God always see Himself through His own eyes? How narrow-minded! And what the hell is this indecision all about? Why isn't it my turn yet? But—leaving the chairman of the local council to one side—who is there on this peninsula who deserves death more than I do? I'm the first among equals . . . Fındık! I tremble with joy. Maybe God too is waiting for Fındık's latest dive . . . The thought mingles with the ecstasy of the dream. If that's so, then I'm in luck. If I can find the dolphin, that is . . .

"Good morning."

I removed my eyes from the darkness of nothingness and opened them to the daylight: at the end of the labyrinth it wasn't Azrael, it was Çiğdem. Like he'd done with the hotel, Sami had handed over my sobering-up ceremony to her as well . . . With this thought on my mind, I sat up. The person there to meet me was standing in front of me like a skein of light, hazy at the edges: shining, striking and ready to scatter . . . How many days had it been now that I'd found her at my bedside when I came to? I tried to count them: eight? Nine? When I got to ten, I gave up counting. She was wearing a thin, see-through sleeveless dress. In the light trickling in through the open blinds, she appeared to be standing there half-naked, with the air of an angelic guardian of life. When she noticed I'd opened my eyes a crack, she raised her voice as though she'd decided she'd waited long enough, and repeated, "Good morning."

If only she had been an angel bringing news from God. "Good

morning," I said. "I see Sami has lumbered you with keeping me under observation! Or I should be calling you partner now?"

Çiğdem wasn't interested in observation or partnership. "You're smiling," she said. "That's fantastic!"

"Bring me a mirror, and I'll take a look," I said, not mentioning the dream I'd had for the past three nights. She leaned forward and stroked my hair. She probably did that every morning. I inhaled the fresh, cool smell that poured like water from her hair. I should have been ashamed of myself: "I reek," I muttered.

"Come on then, get up and have a shower!" Dog days! The ceiling fan wasn't cooling the room, it was milling the screams of the cicadas. "Do you want me to help you?"

I shook my head. I wasn't refusing her offer because I could get up by myself, but to keep away from her provocative smell that faded my dream.

"I'll be on the terrace in ten minutes." She looked at me, apparently with no intention of leaving the room. "You know what Sami does?" I said. "He waits outside . . ."

She smiled. Her smile was singular, for her own consumption; there was no room for anyone else inside her. Did she care about us? Sami, me . . . If I'd been going to say something, that's what I'd have asked. Our eyes met. It wasn't easy to get past the dazzle of her smile and into her eyes. Was she still persisting with that nonsense about love? We hadn't talked about it again since the day she tried to kiss me.

After Çiğdem had gone out, leaving her smell behind, I swung my feet down from the bed. The bottle from yesterday evening was still on the bedside table. A swig? That would have been stupid; I took two. I had to admit, there were advantages to Sami staying out of my room.

I managed to stand up on the first attempt. Even though the fan lopped off the high-pitched screams emanating from the pepper tree, the hum pouring down from the ceiling was still penetrating enough to be annoying. I followed the straight line on the floor to the bathroom. My balance was surprisingly good; I only tottered twice. I turned on the bathroom light. The face in the mirror still didn't look like me, but since I'd dreamed for the third time in one week, I wasn't going to make a big deal out of it. I turned the water on and climbed in. I faffed around for a couple of minutes, then I sniffed my armpits. I'd defeated the sweat; now I only smelled of alcohol. I could finally go out on to the terrace. After a few more swigs, of course . . .

There were no people, no wind; the whole place was empty. I looked at the shadow of the pole like I did every time I went out into daylight. It must have been after twelve. Distancing myself from the amorous cacophony of the cicadas, I went around the back toward the shade of the vine. Sami, along with his newspapers, was beneath the pergola. There were a few Germans at the table at the bottom, and a strange couple I hadn't seen before. The man was completely bald, but a bushy beard covered his face. I pulled out the chair opposite Sami and sat down. When he noticed I was there, he leaned his head forward. "It's still only a quarter past twelve," I said. "That doesn't count as late."

He glanced at his watch without looking up. "Five past one. You're losing your touch."

"Dog days," I said. "The shadows have shrunk in the heat."

"You were supposed to be here at twelve to sign the papers. And Şuayip's busy now."

We didn't speak until Mücella had brought the breakfast tray. Half a slice of bread, cheese, and a few grapes. When I turned away with my plate, Sami put down his crossword, and asked, "So, which mountain did the wolf die on?"[14] When he realized I didn't understand, he

---

[14] "Hangi dağda kurt öldü?" is a Turkish expression used to show surprise when someone behaves unexpectedly.

explained: "You're smiling, get it?" Mountains and death! My face suddenly fell. "What's wrong?" he asked.

"Spot!" I said. "No one's seen him yet, have they?"

He shook his head. "But Mücella's eldest son has gone out to look for him every evening. And you'll have told Çiğdem about it."

"What about Fındık?" I asked.

He shook his head. I chewed the bread. I liked eating bread before drinking. A dog and a dolphin that had turned into ghosts!

"This time he must have dived very deep," he said. "Who knows, maybe he's gone to Chios after a fat sea bream." Was he taking the piss? "Over the water," he said.

He was taking the piss. "You don't believe he can dive," I said.

"Of course I don't," he replied. I ate a few grapes. I actually wanted to tell him he was a total cunt. "Why?"

"Why what?" I asked.

"Why are you grinning?"

"Everyone smiles from time to time, even someone like you," I said. "What's so strange about it?"

"Not you," he said stubbornly. "What's happened?"

I looked around. At the table behind, the short man sitting with the young woman was staring at me intently. I leaned forward. "I'm having dreams."

"Dreams?" Sami asked. I nodded. "They must be really hilarious."

"I've had the same dream three times," I said before falling silent. I expected him to be curious, to ask me more. He didn't. He'd lost interest. Before he went back to the newspaper in front of him, "It's Şafak," I said. "I dreamed about her for the first time in almost two years."

"Really!" His voice was mocking. "Look at you! What were you both doing?"

In the molten silver in the middle of the channel, two ships were about to disappear from sight toward Izmir. "Like I'd tell you!" I said.

"Suit yourself."

He was going to put me in a bad mood, I knew. "Why does Çiğdem come in the mornings to wake me up?"

"She wanted to look after you." He shrugged his shoulders. "And you kept saying you were fed up of seeing my ugly mug."

Lying toad! He just did whatever Çiğdem asked. "Doesn't her behavior seem strange to you?" I asked.

"Strange?" I nodded. "No. She seems to have her head screwed on." Suddenly he raised his voice and said in a high pitch, "I thought you liked younger women? What happened?"

"Shut up." He held up his hands. I was just about to yell at him when a dog barked in the distance. I said nothing and listened to the sound echoing. It didn't bark again. I turned to Sami. He was waiting for me. "Well I think it's very strange," I said. "Some girl suddenly turns up and starts sorting out all our problems. From the root."

"I'm sure she must have her reasons."

I looked at him. I wondered what Çiğdem had told him. "She's as mixed up as a tangled fishing line," I said. "She's obsessed with something called 'self-realization.' If we publish a magazine, if we get the hotel back on its feet, if, if, if . . ."

He raised his hand and interrupted me. "We're all obsessed with something, aren't we?" He was staring straight at me. "Me with my crosswords, İhsan Hoca with pure goodness, Handan with the environment, you with Spot . . ."

"She says she loves me. Isn't that strange?"

"Well, look at you." He wasn't particularly surprised. If he kept on taking the piss, I was going to beat him up. "It seems she really has been out in the sun too long."

We didn't say anything for a while. The heat was draped over the hotel like a wet lace curtain. "Who's that man with the beard behind you?" I asked. "He's been looking at us ever since I arrived."

"Osman Bey, from Ankara," said Sami, without turning around. "He says he's got a restaurant. They've been here for a week, and they're staying another week. I told you about them." The dog barked again. Spot! "When you were with Şafak, you used to grin like that in the morning too. I remember it well."

The man was still looking at us. "Why are you taking her side?" I asked.

I'd finally stumbled on the right question. I could tell from the difference in his voice. "Maybe she'll change you," he said. "That's what I hope."

"I'm happy how I am," I said.

"Crying every night . . ."

He didn't finish what he was saying. His voice was trembling. "You're such a bastard," I said.

"You beg God to take your soul. Constantly, the whole night long."

"Weren't you the one who said you'd be disgusted if I took any notice of what you said when you were drunk?" He was nodding. "You're such a bastard," I said, again.

"I used to keep watch at your door at night." He'd handed over his watch first to Erica, and now to Çiğdem. I was about to swear at him. He got in first. "Do you remember that night?" Here we go! Whenever he wanted to hurt me, he'd always ask in the same way: his eyes, like a murder weapon; his voice, inviting as if he was beginning to tell a fairy tale. I shook my head as if I couldn't remember the story of Nermin. "The night she left." But I could remember every moment of that night. "I was alone in an empty house . . ." He was drunk.

"I was drunk . . ." He was drunk and thinking of putting a bullet in his head. "I was thinking of shooting myself." He had a gun in his hand . . . "I was holding your Browning HP." I'd stopped him . . . "You broke the door down and wrestled the gun out of my hand." He was crying . . . "We were crying our eyes out, you and me. You were slapping me, and shouting at me at the same time . . ."

"I don't remember anything," I said. "I've got a brain like a sieve. The only thing I remember . . ."

He had no intention of listening to what I was going to say. "'Promise! Promise! Promise me!' That's what you were shouting . . ."

I finished the sentence he'd interrupted, ". . . is that you're such a bastard. That's what I remember . . ."

"And that night I promised you."

"I want a drink."

I was probably shouting again like I did that night. Because this time the Germans looked over as well. Sami stubbornly continued: "Now it's your turn."

"There's no gun, there's no nothing in my hand," I said, reaching out both my hands. "Empty, can't you see?"

He didn't look at my hands. Now he was shouting too. "Promise!"

"I can't . . ." I was going to throttle him. "She's gone, do you understand, she's gone. And I'm here. I miss her, you hear me, I miss her. My pain . . ."

If I hadn't noticed his eyes, I was going to mention the unrelenting pain that deepens each morning as dawn breaks, the emptiness in my breast that the tens of drinks I have throughout the day can't fill. Maybe I would have throttled him; that's what I felt like doing.

But when I noticed what Sami was doing, I stopped. It had been such a long time since I'd seen him cry that his tears were like the words of a forgotten language. Like all those years before, he wasn't sobbing, but crying quietly, hiding his pain. I was shamed into silence. He muttered, "If you think my pain . . ."

I'd been a bastard to think my pain was any less curable than his. I didn't let him finish what he was going to say. I was being a bastard, torturing the only person I was going to say good-bye to when the time came. "Okay," I said, hastily. "I promise!" I repeated it: "I promise. Come on, dry your eyes!"

I knew if he'd been able to get up, he would have. Without waiting for him, I got up from the chair and went over to him. It was like returning to the past. We were going to do something we'd forgotten a long time ago even though we used to do it a lot, and it felt strange. I waited for him to dry his eyes. Then we hugged each other. Surprise spread from my arms through my body in cool waves. Hugging him was like looking at an old photo of myself; it was returning to myself again. I took a deep breath. His skin, his sweat, his tears were redolent of friendship. I'd have given a lot for a beer. Still, I didn't let go of him. Who knows when I'd hug him again? Seeing I had the opportunity, I breathed in my past. "I've always been on your side," he said. "Ever since the moment we boarded that ship."

He was right. I could smell the ocean too. "I promise," I said. "I'll give you the gun. Do what you want with it. Bury it, dismantle it, throw it into the sea if you want."

"Give that girl a chance. Maybe she'll get us back on our feet."

And that's when I let go of him. When I realized Sami thought he was as close to death as I was. *Dear God, don't touch him . . .* If I could have prayed, that's what I would have said. But . . . I stopped. And him? "Do you hear it too?"

"What?" he said.

"Barking."

He shook his head, concerned. "It's Necati Bey's kangal." I was about to object, but he said, "Don't argue. I'm sure."

Maybe I would have tried, but just then Çiğdem appeared. She was radiant in the daylight too, just as she had been in my room. Someone had sprinkled her with glitter . . . When she approached, I worked out who the artist was: Satan. That smile that she wasn't going to share with anyone—that she herself was the focus of—was on her lips again. She was walking erect as if she'd swallowed a sword. She came toward us with quick steps and when she reached us, Sami got up like a hapless friend trying to leave two lovers alone together.

"It's so nice to see the two of you like this." She was wearing a swimsuit. A voice inside me said the conversation wouldn't be too drawn out. "What, are you going?"

"I'm going to tell Şuayip to bring the papers," said Sami. He wasn't looking at Çiğdem, but at me. "Seeing we've caught this lanky sleepy-head while he's awake . . ."

As Sami tottered off on his crutches, I followed him with my eyes— as if he'd fall if I didn't look—then I sat down, watching Çiğdem. "Why do you look at him like that, as if he's going to disappear?"

"We should actually look at everyone like that," I said. "Or the next thing you know, you'll never see them again."

"A strange explanation," replied Çiğdem. "Where did that come from?"

I waited until I'd finished the grapes. "He was called Mahler," I said. "I met him a very long time ago. Not the composer. He was a ship's doctor. Late one afternoon, on a hot day just like this, he stood in front of me. 'I'm just going to cool off for a moment,' he said . . . Or something to that effect; he used to speak in a strange language he'd culled from the oceans, you see. I was on deck, in the shadow of lifeboat number two. I was looking down, reading a book. I didn't look up at him. He waited for a moment, then he went. Conrad's

Heart of Darkness . . . Do you know Conrad?" She nodded her head. "He learned English when he was seventeen and went on to become one of the most important stylists in the English language. I had a lot of difficulty reading him . . ."

I lit the first cigarette of the day. The heat was becoming more and more intense and turning into a viscous liquid. We're going to roast, I thought. "What happened then?"

"What do you think, I somehow managed to finish it. I never leave a novel half-finished."

"Mahler," said Çiğdem. "That's what I was asking about."

"He walked thirty feet and threw himself into the sea. No one ever saw him again. The Portuguese had played a trick on him . . . They cooked the rat he'd looked after for three years, and made the poor man eat it thinking it was chicken . . . Whenever I remember it, I say to myself: if only I'd looked at him properly for the last time . . ."

"You're pulling my leg."

"It was a beautiful white rat," I said. "And it was clean. It was called . . ."

Without waiting for me to remember its name, "A correction," she said. "Conrad was much younger when he learned English."

It was obvious: she wasn't going to pay any attention to the poor rat. "Do you want to bet on that?" I asked.

She nodded her head reluctantly. "Why don't you start writing again? You've got so many things to tell."

"But I have no reason to," I said. What I wanted to do . . . "Drinking. That's exactly what I want."

Çiğdem raised her hand. When Mücella's eldest son—or maybe it was her youngest—approached the table, she asked for a bottle of beer. Before the boy left, I corrected that to two bottles. "Did you used to have one?"

"Have one what?" I asked.

"A reason to write?"

I shook my head. I wasn't sure. "Mahler did . . . But instead of writing, he preferred to be shark food. So that means writing's something even worse than dying."

"Is it you saying that? You, who spent virtually your whole youth writing! I don't believe it."

"You make a lot of mistakes when you're young," I said. "And that's one of them." The boy had brought the beers over. "If you can't manage to die, you'll write. That's what I know . . ."

She rubbed her cheeks with the back of her hand. The sun had burnt the top of her cheekbones and turned them red. An enraged bronze-faced goddess, whose eyes had turned into a cascade of light! "Suicide, is that what you're thinking of?"

"I've just promised to leave my death to God's hands," I said.

"You promised Sami?" I nodded. "Promise me too then!"

In for a penny, in for a pound . . . After I'd taken a few swigs from the bottle, "I promise," I said.

"And you keep your promises, I hope."

"I always do," I said.

"Okay then, so what about drinking?"

"Don't push your luck," I said this time.

She shook her head. The sun had really lightened the color of her hair. "I'm unlucky; I was born twenty years too late." Without telling her I'd heard that before, I sipped on my beer. I had to admit that being unlucky suited her too, at least as much as being lucky did. "Don't you want to live? What happened to that unbowed, unflinching voice in your writing? What happened to life . . ."

I shuddered; in her voice was that thing that you don't often hear: the ring of truth. And as that disturbing ring that forces you to return to yourself was echoing in my ears, I thought, what had happened to me? I'd died, but no one was burying me. Death! The loss of our desire to exist, the loss of desire for anything: yes, living was another of the things I'd lost . . .

This was all going through my mind, but, "Nothing," I said. "Nothing happened. Not to me, not to life. Life is a short or long-lasting story of death. And that's exactly what mine is."

"And that's it, is it?"

Instead of saying it was, I took a swig of the beer. The heat had even shut up the cicadas. A jaded day! It somehow wouldn't pass. Our eyes met. I decided to ask the second question: "Do you listen at my door at night?"

"Someone has to look out for you."

"Why don't you find yourself someone else to . . ."

She raised her hand and moved it toward my lips as if she was going to put her finger on them. "For God's sake, do I look like someone who'll be a rich man's girlfriend or wife?"

I thought about saying that men who weren't rich existed too; then I changed my mind. In front of me was a woman who kept Sami away from my room and found me drink whenever I wanted it. I had no intention of making an issue about her being beautiful and rich.

She put her hand down and continued to smile. I turned to the second bottle. At any rate, one day she'd find out her real reason. Maybe she was mad. "Have you ever been to a shrink?" I asked.

"A few times." Her smile wasn't going to wear off. "What about you?"

"Another bottle!"

"They're coming . . ." I looked around. Sami in front and behind him Şuayip, who was following him with respect, were approaching the table.

Two minutes later, Şuayip, in his suit, oppressed by sweat, was explaining the terms of the contract he'd put in front of me. Çiğdem wouldn't be a partner; in return for paying off the debts, she'd have a ten-year lease on the hotel. Sami would still be manager, and the old staff would be kept on. I shook his hand as he was telling me, "It's a very good contract, sir," and I signed. It really was a good contract, for him and me at least. I'd be able to find drink easily, and he'd escape from being imprisoned in his marriage . . . The fire in his eyes was proof of his strong his desire to keep away from his wife. As he handed the pen over, he had something like a lover's excitement in his eyes. He'd managed to save his skin for at least another ten years. Our eyes met. God forbid! I had no intention of living that long.

After Sami and Şuayip had gone, Çiğdem and I sat in the shade without really moving. She was reading a book; I was drinking. From time to time, our eyes would meet, we'd approve our decision to prolong the silence with our glances and we'd smile. The heat was doing us all in—the cicadas first of all. Then, in the middle of the third bottle, I suddenly heard her: "Have you got any photos of her?" I turned to face her. A woman who didn't look like Çiğdem was staring at me. Before I could ask of whom, "Of Şafak," she said.

There's none so curious as a woman in love! And it was that woman asking. That's when I understood I wasn't going to be able to finish my bottle in peace.

May 1998:

Even though anxious shadows have descended, the night has a velvety softness. We're on top of Delikli Burun, listening to the sea rolling coquettishly beneath our feet—the swell pushed by distant winds. Above us, the stars of Homer; opposite us, the lights of Foça.

Suddenly she says, "Tomorrow."

Tomorrow! The word she's squeezed an inexpressible apology, disappointment, desperation and maybe longing into strikes the dark, wavy shawl below and bounces back. She's going! That statue I turn my back to so as not to see it when I pass in front of it soars from inside the darkness like a red ball of flame: the eagle-headed rock at the summit of Değirmen Dağı is coming to life—like an ancient Egyptian god. It's going to take off, plane down the hillside almost without beating its wings and land on my shoulder. Then . . .

I pull my hand away. "Don't," she says.

"Then I'm going to die," I say.

She isn't sobbing. Or is she not crying? No, she's crying, but with her glances, not with sounds. I hug her. "If I don't go back, he'll come here," she says. "You've got to understand! I can't confront him. Least of all here . . ."

Embarrassedly she tells me about how she has more responsibilities. I think about how those in on the secret, those who Fındık has recorded in the Register, die. Tomorrow, after the funeral ceremony peculiar to this peninsula, I shall pass over to eternity like a victim who has accepted his fate.

But I'm not buried yet. I can still speak for the time being. "Okay," I say, with my half-dead body. "You're going tomorrow."

"It's been eight days," she says, apologetically.

What can quell the desire for union of two bodies and two souls?

Days? Months? The woman in my arms gives the answer: only loss of passion . . . "Forget," I say. "Forget you're going tomorrow. You're here now, at least until morning."

She offers me her lips. I kiss her. "Maybe I won't go until the evening."

"Deal," I say. "One more day."

A large wave smashes like a champagne bottle beneath the promontory. We kiss again in the foam that pours down from our heads. The only thing we can do is try and use the kiss of union to forget we're going be apart.

"I won't be coming back . . ." she says. I'll only be losing her body; I know she'll leave her self here. I don't tell her to come back; I don't tell her not to come back . . . She continues, "I won't forget anything: that you can eat sea urchins, that crabs' hearts sound like clocks, that octopuses use shiny sea shells as a lure to catch fish . . ." I'm sucking her lips so she'll stop talking. "And you," she wails.

Not to be forgotten! Is that what being loved is? "And don't forget Spot either," I say.

"I won't forget Spot, or the nests the sea birds make on the hillsides of Büyük Ada." Silence, and then her question: "And you?"

I laugh; actually I don't, but I think I'm laughing. "I don't have any photos of you," I say.

"Very well," she says. "But now tell me. About the oceans, the stars and . . ."

It takes some time for love to mature. Discovering each other's favorite foods, flowers, colors, songs; creating memories; arguments, little break-ups . . . "We've never had an argument," I say. "And we haven't broken up."

"We didn't have time for either," she says. We didn't, she's right. "What are you going to do? Maybe you'll write."

"Maybe," I say.

"And maybe I'll . . ." She doesn't finish her sentence. We both know the other man will see, will change her dreams for the future too. Around us, there is only the sea and the sound of the waves, but I can hear Sibelius. I'm going to die. "If only I'd been born twenty years earlier . . ."

She looks at me with so much regret in her eyes that I laugh. Sibelius returns to where he was born, to Sami's grave. "Maybe it's my parents' fault," I say. "They were in a hurry."

"I'll write to you," she says. "Every week." For the first time in months, I shake with that suffocating desire to drink. "And you?"

I don't reply. Because I'm thinking about alcohol. And why would I write anyway? Can words, which live as long as autumn leaves, span the distance between you and what you miss? When she moves to get up, I jump, thinking she's going to leave immediately. I'm face-to-face with the strongest emotion a man can feel toward a woman: the desire not to lose her, come what may. I shouldn't think anymore. I'll only say something stupid . . .

Three waves that come in one after the other spray foam over our heads. Someone must be celebrating our separation. God? Maybe Fındık. "Tell me then, what are you going to do?"

"I might go to Egypt," I say.

"You're having a laugh!"

"When you go, that's when I'll really laugh."

"Are you drunk, darling?" Not yet, but I'm strolling on the shores of the sea of alcohol. "Come here . . ."

An invitation to sex, to a one-person feast . . . I should tell her. "I should be by the edge of the sea," I say.

"Here?" Why not? Doesn't Fındık always appear here? "But why?"

"They say when someone recorded in the Register dies, if he's near the sea, a large eagle takes him and carries him to heaven . . .”

Her voice is no more than a whisper, but I can make it out in the sound of the waves. “Are there eagles here?”

I point to Değirmen Dağı. “There’s one over there.”

“And heaven?” she asks. “Do you believe in heaven too?” I nod. “What about a heaven for the people who leave?”

“Where we’ll meet again,” I say. “That’s where heaven is.”

Looking down at the little cove where the foam surges up from, “The sea?” she asks. I nod. “In that case, we’ll meet there one day.”

She reaches out her hand. I shake it: we’ve agreed. We get up. It’s time for the feast, the last one . . .

* * *

The next day up top, in the dim shop on the bottom floor of the local council building, I kiss her. Embarrassed, she says, “Shhh.”

Without letting the spotty-faced boy holding the camera see, I kiss her again. She’s leaving in half an hour, and then I’ll lose her lips forever. The mouthpiece of her soul, the first step to pleasure, the taste of her lips needs to be immortalized. “Photo,” I tell the boy.

We’re laughing and kissing. The flash goes off. The boy says, “That’s twelve shots now.”

“One more,” says Şafak.

But her smile doesn’t take shape. It’s feeble; it doesn’t spread to her voice or her eyes. For the final shot, she leaves me and goes to the map of Karaburun in front of the wall. I realize what she’s doing: she’s saying good-bye. To the peninsula and to me. She should look at me. Her smile desperately tries to get out of the indent at the edge of her lips. But it can’t. We breathe in the thickening sorrow.

“Look at me,” I say; the boy presses the button at the same time.

We settle on thirteen shots and go out from the shop, which has turned into an oven in the heat. While the photographs are being developed, I sit her down in the cafe at the edge of the cliff overlooking the gulf. "Why here?" she asks.

"It catches the wind," I say. "You'll cool down."

I light her cigarette. "What are you going to do with the photos?"

"I'm going to keep them," I say. "A souvenir."

"I'd have liked to leave something more permanent." Before I can ask, she tells me what: "A scar. But there's no room on your back or on your arm!"

Without hesitating, I reach out my left wrist. There, a blank page for her. Let her brand it!

August 2003:

"So this one isn't a torture scar."

"No," I said. "A souvenir."

Çiğdem took her finger off the faded cigarette burn on my wrist, like an almost dried-out stain, and turned to the photos. Her face showed only curiosity. Neutral, skeptical. "So you looked at the camera while you were kissing."

I leaned over the photo she held out. She was right; I had looked. "The boy who took them was absolutely useless," I said. "I must have been worried about what he was doing."

"She was attractive."

The thirteenth picture! "Yes, I used to love the way she looked at me."

She nodded as if she had discovered other sources of beauty in Şafak as well. "Now it's easier for me to understand your not being able to forget her." Was that true? What was it I couldn't forget? Her? Or the pain I felt? Did I avoid making too much of a distinction between them? "And you're not looking too bad yourself."

I pushed away the frightening thoughts behind the questions, and replied, "Back then I used to look like myself. Whenever I looked in the mirror, I would always definitely recognize the man who appeared before me."

"And then what happened?" she asked.

"She went away," I said.

"I meant after that."

"She came back," I said this time.

She shrugged her shoulders, "No, after that."

"She went away again."

"I see," said Çiğdem. "You're not going to tell me."

"They were bad days," I said. "Very bad . . ."

"The pain?"

The pain and . . . "Alcohol. I didn't drink in those days . . . How stupid!"

"What's stupid about being in pain?"

"Not accepting the fact you'll start drinking in the end. That's what's stupid."

"You drank instead of dying, that's what happened, isn't it?"

"I drank because that eagle wouldn't come to life."

"Which eagle?" I continued sipping on my beer without telling her. I had proved Fındık wrong . . . Is that what I was going to say? When she realized I wasn't answering, she continued: "Why do you want to go to Delikli Burun? Don't you think it's still very hot?"

"I'm tracking a fugitive."

"Why not wait until the evening?" She pointed at the packet in front of me. "What's that?"

"Something that'll end up at the bottom of the sea," I said. "It's time for it to go."

"Did it belong to Şafak?"

"It's a gun. I promised Sami."

"Have you ever been to Switzerland?" A gun and Switzerland! I shook my head. "What do you think about going to Lausanne?" Lausanne! I wanted to go to Egypt or Delikli Burun. "I know a clinic that overlooks the lake. It has a fantastic view."

I didn't ask how she knew about the clinic! "And alcohol?" I asked.

"You can give up alcohol there, and start writing again if you want."

I shook my head. I'd have shaken it even more vigorously if I'd had the strength. "We should live in accordance with whatever kind of life we believe in . . . and I believe in alcohol."

"I don't know if you realize it, but if you don't hurry up and give up your belief, you'll die."

"We're all going to die," I said. "Even you."

"You can't upset me today . . . By the way, do you know what I was thinking about yesterday evening?" There was no point in her looking at me: I had no intention of asking her. "We could hold a big party on August 27."

August 27? "Whose birthday is it? Yours?"

"Nooo . . . of course not! I'm an Aquarius. It's a party for Mars." Mars! "On August 27, Mars will be the closest to Earth it's been in sixty thousand years . . . Can we watch Mars from this terrace?" When I bowed my head, she continued, "We can invite people we know from Istanbul and from Çeşme. And it would be good publicity for the hotel. What do you say?"

"Ares is on our side," I said. "I like him."

"Ares?"

"Mars."

"Why do you like him then?"

I pointed to Mount Ida. "He supported the Trojans in the war."

We might have spoken more about Mars, about war, about Lausanne or about Delikli Burun, but when we saw the pregnant woman coming toward us with Mücella, we sat up with curiosity. She was in her thirties; she'd put her hand to her forehead as if she was about to faint, and was having difficulty walking, swaying on Mücella's arm to the left and right.

When they got to us, Çiğdem got up to help the woman sit down. I didn't budge; I was feeling very dizzy. The woman was beautiful, but not graceful. Maybe because she was tough: the softness of the soul makes grace appear, you see . . . After the woman, with sweat pouring down her face, said a half-hearted thank you to Çiğdem and Mücella, she turned to me with an air of familiarity and stared straight at me, her eyes demanding an explanation.

"My name's Türkan Demirsoy, Emin Demirsoy's wife. I'm looking for my husband." For her to start the conversation by listing pieces of information about herself one after the other, like she was giving an oral report, was surprising enough, but stranger still was the aridity of her voice, which was devoid of life, and which betrayed the hopelessness of her search. She continued, "I know Emin stayed in your hotel three weeks ago. The driver of the taxi that brought him here told me."

The woman, as if breathing her last, stopped speaking. The silence was like an index finger telling me it was my turn. I waited for a moment, undecided. *Your husband's running away from you . . .* That was the first thing that came to mind. I even thought about saying it. But when I encountered Çiğdem's forbidding glances—she was waiting for my answer with as much curiosity as the woman—I decided not to.

"Captain Emin?" The woman, who was trying to drink the water Çiğdem had given her, nodded excitedly. "He's not here," I said. "He left ten days ago."

"I came here all the way from Bolu—in my state!—to find him! Please, help me!"

She was asking me for help in a heartrending voice that didn't suit her body, but she was looking at Çiğdem. "He's gone," I repeated. "Take a look for yourself if you want."

My beer was finished. Should I get up and get one myself, or should I call Mücella over? I'd have to walk all the way to the kitchen! That was the hard part. While I was thinking about alcohol, it suddenly dawned on me: Sami was the one who'd sent this woman over to plague me.

I was just about to tell her to ask Sami where the captain was when Çiğdem got between my indecision and the woman by saying, "Yes, I remember your husband, but he did leave the hotel ten days ago. I can assure you, we're telling the truth."

"Oh God!"

After a feeble scream, she started crying. Things were even worse now: this time she was looking at me. I thought about telling her she'd screamed for nothing and that God's ears didn't hear particularly well on this peninsula, but Çiğdem got in before me, stood up and walked over to her. I leaned back. First Sami, and now a pregnant woman whose very essence, I could swear, had been formed by living out in the provinces! The day had started with tears. I could hear the cicadas too. Their screams were mingling with the woman's sobs. If only I could go deaf like God . . .

Çiğdem tried to calm the woman down, but it wasn't easy to console someone who'd been saving up her tears since Bolu. As she continued sobbing, the man who'd been looking at me ever since I went out onto the terrace and the woman who was with him stood up and came over to the table. On top of all his strangeness, he had a crooked grin on his face that gave him a foolish look. First the stares, and now this grin that was making his mouth list to the right like a rowing boat taking on water . . . I wasn't going to like him.

"Excuse me, my wife's a nurse. Maybe she can help."

It was even clearer how short he was, now that he had the tall woman standing next to him. What an odd couple! Despite my thoughts, I shrugged my shoulders: I wasn't going to pay any attention. Everything was strange this morning. I left them both to Çiğdem. After the tall woman and Çiğdem had taken Emin's wife between them and departed, the man, without waiting to be invited, went over to the chair across from me. He was still grinning, but there was a definite mismatch between his grin and the way he was looking at me. I could have sworn I'd never seen anyone else in my whole life who suited a smile so badly.

We didn't speak for a while. I declined the cigarette he offered me and sniffed the air; the smell of rotten vegetables wafted from him. He traced an arc with his hand. "It's a very beautiful place."

He was talking nonsense. You couldn't see anything. The mist rising up from the channel had wiped out Foça. It was even difficult to make out Domuz Burnu. "Yes, it is," I said.

"I'm Osman Çileci..." I pretended not to see the hand he stretched out. He was still grinning. "I'd like to get to know the area better. I wonder if you could find a guide to take us around."

I turned to my beer. "I'm just visiting here too, like you."

"Really? I thought you were the owner."

"Not anymore," I said, in the same way I'd say I was sick of him.

He asked a few more questions and went away. Even as he was going, he was grinning. If it were me, I'd have been angry. Then I suddenly worked out why his face was in conflict: his thoughts weren't smiling. His mind must be sulking.

When I was alone, I gestured to Mücella to bring two beers over—as if the man was still there. I actually felt like gin, but I couldn't be bothered to go to my room.

Çiğdem came back fifteen minutes later, as I was about to move on to the second bottle. She approached the table with quick steps; she was like an enraged goddess. As soon as she sat down, she started to speak: "I've put her in seventeen."

What on earth did she expect me to say? "So what? You're the boss," I said. "You can give her whatever room you want."

"Poor woman! As soon as he found out she was pregnant, Emin Bey left her. How can an honorable man do something like that?"

"Didn't anyone ever tell you?" I asked.

"Tell me what?"

"Never to come between husband and wife."

She shook her head. "I promised her." I didn't ask her what. "I promised on your behalf that you'd find her husband."

"Well, it looks like you've promised for nothing," I said. "I don't know where he is. He's a Schoendoerffer soldier."

"And what's that supposed to mean?"

"If men like him don't want to be found, they can't be," I said. "That's what it means."

"Maybe so. But still, I'm sure you can do something."

"I can drink," I offered. "I mean, that's the only thing you can be sure of."

"You're going to make sure that captain comes back here," she repeated. I raised my eyebrows. Why was I going to do that? "Because you're a man who never leaves a woman in the lurch."

I burst out laughing. "I don't leave them in the lurch because I don't get the chance to leave them, full stop. All the women I've known have been quicker off the mark than me."

"You know, I think you can sometimes be as romantic as a knight of old."

Stubborn goddess of the hunt: she was only missing the helmet on her head. "I'm a raving drunk," I said. "Ask whoever you want."

"Snap out of your solitude! You'll see, everything's going to be all right. You just need someone . . . like we all do."

She was mistaken. "I told you I'd read Conrad, didn't I?"

She nodded gently. "I remember your saying you found it difficult."

"Still, I underlined lots of sentences. One of them was, 'We live as we dream—alone.'"

"Do you think we should live our lives like we're characters in a novel? If that's what you're saying, then I'd like to remind you that they're not real people. They're tragic existences made up by writers."

I raised my bottle: "Here's to tragic existences. I prefer them to people."

"Why do you like drinking so much?"

I like it, because . . . "It's the only entertainment I have while I queue up to wait my turn," I said.

"What queue?" She was surprised.

"The one in front of God."

Was she going to give up? No. "Why? Why are you like that? You, that captain?"

I thought for a moment. Actually it was obvious. "Probably because we're human," I said. "Humans are the most messed-up species on our planet."

At a certain point in life, you become your own worst enemy. I'd reached that stage. That's what had happened. Çiğdem stood up. Her shoulders were straight. She was angry, but it was an anger she could keep under control. "If you don't mind, I'm going to the sea; by the way, I still think you're going to find Emin Bey."

As soon as she finished what she was saying, she turned and went away. I followed her shapely young body with my eyes for a moment. Who was it that was going away? An essence that hadn't come into being, or an existence that hadn't realized itself? Which one? Essence or existence, maybe she wasn't whatever she was through her own desire . . . She'd given up, and I'd given up on thinking. Anyway, I was off my head.

It was hot; over the channel, the mist was slowly bearing down on Uzunada like a plump caterpillar; in the back garden, the Germans were cheerfully shouting to each other; in number seventeen, a woman whose sorrow I didn't share was crying; the prostitutes of the pepper tree were lustfully mating to give birth to cicadas that wouldn't go to Chios or Mytilene; in the distance, a dog—one that I wasn't looking for—was barking; and Fındık and God were still being stubborn. I returned to my beer.

When I got to the end of the bottle, I noticed I couldn't swallow. Like I was being crushed by giant gills. Still, I didn't give up immediately. After resisting until my stomach was really upset—just before vomiting—I got up, taking the packet with the gun with me. God had decided to begrudge me the only—and the final—thing I took pleasure in. After lurching a little, I managed to stand up straight. Mücella's son—I somehow hadn't been able to learn which one he was—took care of the rest. I took his arm and said, "To the kitchen."

Şükrü wasn't there. We found him in the back garden, in the recess between the jasmine and the pepper tree, smoking a cigarette. He was in a silence that belonged only to him, which the screams of the cicadas didn't encroach on. When he saw us approaching, he stood up. I didn't spin things out because I was on the verge of vomiting. "Get me Ahmet," I said.

"Has something happened, boss?"

"I want a word with him," I said. "And don't call me boss anymore." Then I turned to the boy. "Take me to my room, son."

The boy laughed, and so did I. But there was a sorrowful expression of surprise on Şükrü's face. I found out the lad's name at the door to my room: Veli. Veli put me to bed. My stomach seemed to have calmed down. I could pass out for a few hours. I left the packet on top of the bed.

* * *

I passed out. I had no idea how long for, of course. When I opened my eyes, Sami was standing at my bedside—at my feet actually. I shuddered in pain. My hands, my ankles were itching. The monsters were coming out of their nest! Sami said, "You need a shave."

"Have you taken the hotel back?" I asked.

He shook his head. "Ahmet's outside. He says you sent for him."

"Good," I said. "We'll have a chat." He was going to ask what about, but I got in first: "Emin . . . Who was it that unleashed his wife on me?"

I sent him on ahead of me. I didn't have much time. I had to get a move on and act before the ants did. I opened the bedside cabinet. The bottle of gin was in its place. I swiftly downed two glasses and went out onto the terrace. It was a little cooler now; Foça, which had been vaporized and dispersed by the noontime heat, was back in its rightful place. The channel was empty; the caterpillar must have made it to Uzunada. The time? I'd say half past four!

If it had been five, half past five or six, what difference would it have made? Sami and Ahmet were at the table that looked out onto Küçük Ada. I sat down across from Ahmet. Because a mine had exploded underneath the vehicle he was driving on the way back from an operation in Bitlis, he was practically deaf; to understand what was being said, he had to lip-read. Still, he was lucky. Three of the soldiers in the truck had died.

"How are you?" I asked. He nodded. "When's the big day?"

"Before Bayram. But I dunno when exactly. Me dad knows though."

I turned to Sami. He looked down. I looked at Ahmet again. "That CO of yours," I said. "Are you in touch with him?"

His eyes went blank. I'd gone too fast. "What?"

I asked again.

"What?" he said again.

He was trying it on! "Look," I said finally. "I know you're only pretending to be deaf."

I offered him a cigarette. He took it. His indecision was wearing off. "We'll call your dad in if you want."

We both turned to Sami, who was shouting. He always knew just where to strike. Mentioning Şükrü had opened Ahmet's ears. And his tongue was loosed. "He calls from time to time."

"Good," I said. "In that case, tell your captain his wife's here. She says she's not going to go without seeing him."

His eyes went dark once more. He was surprised. "The CO's got a wife?"

"Pregnant too. And the way things are going, she'll be having it here."

While Ahmet was looking open-mouthed at Sami, who was touching his shoulder, I raised my hand. He turned to me. "Are we agreed? Are you going to call him?" He hung his head. "Why did he retire so early, your CO?"

"I dunno . . . they say he didn't come down from the mountain for two months after the skirmish in the village. He went on every operation. Not long after I'd gone, they say the general called him down one day and retired him. I . . ." he pointed to his ears, "were discharged."

Sami asked, "What happened in the village?"

Ahmet waited undecided for a moment. He was apprehensive, as if he was revealing the secrets of the southeastern front.

"It were a Friday. As soon as our team entered the village, it were caught in crossfire; we lost four men. Then the CO and a sergeant dived into an house . . . they brought out three bodies . . ." Ahmet, as if it proved the bravery of his CO, repeated the number three with emphasis. "Three of 'em."

I needed a bit more to drink. When sober, it was difficult to cope with a world where bravery was measured in dead bodies.

Sami said, "Okay. Now your CO has to prove his bravery again."

"And this time, he doesn't have to kill anyone," I said to Ahmet. "It's enough for him to come here."

I left them both and walked to beneath the vine. To watch the final rays of sunlight in the west. Just like I did five years ago with the woman I love, that day when the sun lit all the windows facing Hisarcık Kayası with ruby-colored flames.

June 1998:

Cottony clouds tossed into the sky . . . We're watching the sunset from beneath the vine. Or rather, I'm looking at the horizon smoldering away beneath the sunlight, and she's looking at me. Her gaze is like an arrow of longing: as she looks at me, it sinks in deeper. I reach for her hand. It's not where I expect it; her inquisitive fingers are wandering over my face, my shoulders, my arms.

"It still hasn't healed." She takes my wrist—as if she wants to reread a verse she's written in her diary—into her lap. "I can't believe I did something like that," she says afterward. "How could I have asked this from you?" It's unbelievable, but what's really unbelievable is that she's back. "Does it hurt?"

"Not anymore," I say.

She smiles, but on her lips, it's not that old smile. Her smile has changed: it's wounded and bruised . . . I don't dwell on her smile. As we wash our faces in the golden rays of the western sun, which is reclining on the horizon, I'm all ears, listening to the song, the song her body is singing, the song that only I can hear. It has a simple tone . . . It's the melody of a pitiful meeting. At the same time, it's a parting lament announcing her departure while she's still arriving.

"I couldn't take it anymore," she says after a long while. The melody weakens; the tone of her voice darkens. Her question has a ring of anger that she doesn't want to conceal. "How did you manage?"

I whisper in her ear what I told Sami: "The secret's in my doggy nature," I say. "When I get hurt, I disappear off somewhere and lick my wounds better."

She laughs and strokes my hair. "You're my favorite dog," she says. Then she points at Spot, lying at her feet, and continues, "I like him too, but if I had to choose between you two, I'd choose you."

"Thanks," I say. "To be the first among dogs makes me happy."

She leans her head back and I kiss her. There's a French couple on the terrace, but no one's paying any attention to them. Her lips are harbingers of a late summer: hot and burning. Responding with desire, she mutters, "It's been seventeen days . . ." As soon as she says seventeen days, I remember the nights as well. Seventeen nights of seventeen days. The truth, as black as night, as heavy as seventeen nights, slaps me in the face. For seventeen days and seventeen nights she was together with a young man. How many times did she have sex with him? And then, an even more terrifying question: does she come when she's with him? I'm going to leap up . . . "What's wrong?" she asks.

I push the embarrassing questions, all those nights when anything could have happened, down to the depths and say, "Nothing. Nothing's wrong."

"I've been doing a lot of thinking," she says, without suspecting anything. "About love . . . Why do you think we love someone?"

It's not a question; it's clearly a confession meaning, *I can't seem to find the answer to why I've fallen in love with you.* "It depends on the person," I say.

She launches in excitedly: "How do you mean?"

"A young person always loves for themselves."

She thinks for a moment. Then asks, "What about an old person?"

We're looking into each other's eyes; she's weighing me up. "And an old person, well, an old person loves the other person for being who they are," I say.

She murmurs again in a non-committal voice. "Does love change with age?" I nod. Then there's another question: "Do you think young people are selfish when they love?"

"When you're young, you want more than you love, more than you can give. If that's selfishness, then yes."

"So that's youth?"

"That and making the same mistakes over again," I say. "Youth is mostly that."

She pauses for a short moment, and then says, "All I want is a few days. Apart from that, I'm old."

I want all her days. Seventeen of her days, seventeen of her months, seventeen of her years . . . The years make me stop. I'm talking nonsense. "I think I'm probably the youngster," I say.

"Come," she says, as if in pain. "Let's swim to Küçük Ada. And then . . ."

Ten minutes later we're flinging ourselves from the rocks into the sea. The shadows have receded like mist, but still, the water's so clear and smooth that we have the sensation we're swimming inside liquid glass. Maybe that's why our strokes slow down. We stop when we're half way there. She's on my right; on my left, there's a rueful, red horizon. And in front of me? In front of me, there's a misty uncertainty whispering to me to forget everything. To forget she'll go again, to forget her body that turns me into a voluptuary, her lips that I won't be able to kiss—that I won't be able to taste heaven and hell on—my sleep, the future, maybe even living . . . I need to forget everything.

I turn to Şafak; I was going to say, *Come on, let's swim to our island and destroy the seeds of this doubt that envelops my brain and my heart.*

But she's not next to me! Has she sunk? The terrifying thought makes me shudder. I can't find her; I'm not a dolphin. I'm going to scream, but water gets into my throat. But then I suddenly see her. Ten meters ahead, she's waiting for me. I'm spitting out the water; the salt that clings to my nasal passages sears my flesh. I'm taking my strokes slowly. Her disappearance is instructive: her presence at my side is fleeting. She might come back, but each time she'll go again . . . and then one day she won't come back.

If love means planning for the future, I won't even try because my future has already been planned out: the future, my future, is now merely a journey for me where I'll discover the bounds of pain. And it's up to the present to be a rehearsal for this separation. Because if I do survive, I only have one thing to learn: how to cope with separation.

Two more strokes and then I reach her. "Come on, let's dive down to take a look at that treasure of yours," she says. No, she must stay with me forever, where I can see her. I mustn't lose sight of her. Just then it occurs to me, I mustn't sleep anymore. "Okay?" she repeats.

I shake my head. "We're late for rehearsals."

She's surprised, but I ignore it, I look at the organ that belongs to me the most, her eyes, which she gave me weeks ago. "What rehearsals?" she asks.

I don't say for my death. A few more strokes and we'll reach the island . . .

That night in the room, as I lie on top of her, I don't look at her naked body; I look at her eyes. She's got them tightly closed. What doesn't she want to see? It's as if we're in the season of dried leaves; her skin smells of sorrow. I'd have liked to live with her in a time that's not measured or divided, to wake up to a day that doesn't have a nighttime and a daytime. As I set off inside her, toward the depths of her intimacy, that's what I'm thinking about. Her sighs very soon turn into delayed, fruitless moans. Does she really want me? Or is us having sex just a stop she has to pass through on the path of love?

A long time after she's rolled over onto her back, she asks for cigarette. I give her one and light it. The match flame reveals a matte, pallid and distant face. She's unhappy.

She only lasts until the second puff. As the smoke melts the silence away, she reaches that salutary twist in unhappiness: the moment of truth.

"I don't know what to do." She's not sobbing, and she's not complaining. "Does love mean having to choose?" No, it doesn't mean that; it means not being able to choose, but I don't tell her that. "It's painful for me. When I go, I miss you. And when I come back, I'm crushed by guilt."

I look into her face. Her sinful face is suffering. But hers is a virtuous sinfulness, if only I told her that! But it's no use, I know. The problem isn't the past or the present. The shame of the past can be covered up, but fear of the future can never be destroyed. We'll never have a heaven. Ours is a spent dream. We're on the threshold of a frightening door that opens onto hell. As we lie side by side, as I feel the moisture on her skin, that's what I'm thinking about. I have to help her, whatever the cost. If she can't leave me, maybe I should do it for her . . . I'm thinking about that too.

"What are you thinking about?" she asks.

"Nothing," I say. "I'm not thinking about anything."

"I wanted to travel the world," she says. "Australia, Asia, Africa . . ." Her voice drifts away as if it's already arrived in Africa. "No, I'm not even sure about that anymore."

The desire to go far away. And me? "I've been on this peninsula for two years," I say. "I haven't been anywhere."

"Nowhere at all?" she asks. She's surprised, and it's a sincere surprise.

"That's right," I say. "I'm finished. And I hadn't even noticed."

"Don't be stupid," she says.

"Okay," I say. "I won't."

To think that someone who's contemplating waving to himself

from the wharf of her soul can live at the bottom of a well, on this peninsula. If that's not being stupid, then what is?

I shake my head. Maybe my head is shaking by itself. I didn't used to be like that. "This time you are thinking something," she says. "Don't try denying it. What's on your mind?"

"That I used to be a knight in shining armor, once upon a time." She sits up on her left elbow. Before she can ask me, I ask her, "Why do you close your eyes?"

"When do I close them?"

"When we're having sex."

She lets herself fall back onto the bed again. So she didn't realize she'd been doing it. The answer remains behind her shame or her indecision, and I don't insist. She too has things she's curious about. "What is there here? I mean, what's kept you here for two years?"

What? Instead of saying that this peninsula is a wall separating me from my past, a trench that I dug with broken bottles of alcohol, I say, "Old age. It must be old age."

"You see, now you're being stupid," she says. "Men like you don't have an age; you never grow old."

"Old age is when the dimensions of life shrink," I reply.

"Really? Who said that?"

I tell her the truth. "I've only just realized it."

She says nothing for a moment, then she asks me something. This time her question is like a knife. It's sharp and targeted: "Are you in love with me?"

She waits, then I tell her the truth: "We're always tempted by someone we can possess completely."

She hands over her cigarette; I put it out together with mine. "That's not answering my question."

Let's try this: "The fact is we're always taken in by probabilities."

"Love isn't a probability for me," she says angrily. My poor darling. Will she understand that I'm talking about myself? "You're not in love with me." No, she hasn't understood. "Love is the most magnificent thing a man and woman can form together, the most sublime position they can reach, the farthest land they can go to, the land of dreams . . ."

The land of dreams! Ah, if only I could tell her that dreams end no matter what we do! Has she ever thought about why she feels guilty? If one half of love is probability, the other half is fooling yourself. And she's the one who shouldn't be fooling herself, not me.

August 2003:

"I don't think you were in love with her." I was still looking out toward the west. But now, instead of the sun, there was a black lace curtain. And it wasn't Şafak with me; it was Çiğdem. "If you'd really been in love with her, you wouldn't have let her go."

"But sometimes loving someone means letting them go," I said.

"Precisely," said Çiğdem excitedly. "That's what I meant. She was *in love* with you, but you just *loved* her."

I sniffed. "You're playing with words."

"If a woman really is *in love*, she won't stand for only being *loved*."

"That's not very sensible . . ."

"Why not?" she asked.

"Because being in love, in other words, desiring a fiery union, never lasts . . . Once one of the egos possesses the other completely, desire subsides, and being in love comes to an end. Just love, on the other hand, is long-term; it's not invasive . . ." I gulped, the words I hadn't been able to stir from the tip of my tongue five years ago were now pouring from my lips one after the other. "And being in love needs a lot of care and attention; where love is flexible and durable, being in love is fragile."

She was listening attentively. "I see which side you're on," she said. "So what else?"

"Actually, I'm neutral," I replied. "But I can't ignore the fact that being in love is full of the desire for freedom. It needs to subside and be saved from passion; it needs to go right to the end, consume and be consumed. It's hasty, it's willing to go all the way; and if it can't do that, it's ready to give up. But love is a voluntary captivity; it's dedicating yourself to someone else."

She shook her head as if she didn't agree. "You're scared of being in love! That's what I think when I listen to you."

Now it was time to explain what being in love meant to a woman who'd never been in love before. "If you're seeking belief, it means you're without belief. And if you're seeking love, it means you'll never fall in love. Because if you've been in love, you'd never attempt it again . . ."

I wasn't going to say anything more. She reached out her hand and wiped my cheeks. "Okay, I'll shut up now. Come, have something to eat."

"Sleeping with a young woman, waking up with her, going off on journeys with her, living with her . . . it was all a seductive dream," I said. "But a low probability . . . I didn't get taken in by probabilities."

"But why on earth were you afraid of a dream?"

Was it a dream I was afraid of? No, it was a reality. "We were going in different directions," I said. "I was going to grow old; she was going to grow up. I was like a cane. One that they stick in the ground to support flowers so they don't droop . . ."

She was surprised. She waited a moment; then, "Like it says on the packet," she said, "a supporting cane. What's wrong with that?"

"Maybe nothing in the beginning. But then? The flower grows, blossoms, turns its face to the sun . . . But the cane, it stays in the same place. Unless the tie between them is undone, it's inevitable that the stem of the flower will get damaged."

She reached out her hand to my face again. Then we started copying each other. She gently cried; I reached out my hand and wiped away the tears that fell on her cheeks. As she was crying, she kept looking at my face. Even though it was five years too late, a young woman finally understood me.

I didn't really eat very much. And she didn't really insist. Half an hour later, when Sami came out onto the terrace, I told Çiğdem to take me to Delikli Burun. But we didn't go. I got dizzy and it was decided we wouldn't go. They both probably suspected I wouldn't be able to walk.

When I wanted to sleep—the time to pass out had come—I went to my room with Çiğdem. Our tears had dried. It was surprising how the sorrow had been so short-lived. I had one or two sips of gin. Çiğdem leaned over to my ear and whispered with the tenderness of a mother putting her child to sleep: "Good night, Mr. Cane."

She wasn't smiling. I was drunk. When you're drunk, you either smile or cry: I smiled.

"Good night, crocus[15] flower," I said. She held my hands. Both of them at once. First the right, then the left. Then she began to twist my body left and right. When I understood what she was trying to do, "It's no use," I whispered. "You can't get it out . . . I haven't moved for seven years. Fındık, only him . . ."

---

[15] *Çiğdem* means "crocus" in Turkish.

Sami Çetin, August 10, 2004:

"No, Çiğdem twisting him like that as if he was a garden cane apparently wasn't her trying to pull him out from where he was stuck . . . She wanted to stop me laddo from getting buried in the soil and completely disappearing. I think she realized he was re-staging the performance he'd put on for Şafak five years earlier. That night, after she'd put him to bed, she told me these exact words: 'Au revoir, arrivederci, bye bye, sayonara . . . Yes, those words exactly. The honorable gentleman was bidding me farewell. And he managed to do it so masterfully that I might not even have noticed he was saying good-bye . . . Wrong-footing women who love him, that's exactly that what your friend's doing, Sami Bey . . . Now it's easier for me to understand Şafak's desperation.'

"I think Çiğdem was right to get angry: Şafak came here at least five times that summer. Kuzey must have begun thinking about breaking up with her—he apparently told Çiğdem it wasn't breaking up, it was 'freeing the one he loved'—during their third meeting. In other words, before Şafak's big sister and her fiancé came to see him. Anyway, that's why I don't agree with Çiğdem when she says this visit, which embarrassed Kuzey and made him feel even guiltier, was the fundamental reason for the breakup. I should also add at this point that I'm doubtful about whether that visit ever took place. Strangely enough, no one saw Şafak's sister or her fiancé. Kuzey, if we take his version of events, bumped into them by chance up top, in the town center, and they spoke for about an hour. I asked the owner of the cafe over by the bust, and he said on that day Kuzey had sat there alone the whole morning. So I don't think that meeting ever happened. It was more of a mental meeting, in other words, a figment created by Kuzey's own guilt. Maybe they spoke on the phone.

"If you ask me, Kuzey's talent played the lead role in them break-ing up. His talent for dramatizing, that is. His habit of always seeing life, events, people not as they are, but as if they were from a novel. You could call it his affliction if you like. Kuzey had transformed his relationship with Şafak from the passion, the love, the friendship—call it what you will—between a man and a woman, to a display of self-sacrifice between a savior and a victim waiting to be saved. He fell in love as he lived: he couldn't put himself in his own shoes; he always became the other. He couldn't swap his role of knight in shining armor for that of lover. As İhsan Hoca put it, 'If love doesn't change you and make you someone else, it's not love.' And that's what it all boils down to . . . Why do you think he liked me so much? Because I was a victim for him, always in season, always ready, always at hand. He saved me on the ship from the Portuguese sailor, in Laleli from the fascists, and then from Azrael . . . Yes, you're right. I should be ashamed of what I did, but I don't care if it's appropriate or not, I'm angry with him. Very angry . . .

"The second week of August 2003? In spite of all the warning signs, who could have guessed that week was the beginning of the first act of a well-scripted tragedy? It was as if Kuzey had reached the end of the road. He could only stand up with difficulty by then; he couldn't walk unaided. He'd almost completely stopped eating. Even though his cheeks were often wet, he'd say he was happy. He owed his happiness to God: because He'd lifted the ban on him dreaming at night. Did I laugh? Maybe. Let's just say it's because I managed to work out where his dreams came from . . . No, I only knew for sure later, of course, along with everyone else. When Çiğdem got to the point where she couldn't hide things anymore . . .

"Kuzey never found out Çiğdem's true identity. He had no idea Vildan was the mother of the girl who watched over him. I don't

think Çiğdem showed him the answers she wrote to his letters . . .
The interest Çiğdem had in Kuzey . . . okay, if you want to call it love,
let's call it love, but it's still a question mark for me. Longing for her
father? Punishing her mother? Her quixotic nature? I can't think of
anyone less like a father than Kuzey, so you can leave the father idea
to one side. Her mother? If Çiğdem wanted to take revenge, wouldn't
Vildan have had a part to play in the drama? Vildan had no inkling
about anything. Yes, her quixotic nature. If you're unhappy and long
for other lives, you just might fall in love with a fairy-tale hero. Fairy-
tale heroes are the people who are the furthest removed from reality . . . In other words? In other words, you can leave them whenever
you want. If you don't want attachments, go and find a hero from
a fairy tale or a novel. And even if you can't manage to leave them
yourself, they'll leave you in the end . . . Whatever Çiğdem's reason
was, I still think it's impossible to understand. Maybe she was sick in
the head, like Kuzey said; maybe she was punishing her ego, which
had always plagued her. Yes, why not? Did she tell you as well that
in every period of her life, she found a way to start a fight with her
best friend, and each time that happened, she broke off the friendship? Why? That's a good question. Because of her ego perhaps? An
ego that can't tolerate the existence of any love that could be a rival to
itself . . . I think that's also why she'd never managed to fall in love so
far. So maybe she wanted to punish that meddlesome, troublesome
ego of hers . . .

"Us? Who's us? I can only tell you a few things about myself: I
don't have much of a clue about plants; the only thing I sow and reap
is sorrow. I'm a gardener who cultivates sorrow. And what's more,
I've got a gloomy mind. And that darkens everything I look at . . .
It's obvious my memory's lost the fight; it's given up trying to resist
forgetting. But memory is courage. Now I'm such a coward. What's

a coward? Someone who doesn't go beyond the boundaries of his mind . . . Kuzey attempted to love a young woman. Even if I don't approve, I have to admit, it takes the heart of a lion."

From the diary of an itinerant drunkard, page 51:

Disaster reveals the meaningless inherent in life.
—Kuzey Erkil

Oh stained memory of mine, do not cover your face, open the veil of your shame; there is no such thing as a guiltless memory. As my regret flows toward the future, like a cursed river, the traveler of death, this man who has thrown the sounds of the sea like a cloak around his shoulders, begs you: Tell me! Who can know what happens in the heart of a woman in love? They said that doubt would light the way to the pinnacles of the mind. My doubt casts no light; it buries me in darknesses that no scream can penetrate: Could I have known? Am I guilty? Yes, I am guilty. Because love most often means pure, unadulterated guilt. Very well, but who will judge me? God? No, I do not want forgiveness. Behind God's indulgence there always lies a deep disdain. Besides, He is the most guilty.

Love, in fact, means love; me means me; my regret taught me that. I wait, thinking my honor will be a consolation, but it is not; my pain brings shame. Therefore my story shall not be a story of the birth of anything, but of its coming to an end. A story written in consciousness of death . . .

The great lie: 'If you want to be a great discoverer, discover love.' You grasp love only when you lose it, when disaster reveals the meaningless inherent in life, when its pain brings shame . . .

CHAPTER V

There is no such thing as a guiltless memory . . .
—Kuzey Erkil

August 2003:

The next morning when I opened my eyes, I found not Çiğdem, but Sami at my bedside, examining the razor blade in his hand. A crippled Azrael instead of a goddess! I opened my lips a crack, but God's bailiff acted before I could: "You need to have a shave, mate."

Was that why he was here? I pointed at the packet that was still on the bed: "I'd prefer the gun."

He waved the razor blade. "I'm only going to cut out your tongue for now. Your throat can wait."

We both pretended to laugh. My head was still muddled from the drink, and he was tired. First, I needed a shower, but I didn't have it in me to walk the length of the bathroom and back. Being sober made me lazy. I lowered my feet down from the bed. I took out the gin from the bedside cabinet. It was full. That put me back in high spirits. I raised the bottle and said, "It never ends."

"The angels must be filling it up," said Sami.

Angels! "Maybe it's a houri," I said.

"Houris only serve the drink of the gods," he said. "And that's if you can get into heaven! They wouldn't touch filth like that with a barge pole."

Houri, angel or goddess, it made no difference to me. I took a few deep swigs from the bottle. I stretched contentedly. Soon the rust accumulating in the pipe going down to my stomach would dissolve. Sami was looking blankly at the bottle, with indifferent eyes. When it came to alcohol, he was a complete ignoramus.

"If the still had been invented when the gods held sway, they'd all have drunk real alcohol," I said. He grinned with a smile that wasn't going to bloom on his lips and that made it obvious he wasn't going to put up with me being so full of myself. "How do you do that?"

"How do I do what?" he asked, just as he turned his eyes toward the razor blade.

"Pretend to smile but sulk at the same time." He shook his head, unconcerned. "All right," I said. "I don't know about the gods, but you were right. Us handing over the hotel turned out well. There's more alcohol than ever."

He'd approached the bed and was leaning his shoulder slightly forward for me to get up. I held on to it and got to my feet. We came face-to-face. He was as bleary-eyed as I was. I mustn't have seen him so close-up for a long time. He looked away. "Emin's here," he said.

I let go of his shoulder and listened. Shadows, heat . . . Then I gave up and asked, "What time is it?"

He looked at me for a long time before saying, "Two."

I'd escaped one meal. "Good," I said. "Breakfast time precisely."

Twenty minutes later, we went out onto the terrace. The heat, the cicadas, Küçük Ada were all there. Emin, his wife and Çiğdem were nowhere to be seen.

We walked to the far end. People! The man from Ankara and his young wife, and a few Germans were eating at the tables in the shade of the vine. We went over to Sami's crossword corner. From the tray Mücella had brought, I ate a bit of fruit, half a slice of bread and of course, out of my fear of her, some cheese. She said Emin was upstairs, with his wife. And Çiğdem had gone for a swim.

Sami waited until I'd taken the final mouthful. Once I'd finished chewing on the dry corner of the bread, he started to speak.

"You know what I've been thinking recently?" From the way he was looking at me, I could tell that he already knew he wasn't going to like my answer. I shrugged my shoulders. "Here's what: What have I done that's memorable?" He'd leaned forward as he does when he wants to be persuasive. "Yes, I'm past fifty and what have I done that's memorable? That is the question. I keep thinking about it."

When he finished speaking, he leaned back. He was looking at me with a hostile rage implying that I had done something memorable. I defended myself. "I wouldn't worry about it. The things I remember just mess me up."

"That doesn't matter," he persisted. "To have done something memorable, good or bad . . . Nothing will be left after I'm gone. My life's like a water stain that vanishes without a trace. Half a glass of water spilled on the floor that will end up disappearing and going . . ."

He was going to go senile before I did. "You used to have an Italian girlfriend," I said, skipping his wife. "Why don't you remember her?"

He shook his head stubbornly. His anger had darkened his eyes. "The other day I had to think for twenty minutes to remember her name."

"You're getting old," I said. "It was Lola."

"Madame Lola was her landlady, you fool. The girl was called Laura."

"Okay," I said. "Don't get angry. I'm getting old too."

He thought for a moment. "In fact, I've spent practically all of my adult life with you."

"Is that a bad thing?" I asked.

"I can't say it's good," he said. His pupils went from side to side, and then he shook his head. "Except for our time on the ship. You see, even though I was seasick, it was fun cruising on the ocean." He remembered his seasickness; I remembered the Hausa women Mahler had screwed. "The bad thing is that for some reason I always remember the arguments, and the fights more than anything else. Especially the ones with you."

I took the words out of his mouth. "Okay, I admit it. When we first met, for a time, I did think I'd end up shooting you," I said. "Seriously."

"So you'd have shot me over Stalin! Shame on you." He was looking at me like I actually did have a gun in my hand. "You were yelling at the top of your voice, 'Say Trotsky's a traitor!'"

"I was a complete idiot when I was young, comrade." I waited for him to laugh. He didn't. He was even unhappier than I'd thought. "You're talking rubbish," I continued. "You know what you should do? Eat lots of fish; it's good for the brain. You'll see, you'll remember lots of good things."

He waited for a moment without saying anything. "I always end up remembering my unhappinesses," he said, after a while.

If I ever had the chance, I'd erase the word happiness from the dictionary. "Ignore it," I said. "Don't dwell on it. And who knows, maybe unhappiness is what's really valuable."

"You're trying to die. But what about me? I haven't done anything. I've got nothing left to strive for." Any other time, I'd have said, *You die too, comrade,* but he had to stay behind and keep an eye on things. "A life with no taste, no smell, no color, no goal . . . You know, I sometimes wonder if I've died without noticing it."

Beer time was approaching, but instead of calling Veli over, I reached out my hand and touched Sami on the shoulder. "What's the matter? Just as everything was starting to go your way . . ."

He lifted his hand for me to be quiet. He was staring into my eyes, right into their depths. I thought he was going to confess something. What I wanted was one, maybe two beers.

"It was probably the first time I was scared shitless," he said. Then, without pausing, he thrust forward his sharpened voice threateningly, like a knife. "Don't even think about dying before me . . . I've followed you my whole life. This time, it's my turn to go first. I refuse to be left alone in this shitty world that doesn't want us, that screws us up and throws us away. Do you understand?"

He was waving his hands around spitefully, whining like an abandoned child. Okay, so he had been orphaned by the revolution, but I didn't have to put up with his shouting and screaming. "I can't make any promises, comrade," I said. "But if you buy me a beer, I'll think about it."

"You've got to stop drinking," he said. "Or else you'll die." Without waiting, he gave me the news: "We'll use force if necessary . . ."

We? "And who might your accomplice be?" He didn't reply. It was a stupid question anyway. The chaste goddess! Who the fuck else could it be? "That girl's a bloody maniac," I said. "She's obsessed with me . . . and she's got you wrapped round her little finger . . ." He was shaking his head as though it was empty. I was losing him. "You can't do anything to me. I'm not going to the loony bin again . . ." The way he looked at me seemed to suggest otherwise, so I presented my coup de grace: "If I don't consent, you'll need a court order for that, comrade."

"Maybe we'll have a chat with your big brother . . ."

I tried to raise my hand, but couldn't manage it. I was going to shout, but I couldn't move my lips either. That's when I understood. It was August, but I was frozen. A fossil trapped in ice . . . I did the only thing I could do: without being able to move even an eyelash, I just thought. If they asked Salim, I was sure that bastard would have me sectioned, just like last time. The first thought came dragging the second, even more frightening one behind it: maybe they'd already spoken about to him it . . . My stomach was burning; it felt like I'd swallowed poison. Suddenly a bad smell reached my nose. I'd probably shat myself. I was shafted . . .

It was this silent scream that melted the ice covering my skin like plaster. First I felt the pain on my lips, then I heard my voice, except it didn't sound like mine. "Bastard!"

The bastard didn't reply. I picked up the fruit plate in front of me and flung it, aiming for his face. My movements were slow; Sami ducked; the plate traced a short arc in the air and smashed at the feet of the bald man with the head that shone like a mirror. The tall woman jumped to her feet with a short scream. But the man managed to keep his cool. After the almighty crash, Veli was the first to make a move; as the man was sitting his wife back down at the table, Veli had already started gathering up the grapes strewn over the ground.

Sami used hand gestures to calm down the startled, worried Germans. He wasn't surprised or angry. When everyone had started eating again, he went off grumbling. Senile twat! Did he honestly think because he'd realized he hadn't done anything memorable after all these years that he was going to send me back to the funny farm?

If I'd had the strength to go after him, I would have. But I didn't, and this left me no other choice but to cool my anger down with beer. I called Veli, who had finished what he was doing, and told him to bring me a few bottles. That bad smell was still in my nose. I sniffed my arm: it smelled like rotten meat. It seemed there was no point in me begging God to let me die. I was already a dead body, but I hadn't been buried.

Fifteen minutes later, as I was finishing off the second bottle of the second round, Çiğdem returned from the sea. The ice had melted; I'd warmed up a bit. She was in a good mood. The wet, white dress she was wearing wound around her body like a spider's web and accentuated her curves. As soon as she sat down across from me, she asked with a cheerful smile that bore hope for the future, "How are you?"

Without mincing my words, "You'll be left with egg on your face," I said.

The light immediately went out of her eyes. Her smile had been as short-lived as the éclat of spring. "What's happened now?"

"You go to the funny farm," I said. "Because you're the one who needs your head examined."

She was looking at me now with blank eyes that had lost their sparkle, their color. Completely blank, as if the only thing that occurred to her was to keep quiet. When she regained her composure, she took refuge in her politeness and muttered, "I'm afraid I don't understand what you mean."

"Here's what I mean: find someone who'll fuck you and quit interfering with me."

She blushed, and I calmed down a little. At least there was one realm where I had the upper hand: shamelessness.

"What are you trying to conceal behind your rudeness? Your fears?" I didn't reply; I was happy with the superiority I'd acquired. "And you never know, maybe I have found someone."

Now she was looking at me, sure of herself, almost challenging me. "So stop interfering with us then," I said.

"Us?"

"Me and my drink."

"I see!" She was staring straight into my eyes, oblivious to the bottle I was pointing in her face. "So that's the reason for your absurd rudeness."

"If you plot behind my back, I won't be held responsible for my actions. Just now, I threw a plate at the head of your partner in crime. He was sitting right where you are now."

She thought for a moment. "How can you think I could ever do something against your will?"

Was she telling the truth? I didn't let up. "I don't trust you. I think you're hiding things from me and . . ." I laughed; I had to draw a line between her sidekick and me; she could have told him. "I think you're hiding things from me. I'd bet on it."

She was still blushing. She thought for a moment. "Very well then, let's say I was prepared to tell you what you want to know. Would you give up alcohol for it?"

She was being sanctimonious and funny at the same time. But more than anything else, she was being foolish. Optimistically foolish at that. "There's nothing important enough to make me give up alcohol," I said. "And if you think I'll go to hospital for that, you're stupid."

"Maybe we can find a middle path."

"Through the middle, around the side or up the front . . . I'm not going anywhere. I'm going to stay here and I'm going to drink. If you say the hotel's yours, I'll find somewhere else."

She squirmed for a while in an intense silence that was as malleable as dough, and then asked in a lifeless voice, "But why?"

"I can't leave this place. I've got a date."

She didn't ask with whom. "Why don't we do this: I've invited a friend of mine here, actually he's my old doctor. Why don't you have a chat with him?"

Her shrink. "I'll chat with anyone," I said. I put my right index finger on the table, and traced a circle around it with my middle finger. "As long as I don't have to move from where I am."

She was curious. "What have you drawn?"

"A circle," I said. "Inside is real life. Because that life is my life."

"But there's life outside that circle too."

"There's a desert outside," I said. "Piles of sand under the command of a deaf God. A world of scorpions and snakes."

Again she took refuge in that silence, which was rising like dough. When she returned, she had lost hope.

"Your problem is that you do everything to excess . . . Your drinking, your sorrow, your regret—they're all excessive. You want to imprison yourself on a desert island, but there's no such place." She thought for a moment and repeated: "I'm sure of it; there's no such place. Don't you understand? There's nowhere you can be alive and alone, by yourself . . ."

"Yes, there is." Then I said what sprung to mind: "In the womb."

Her face lit up as though it had re-established contact with life. "But it's been a long time since you were born." She leaned forward. She was excited. "Maybe a child . . . That could solve everything." She was practically clapping her hands. "Come on, perk yourself up a bit. Take a look around. Come out from that circle!"

"I'm not an exhibitionist. I don't need people to see that I'm alive . . ."

Then I gulped down the beer. Just when I'd managed to forget how to live, when I'd stopped being curious about people, I had no intention of starting everything again from scratch . . . Do birds die while they're flying or while they're on the ground? Maybe it was nonsense, but that's what I was actually curious about.

As I reached for the third bottle, I noticed there was something different. I waited a few moments, and it became clear. The silence: it had changed form. It was a silence that belonged to the terrace, a silence of the kind Çiğdem didn't emit. I turned to the woman opposite from me, who was inside life, still waiting for me, full of hope. "Have you noticed?"

"Noticed what?" she asked.

Her disappointment spread like a shadow across her tanned face, which men found arousing. We weren't in the same place. She was on the train that was getting ready to depart; I was waiting on the platform. "The cicadas," I said, after I had grasped the silence as a whole. "They're not chirruping."

"So?"

"They're randy," I said. "They don't just stop making noise. And certainly not while they're on the job."

We sent Veli around the back, to the pepper tree. Three minutes later the boy appeared at the corner; next to him was a formless creature glistening brightly under the sun. My arms spread out, and I slowly tilted backward, like a tree trunk that had been cut off from its roots. Fındık! After days, the cursed dolphin had finally surfaced.

On land—if he wasn't slithering along the ground—Fındık would shuffle along without lifting his feet and wobble from side to side. And that's how he walked. Leaning back in the plastic chair, I waited for him to get to our table. Once he was directly in front of me, he stopped. He'd raised his shoulders in the air as though issuing a challenge. I sat up and offered him the packet. He took two cigarettes after he'd handled them all one by one, the way he might select fruit. He put the first one to his lips, and placed the other one carefully behind his ear. I was engrossed in watching him. With the first smoke he puffed out into the air, he lowered his shoulders.

That was the sign I'd been waiting for. We were friends again. I pointed to the empty chair. Slowly—was he afraid of slipping?—he sat down on the chair in two actions. Once he was in his place, like a tired acrobat who had reached the other end of the tightrope safe and sound, he smiled happily. Had he dived? What had he found? When the silence became a fence between us, I turned to Çiğdem.

"It seems I'm no longer wanted," she said, without smiling.

She wasn't mistaken: as soon as she'd gone, the happy dolphin started to speak. He was as impatient as I was. "The commander's come . . . Did 'e bring it? Well?"

He stared directly at me with his lashless eyes—if you could call them eyes. As he looked at me, I heard an alarm go off in my head: decision time! If I told him the truth, I'd never see him again. That was certain. The other option? If I lied, I'd have deceived the only being on the peninsula that resembled me. I gulped. Would he understand me? I was late for the meeting. If there was only one word between God's forgetfulness and His grace, I could lie. The distant alarm, like my resistance, was getting weaker. *H* one, *o* two, *n* three, *e* four, *s* five, *t* six, *y* seven! I wasn't going to yield to a seven-letter word. I gulped again, and snapped the barbed wire that was in my throat. Then, "Yes, he did," I said.

"What do it be like?" His eyes had gotten even bigger.

Without letting go of the bottle, I spread my hands out. At the same time, I was saying to myself, *Relax, you charlatan: you're not going to blush. Your cheeks are bright red anyway.* "A huge Kalashnikov," I said. "This big."

"Zwo, an AK?"

"An AK," I said. "Double magazine, too."

"Double, eh?" I nodded. "Well done!"

Like his eyes, his face had broadened too. Alcohol made me happy; lies made him happy. I was deceiving a fish who knew how to have a laugh, who didn't hesitate to put his life in danger with me, who had shed a tear after a woman crying "my daughter, my daughter," a friend, a wonder of nature, and I was betraying the sacredness of the peninsula, of the Register. It was all I could do not to tell him to erase me from the Register. Beer came to my aid. I swiftly downed what was left at the bottom of the third bottle. Now it was time for the question whose answer I'd risked being a bastard and a liar for.

"What about you?" I asked. "Did you dive where I said?" He nodded his head, or the part of him I fancied to be his head. "Is it there?"

He didn't answer immediately. First he took a long drag on his cigarette, which was about to go out because of the water flowing from his forehead.

Then, "There do be zometh'n there . . ." he drawled. "But I doesn't know what, zee; it be under the zand, I can't make it out . . ." I tried to stand up, but I couldn't. Fındık continued. "But it don't be where thee said . . . It be about two 'undred vathoms toward Uzunada . . . Thee knows tharn juniper tree? Well, it be level with that."

I lifted my empty bottle and showed it to Veli. "Are you sure?"

"Very deep," he said. "There be a current too."

I looked into his glassy eyes; he was sure. I took a deep, long breath, as if it was my last. I was about to reach that point when the compass of time would narrow, when it wouldn't have such a thing as "the future." "Juniper tree," I muttered.

"What be the date today?" What was it? "Thee 'asn't vorgwodden, 'as thee?"

"The 15th," I told him.

"And on the 17th of Zeptember . . ."

He was an incorrigible maniac! "I know," I said. "On September 17th we're going to Mytilene."

He chuckled with joy. And I responded, as if he'd reached out his hand, with a smile. If I was going to die, it wasn't going to be this lie that killed me. I pointed to the bottle that Veli had brought. Fındık shook his head. "Dwon't drink neither. Thy 'and do shake, and then . . ."

"Don't worry," I said. "I'll be sober by the 17th . . . Anyway, tell me! How deep is it?"

He shrugged his shoulders. "'Ow do I know? Like I zays, it do be very deep."

"Right under the cliff? How close is it to the shore?"

He pursed his lips. "Thirty?"

Thirty fathoms! "And exactly level with the juniper tree, yes?"

He nodded. As I was trying to summon up an image of the juniper tree before my eyes, something strange happened. My thoughts started turning into a picture . . . To the right, on the road that looked like a tunnel carved into the hillside, I could see a red car. The sky at the top of the slope was about to turn from gray to black; the evening star was getting ready to descend from between the hilltops toward the valley . . . Okay, so when was I going to go there? A voice yelled, "Right now." And then, "Tomorrow!" And tomorrow had turned into a picture: a view of the sea with a single tree in the middle.

"Thee really be com'n, ain't thee?" Where was I going? Without raising my head from the view I was focusing on, I nodded. "Okay, let's vorgive each other in the next life?"

So dolphins had a heaven too? "If you want us to forgive each other in the next life, then let's do it," I said.

"I can't pull the wool over thy eyes anymore."

So a lie didn't kill him either. "Pulling what wool?" I asked.

"That pup of thine . . ." I was in a daze from the throng of pictures one after the other—of course, there were four bottles of beer next to the pictures too. When Fındık saw I was staring blankly, he started explaining: "Thee knows, its mother gwot mangled by a bus . . ."

"Spot," I said, excitedly.

"Ah, Spot, Scott, whadever, that one. Anyway, it died last winter . . . I was gwo'n to tell thee, but Miss Handan twold me not to."

For a moment, neither of us could speak. After a long while, I tore through the silence that hung like the reticulations of a spider's web. "How did it happen?"

"Who knows! It just died . . ." I reached for the beer. "I vound it on the ridge of Alman Koyu. Thee knows, over where the rubbish bins do be. I buried it past the dry well be'ind there . . . deep. And I put a whopp'n great stwone on twop."

"Tomorrow," I said.

"What did thee zay?"

"Nothing."

"'As thee gwot zometh'n in thy eye?"

I was sobbing gently, but, "No," I said. "There's nothing in my eye."

The reclusive fugitive, Schoendoerfffer's dog, my unborn child, the poor creature I'd abandoned to the night, to the darkness, to hunger, to snakes, to poisons, even though I'd promised to look after him until I died . . . I reached for the beer: what was I going to do? In my memory there was a huge, cliff-like abyss. I was lost in the pages of the story I was telling—or maybe I wasn't telling it, I was reading it—I was someone puzzled to find he's lost his page! Could I have been one of the heroes in that story? Everything was muddled. I laughed. Was I alive? If I wasn't even sure of that, what was so strange about being puzzled? I closed my eyes to hold back my tears. Then I wished someone would come up, open the book and show me the place I wouldn't be able to find by myself: a guide.

When I opened my eyes, I saw that man. Every time I met him, I thought his face had been turned upside down. He was still grinning. Was it a sign? "How are you?" said the man.

I turned to Fındık. He got up as Çiğdem had done half an hour earlier. "I'll be off then . . ." I raised my hand. "When be I gwo'n to zee what the cwommander brought?" When? "Raise the zailor's ghwost . . ."

"Okay," I said. "I will."

Fındık waddled off. The man asked, "The sailor's ghost?"

"Whistling," I said.

He'd sat down across from me without waiting to be invited. I'd asked God for a guide, and He'd sent me a churlish charlatan.

"I've done a little research. It seems you haven't sold the hotel." Our charlatan wasn't just churlish; he was a curious bastard too. "Actually, there's a group of us thinking of investing here. Close friends. You might be interested."

"Are they restaurant owners? Or cooks?"

He wasn't offended by having the piss taken out of him. "Shipping agents, but they have investments in the tourism sector too. They might be interested in your hotel."

"Really?" I said.

"They'll be generous. I can guarantee that."

Things were getting more and more interesting. "How generous?" I asked.

"Name your price . . ." His eyes quickly narrowed, suggesting he had no intention of haggling back and forth. "And they'll put you up abroad for a while too. With whoever you want. That friend of yours who was raising the sailor's ghost just now, for instance." To go abroad with Fındık! I had to try hard not to burst out laughing. "We've got very good facilities abroad."

Had I been mistaken about the guide? Or had God regained his hearing? I took the cigarette the man offered and lit it. The bastard restaurateur wants to buy up the hotel, and get me and Fındık out of the way! Why? I shuddered. It was all falling into place. I was going to say, "Okay, I'll think about it." But no sound came out. I reached out my hand in desperation.

He shook my hand quickly, as if he'd understood that it was his turn to leave the table. "What shall I tell my friends?"

For a moment—beneath the dark shadow reminiscent of death—I thought about what to say. I was at the edge of the cliff in the middle of my memory; I seemed to be tongue-tied. But anyway, I remembered that view, the picture I'd put the juniper tree in the middle of, the picture I called *Tomorrow* . . . Without stammering, I said, "Tomorrow. We'll talk in the morning."

Once he'd stood up as though he'd got what he wanted, the tall woman appeared at the corner. He scurried off toward her.

Tomorrow! The end of my future. The big reunion . . .

I called Veli over and asked him how long I'd been sitting there. "Two hours," he said.

I left the most important two hours of my life there, on the table looking out to Küçük Ada, and I got up. "To my room," I said to Veli, who took my arm. I guess in the end God was willing to keep rolling snake eyes.

Once in the room, I turned on the fan and lay down on the bed. I took a deep breath. If I was going to stand up on my own two feet tomorrow, when the dice were scattered, I was going to have to drink as little as possible.

July 1998:

"How many times has it been?" she asks.

We're face-to-face, eye-to-eye. There's a strange, out-of-place darkness in her eyes: the shadow of nothing. If I could see them, I'd say there's indecision and shame in mine. As the moisture between our tired, satisfied bodies cools, it turns into a fine film. A film that keeps the realities of life and the realities that have gotten stuck in this room—our reality—separate from one another, but which, no matter what we do, will eventually evaporate and disappear.

"Why won't you answer me?"

"How many times has what been?" I ask. "That we've had sex?"

"How many times have I come here?"

The other name for waiting: her coming, then her going. Painful memories I'd like to forget. "Five, maybe six," I say.

"Five," she says. "I've come here exactly five times, and each time I've told myself it would be the last."

Does that make her angry? Her eyes are deaf; they don't reply, like a dark blackout curtain. "Is everything ready?" I ask.

Should I tell her about her sister? No, this is her last visit. This time she's going. Didn't she say her passport and ticket are ready? Questions in my mind . . . How did her family take her sudden decision? And me? I have to wait in silence. "What are you thinking about?" she suddenly asks.

"Nothing," I say. "I'm not thinking about anything."

"Liar," she says.

"And you?" I ask.

She doesn't reply. Not with her lips, not with her eyes: both are mute. I stand up and go to the window to watch what's happening outside. It's July, but it's a strange day. A storm has been brewing on the western horizon since morning. In the middle of the sea, shadows of clouds that make you think of laden rafts buried in the water: some of them pigeon gray, some of them seagull white. I should close the window. There's an oceanic splendor on the darkening horizon: unreachable and eerie . . .

"Life is the story of whether or not we can change ourselves," she says, out of the blue. I turn to the room without closing the window: her body, which has now shed the red cloak of lust, is lying—still half-naked—on the bed; her eyes are large enough to take in the world, the continents. God, how can I part with her? Her words have a follow-up: "Interesting lives are the stories of people who've been able to change themselves . . ." Then she drops a bomb in the middle of the room. "Come with me!" Where? "To Africa." To go to Africa with her. I remember the heat, the damp, the ocean and Mahler. I remember these things; she repeats the most tempting invitation I've ever received. "Come with me!"

"I had my turn thirty years ago," I say.

"But I wasn't even born then," she says.

"And that's precisely the problem," I say. "Bad timing."

"Stubborn!" She continues, "Because you're intent on staying how you are . . . Is it really so difficult to change?"

I don't know, but I do know that when you still haven't got a grown-up life to change, you think it's easy. "We've rewritten our story from scratch at least three times already," I say. "The next time would be a boring repetition."

"So be it, take that chance! Take a risk! Isn't that what love is?"

She's looking at me now like she's an accident victim: with the hope of being saved. I shake my head. Our love is like the light that strikes the wall from a torch lit in this room at night: enchanting but ephemeral . . . I want to bellow that I'll come: "I can't come," I say instead.

"Why not?" she asks. "I'm ready to risk everything."

She's ready because she has time. But me . . . I promised I wouldn't get between her and her future. If I knew I could get used to betrayal, if I believed in myself a little, maybe I would have tried. "I won't be in your future," I say. "Not because I don't want to, but because I can't; nature won't allow it."

She says nothing for a moment. We're both helpless. Which one of us can oppose the real God, nature, which parades its cruelty with an obscene impartiality? The whoosh of the match ignites the silence too; we size each other up skeptically in a dirty, ashen silence that flutters in the air.

"I'm not looking for the future," she says, once she's halfway through her cigarette. "I'm happy with the present, and with today. No matter how long it lasts, whatever I can get from the moment I'm living in is enough for me." I say nothing. My silence is my reply. But she's deaf. She can't hear what I say; she suddenly leaps up: from disappointment to anger. "I'd like to know if you're really in love with me. Madly, like I am with you." Madly? How can you tell if you're in love with someone like that? The answer rattles in the silence like a choked scream: with us no longer sparing the fact that we're in love . . . Do I feel sorry for her? I'm not sure. Maybe the person I feel sorry for . . . Her trembling voice interrupts my wavering thoughts. "It's not love you don't believe in, it's yourself. You don't believe in yourself. You're the only reason for your lack of belief. Because you don't want to admit that someone could be madly in love with you; is it because you hate yourself? Why?"

Why! There always has to be a reason . . . But often what we posit as a reason is only an excuse; an excuse we've invented because we can't refuse something we don't want to accept . . . *You'll never be able to understand women!* I know that to be a lie invented by women who don't want to be understood, who want to hide their foolishness. I understand all too well what the woman in front of me wants . . . "Madly!" I say. "I haven't done anything like that for a long time."

"What would you do for me?" She returns from anger to disappointment. She's falling, onto her back. "Would you die for me?"

"Hush," I say. "Don't tempt death!"

She has more to say, but she decides not to. She scowls, eyeing me like I'm a coward. Then, "Fine," she says. "Off you go. I'm going to sleep for a bit."

I get dressed and go out. The daylight seeping from the clouds looks like a golden sword that has been plunged into the darkness of the storm in the west. The islands complete the bleak but magical scene. How can I explain to her that real love is being able to let go? I can't. I light a cigarette. Sami approaches; no, it's not him approaching, it's his crutches, the noise his crutches make on the concrete. The smoke I blow out drifts off toward the islands. Sami, once he himself has arrived, asks, "What's happened?"

"Nothing," I say. "It's painful for her."

"You're not going to change your mind, are you?" I shake my head. "It must be difficult."

I'm thinking. Was it difficult? I'm engrossed in myself. "Watching someone in pain! That's what's difficult," I say. "Being able to bear the shame of causing pain to someone you really love . . ."

"You're doing it for her own good."

Good . . . Should I say I hate being good, that the mere mention of the word good makes me feel sick now?

"What I wouldn't give to be bad, to be a bastard." My head is shaking by itself. "Renouncing what I want for the good of someone else; I'd say that pretty much sums up my life. How soul destroying! We've never ever indulged ourselves. We've always renounced. Someone once said we valued virtue too much. Was it Mahler? Whoever said it, they were right."

Sami says, "Sit down." I've got nothing else to do apart from smoking and feeling ashamed; I can sit down. So I do. He continues trying to console me: "Maybe we really are as good and as soul-destroyed as you say. But what else could we have done? Our badness was stolen from us; they destroyed our ability to be bad and condemned us to be good. What do you think? Did they erase and destroy our egos with humanitarianism and revolutionary marches when we were still young?" I laugh. He silences me by saying, "Don't laugh. I'm being serious. Look at us! Always us, whatever the weather, *us*! We forgot how to say *me*."

Then he falls silent. We eye each other. Our lips open a crack. At exactly the same time, lightning strikes off the shore of Mytilene. "Someone's telling us to shut up," I say.

Sami smiles. I'd cry if I weren't embarrassed to.

One hour later, when I return to the room, I find her dressed and in front of the window watching the wind approaching the peninsula, leaving a trail of black on the sea. She's smoking. I shudder. She's so beautiful that I can't help loving her. When I get close to her, she turns around. Her eyes and the light of love are extinguished: there's no light on her face or on the wall.

"I didn't sleep; I was thinking. Maybe there's another way." She pauses and waits for me to ask, but I don't. "Seeing you won't come, I'll stay. Here with you . . . All you have to do is say 'stay;' what I want to hear is one short little word." I bite my lips not to shout out that short little word over and over again. Resist; keep quiet for a few more minutes. That's what I have to do. I avoid her eyes. "My God, you're not even going to tell me to stay."

When she starts sobbing, I hold her. She shakes me off and escapes from my arms. I follow her as far as the bed, then leave her alone with her sorrow. If you're in pain, you cry out; if you're ashamed, you stay silent. I'm buried in a silence futile enough for me to drown in. Ten minutes later the wind that has been dallying in the west since morning bursts in through the open window, full of enmity.

As I close the window, I hear her. Depending on whether she's feeling angry or despondent, the sounds that structure her sentences sometimes fall from a high pitch to a low one, and sometimes climb from a low to a high, like in a jazz improvisation. She's not speaking; she's singing the song of her sorrow. That's why it's sincere; that's why it's convincing.

"I'm not you. I can't lick my wounds better like a dog. My blood doesn't clot."

She's speaking; I'm muttering silently like a mouse, afraid even of letting myself hear: "I love you; if death's what you want, I welcome death . . ."

"You know what your problem is? There's an impassable wall between dreams and you: your mind . . ."

I was still muttering: "If I'd been a tree, I'd have pruned myself down to the same height as you . . ."

"But you know what's funny? What you think is your mind is actually your cowardice."

That's when I work out the secret of that strange shadow in her eyes: despair. I can't do it! Letting her stay means spending the rest of my life proving how brave I am. And that's something too grueling for me to risk . . .

She stops speaking and I listen to her: her voice is staid and without vigor now. Her sentences flow with crystallized words between the smooth walls of logic, but her eyes are like the faded sign of a clouded, shadowy consciousness. Her short sentences, the words she's chosen, her voice—they're all messengers of exile. Her sorrow has no smell anymore. "Soon I'll be gone . . ." She continues as if putting a curse on me: "I hope one day you'll find out what being in love means."

I don't even tell her to stay until the morning.

An hour later, she's walking toward her car. We don't say good-bye; we both realize we're seeing each other for the last time. Her eyes are dry, as though she's lost the ability to cry. They're focused on somewhere in the distance that I can't see, that I won't be able to reach. Her blood-colored mouth, shriveled up with contempt, has turned into a full stop marking the end of everything. I've stabbed her. She's bleeding from every part: her eyes, her mouth, her hands, all over her body . . . and, of course, her soul. I take a step toward her; my feet are sticky; I feel the wetness of the blood on the ground . . .

The murmur that remains in my ears, in the fig-tree cove on Küçük Ada, in the top-floor room she's emptied out repeats like a chorus: "Go, my darling, your future now belongs to you alone . . ."

August 2003:

"Are you going to wake up?"

I wasn't sleeping; I was remembering . . . I opened my eyes and there was an itching on my fingertips. Çiğdem was leaning over the bed, smiling. What a contrast! There she was, the goddess of the hunt, the appetite for life bursting from her eyes, from her skin, and there I was, a corpse doubtful about whether or not I'd be able to sit up. I couldn't move, but at least I remembered I could speak. "What time is it?"

"Going on eight . . . What? Can't we work out the time anymore?"

She was being cheeky, like a child. "It's because of the dog days," I said.

She sat at the edge of the bed. I gripped the sheet to stop my hands from trembling. I had no choice: *I have to drink a little* . . .

"I've got some news . . ." *I'm going to drink half as much as I used to* . . . After telling myself this once more, I reached out my left hand to the gin standing on top of the bedside table. Çiğdem waited for me to take the bottle, then continued: "We've got guests the day after tomorrow . . . a few friends from Istanbul are coming and so's Rana. I've decided to accept her offer of peace after all . . . It's great, isn't it? We're going to be holding a big party for Mars . . ." The day after tomorrow! The future I pledged to the love of my life five years ago might not extend that far . . . Still, instead of saying so, I took two swigs of the gin. "Why aren't you saying anything?"

"It's obvious it's a good idea," I said.

Skeptically, she scrutinized my face. "Maybe we'll dance."

Two swigs weren't going to be enough. I took one more. "You dance; whenever there's dancing, I just watch."

"Come on! Be serious. Stop talking like an old man."

"Fine," I said. "I won't talk."

She looked at my face for a moment, then asked: "What is being old?"

"Always talking about your illnesses," I said.

"In that case, you're not old. Come on, get up!"

I tried to get up unassisted. And I succeeded. I took a pair of trousers from the cupboard and went into the bathroom and washed my face. The water wasn't cold, but it took away some of the heaviness in my head. When I came back, I asked, "What's Emin doing?"

"He's on the terrace; I think he's waiting for you."

Without wasting any time, I went out onto the terrace. The sun had drawn back to behind Hisarcık Kayası, but the heat was still there. The cicadas had shut up. Beneath the pergola, it was deserted. The Germans hadn't rendezvoused with their beer yet. As Çiğdem headed over to Sami, who was sitting on his own, I went to Emin's table.

He waved. I said hello.

He still looked like a statue, a devilish demigod who had withdrawn into the shadows. Our eyes met. The never eroding expressionlessness of his face must have been a reflection of his irreparably wounded soul. With the embarrassment characteristic of those who live alone, "Thanks for your help," he said.

I pointed to Çiğdem. "Thank her."

He nodded his head and squirmed awkwardly in his chair. "She'll come back when she's gotten over it," he said. "I'll cope."

We stopped speaking as if the conversation was over. I made a sign to Veli, who had been watching my movements since I came out onto the terrace. He came up to the table. I was going to say two, but then I decided on one bottle. As the silence lengthened, "It's hot," I said.

"Look. Don't think I'm some sort of shitty bastard who abandons his wife in her state."

I understood him. He didn't care about being good or bad. What shamed him was leaving someone behind. "Very well then, what sort of bastard are you?" I asked.

He paused. His eyes had frozen too. He had a toughness that stemmed not from his strength, but from his nature.

"I can't say I'm a good person." Then he started to tell his story. "Years ago, we were on an operation in Bitlis, when they opened fire on my men in some god-awful village. We lost three men, one of them a lieutenant. I took the sergeant with me and went into the house where the shooting was coming from. The men were on the bottom floor of the stone house . . ." His voice had lost its fluency; it had turned into paste; the words were getting more and more drawn out, and as they got drawn out, they solidified. "The skirmish lasted all of five minutes. Then we went downstairs . . . there were three carcasses behind some sacks . . ." He fell silent for a moment, as though counting the dead bodies, which he referred to as carcasses, again. That wasn't all he saw behind the sacks. "To the side, there were two women lying on the floor too. Pregnant women, practically full-term . . . They'd been caught in the crossfire. Their stomachs were riddled with holes. Their babies too, they'd come out . . ." He took a long gulp and cleared his throat. His words were pieces of stone now. "Once you've killed someone, you become isolated; then comes the second one, the third one . . . I'd kept telling Türkan I didn't want a child. Over and over again . . ."

If you can't console someone, it's best just to keep quiet. I opened the bottle Veli brought. The beer numbed the silence and made it bearable.

I understood his story: maybe because I still hadn't forgotten the language peculiar to those who've killed. After waiting half a bottle,

I told him what I'd learned in the watery deserts thousands of miles away from here: "Regret is much bigger and heavier than we think."

"If only it had been me . . ."

. . . *who had died*, was what he was going to say. But he stopped short. Maybe because he understood it was an empty phrase. Still, he must have had lots of opportunities to die in those mountains. I knew; there was nothing strange in it. If I'd been fighting, I would have done the same as he did too. I would have wanted to live like he did too. Because war makes life more attractive.

"Anyway, you're going to have to decide . . ." I offered him a cigarette. "Why don't you wait until after the birth?" Was he going to answer? No. He couldn't get beyond the "if only;" he said nothing. He thought about those pregnant women, and I took small sips of the beer. Once I'd taken a break from drinking, "Spot's dead," I said. "Months ago apparently. They hid it from me."

"That dog you were looking for?" he asked.

Surprise had quickened a small band of his frozen face, his eyes. I nodded. He mustn't have understood how I'd gone from the lifeless pregnant women lying on the ground to Spot.

"I've never had any children," I said. "Maybe it does you good to have children."

He raised his head and shrugged his shoulders. He couldn't make up his mind if it would be good or bad. We withdrew into silence once more. The sun had set; twilight, like fast-growing flowers, was spreading across the terrace. "That strange thing, the insect hater, why's he looking at us?"

I turned to where he was pointing. From behind the vine, Fındık had fixed his glassy eyes on us, like a double barrel, and was scrutinizing us. "He thinks you've brought him a gun," I said.

"What gun?"

"The one we're taking with us when we go to invade Mytilene," I said. "An AK-47. On September 17th." He tried to raise his eyebrows in an expression of understanding, but he couldn't. His forehead was still lifeless. "Of course, we're not going anywhere. I'm tricking him." He didn't ask why. "If you're here on September 17th, will you keep an eye on him?"

He paused for a moment. "Why won't you?"

"You never know, I might go on a trip."

"A long one?" he asked.

Forty or fifty fathoms. Maybe a hundred . . . "Pretty short," I said.

He raised his hand. We were agreed. "I hear you've handed over the hotel." I nodded. "Çiğdem . . ." He thought for a moment about what to say, then continued decisively. ". . . Hanım seems to be taking it seriously . . ."

He must have heard the rest of the story from Ahmet. "She's a good girl," I said. "But a bit crazy . . . she thinks I'm her boyfriend." I wasn't going to be able to hold out any longer; I took long sips of beer one after the other. "And there's something else I want you to do for me."

"What?"

"We're going to dig up a grave," I said. "I can't do it by myself. I need your help."

He stared into my face. I drank a little more beer. All of a sudden, as if they'd been waiting for Çiğdem's cheerful laughter, Germans filled the terrace. "We'll need a shovel," he said.

I looked at his watch. It was a quarter past eight. So . . . "Let's go before it gets too dark," I said.

Çiğdem didn't ask why we wanted her car keys. The happiness she got from me being on my feet had destroyed her curiosity. She said Rana might come tonight; when she reminded me we were going to have dinner together, I said we wouldn't be late. Ignoring Sami's suspicious glances, I went around the back with Emin. Veli brought a pickax, shovel, sack and torch. Without being seen by anyone apart from Fındık, who was still observing us, we got in the car and went out onto the road that went down to Bodrum. A few minutes later, when we reached the hill that looked out onto the cove, I motioned for Emin to stop. We got out of the car. To our right, the tall, saw-toothed Akdağlar; in front of us, Domuz Burnu; at the bottom left of the frame, the bottom of the bay, which was turning navy, and a smooth sea. After drinking what was left in the bottle, I turned to Emin. "We're going to have to go into the bushes."

Except for his eyes, his face was still lifeless.

We left the road and entered the bushes on the southern slope of Değirmen Dağı. Emin was walking in front; he found the well as easily as if he'd put it there himself. Among the brushwood, we came across the large rock that Fındık had mentioned. The clever dolphin, like an Egyptian priest, had chosen a perfect place for the grave that predators wouldn't be able to find easily.

Everything was different on this hillside that had its back turned to the sea. A strange sky that bore the tracks of the devil was suspended above: ghost-like shadows on the half-dark horizon, an orange belt of distant lights that had descended on the peaks like mist . . . The heat was leaning against the mountains, pushing against the night, delaying it. The peaks had melted, and were about to drip down onto the plain . . .

Before the final light of the day disappeared, Emin pushed the stone to one side and started digging the earth. At first I was calm, but once the pile of soil at my feet started to get high, I began to cry. Each shovel load noisily crumpled up another picture of Spot and flung it into the void: on Şafak's lap kissing her, sleeping at the foot of the bed, playing with the waves on Küçük Ada, chasing after crabs that were sunbathing on the rocks, hunting grasshoppers, hiding inside an empty jar in the yard when he got scared of the cats, turning and running away when I went near him after I'd started drinking . . . Each time the shovel went into the soil, my understanding became clearer: the photographs I was losing, that were being buried one by one in the earth beneath my feet, were not individual memories— they were the illustrated story of the last five years.

Six inches down, we encountered the first trace of Spot. Emin paused and leaned over, and I turned on the torch and hung it on the bush at the side. There was a sack about sixty or seventy centimeters long in the hole that had opened up. Emin put down the shovel, and as he pulled at the perished sack, it crumbled apart like a snake's skin. Fındık hadn't taken as much care in choosing the shroud as he had done in choosing the place.

After working for a few minutes, he got up. He had something to say. "There's nothing holding the bones together. I'm going to take them out one by one." I didn't reply; I sobbed. As if it would comfort me, while thrusting the dusty head into my hand, he explained: "The skull's complete; there's no damage to it."

He took the torch and placed it at the top of the hole. I shook the skull in my hand. There was no brain inside it. Even when he was alive, you couldn't have called him particularly clever. "He couldn't stand the smell of alcohol . . . he ran away," I said. "That's why he died."

"So he had a sensitive nose then."

Mine's sensitive too . . . "I want a beer," I said.

He didn't turn around. I was by myself, holding a head I used to kiss. There was only one thing that thinned the sorrow. The picture called *Tomorrow*.

It took fifteen minutes to transfer Spot's bones to the sack. I didn't touch any other bones apart from the skull. As Emin stood up and handed me each bone from the shallow grave, I opened the mouth of the sack. When it was over, he got out of the knee-deep hole. He stamped his feet to shake off the soil that had got on his trousers. His breathing was regular, and he didn't seem to think there was anything strange about what he'd done. Maybe because he was used to dead bodies, regardless of species.

Before returning, we waited for a moment in the opening between the bushes. One by one, the stars took up their positions in the sky. Emin was hanging around instead of coming out; I thought he wanted to smoke a cigarette. I was wrong. He was looking deep into the bushes, scraping his feet on the ground like he was searching for something. I suddenly realized: he wasn't really there in front of me; he still hadn't returned from the war he'd gone to.

When he noticed I was observing him, he explained in a neutral voice as though talking about someone else: "When I came to the hotel, I slept on this hillside for the first week." He shrugged his shoulders: "Whenever I see a sheltered hill that's quite high, I can't help myself."

There are two kinds of people: those who manage to escape from their past, and those who never do . . . I didn't tell him that. He already knew anyway. Besides, I needed to drink immediately, like there was no tomorrow . . . no tomorrow! I left the thought that scared me shit-less where it was, next to the sobs that were building up in my throat. I vocalized a new thought like a prayer: *I'm not going to drink; I have to last until tomorrow* . . . "With half of what I want . . ."

"Half of what?" asked Emin. "We've got all the bones."

"Okay," I said. "Say good-bye to your bed; we're going."

He paused as though he really was saying good-bye. Then he put his hands up. He had something to say, his last words: "When you're trying to decide about me, don't forget this: when you're making war, you can't remain good . . ."

While he was emptying out the grave, he must have been thinking about the trenches. The badness that he'd acquired after the fact. I didn't reply. Even if I'd wanted to, I had nothing to say. He swung the sack onto his back with ease. Slowly, we walked away from nature's frightening face, toward our side, the friendly side.

Sami Çetin, August 10, 2004:

"That strange, stormy evening, after Şafak had gotten into her car and driven off, Kuzey imprisoned himself in a strange cocoon—a deep, coffin-like silence. And from that moment, we couldn't get through to him anymore. It was as though his life span wasn't complete, as though he was on the verge of passing on to another stage in his life cycle, and he was waiting for his time to come. He was both deaf and mute now. He didn't speak and he didn't hear. We begged him to eat, to drink some water even . . . Me and Handan.

"Then? Then that phone call came. From her big sister. That fateful phone call saying they hadn't heard from her for a week. And the next day the whole family turned up . . . We were all in shock. The search lasted a whole ten days. One by one, every road, every track, every valley, every hill on the peninsula was searched. The ground had opened up; Şafak had disappeared. The family gave up at the end of the first week and went home. The Gendarmerie carried on searching for three more days. No one had seen her car. No one knew, no one had seen if she'd gone down in the direction of Mordoğan, or to the north toward Yeniliman. The storm seemed to have wiped away every trace of her. Kuzey and Fındık searched the whole coast from the sea in a boat. There was no trace, no remnant. Kuzey came back on the fifteenth day. His face wasn't alive; it was a mask: the mask of a bearded idolater . . . As soon as he set foot on dry land, he came straight up to me. He had a strange expression on his face. 'I'm a writer now,' he said. 'Because I've left death to my lover.' Then he started to drink. I told him Şafak could have gone abroad without telling anyone. It was a possibility . . .

"We heard it in the middle of the night. It sounded like something a species not of this world would make. It was like howling. I came out of my room; it was coming from the top floor. Kuzey was staying on the first floor at that time, in the corner room. Everyone rushed out. Spot, out of his mind with fear, was whimpering beneath the stairs. We entered Kuzey's room and found him sitting in bed. That's when I understood: what we'd thought was howling was actually pure pain that had turned into sound. I went up to him, and when I touched his arm, he opened his eyes as if he'd woken up from sleep . . . then he went silent. I'd never seen him looking so shocked before. As he reached out his hands beseechingly, he was muttering: 'I never thought anyone would love me so much.' I realized while he was still holding my hands: from now on his whole life would be made up of the indescribable sorrow of that moment . . .

"In the morning, he started howling again. It was unbearable to hear. It was as though he'd swallowed barbed wire and an invisible hand was pulling it out from his throat, plucking out his internal organs one by one. Anyway, on that day, first the Germans transferred to the hotels down the road, and after that, the cicadas migrated to another pepper tree in Bodrum. Kuzey's shock lasted the whole day; whenever he stopped howling, he'd repeat the same thing over and over again without stopping: 'I never thought she'd love me so much, I never thought . . .'

"That night, when we'd run out of patience, when we'd finally reached the threshold of madness ourselves, Handan eventually managed to shut him up . . . easily too: by hugging him, by making him her son. The next morning, I went into his room to see how he was. The man lying exhausted in Handan's arms was very different from the Kuzey of a fortnight earlier. Actually, there was nothing strange about that. In those two weeks, he'd consumed what was left of his life.

"Ten days later, Şafak's sister phoned again. To get closure. There was news from Holland. Şafak hadn't turned up at the HQ of the charity where she was going to get training before going out to Africa by the deadline given in the contract . . . Kuzey? He never did get closure; he couldn't. Not until the morning he decided to scratch out the stamp of guilt from his soul . . ."

August 2003:

There's a day ahead of us like one of Manet's pictures: a day when black is forbidden . . . The boat, cutting through the waters in front of a low humming of the motor, advances to the final scene, toward "tomorrow." It's time to experience the mystery of rebirth. According to Sami, that's the reason for the morbid hunger I have for my end: the belief that you can be reborn after you die. It's not a particularly complicated, nonsensical desire. My goal is to live long enough to be able to speak with her after I die! If the nails and hair of dead bodies can grow, why shouldn't it be possible?

I have not fear, joy nor hope inside me. Not to be any later than I already am: that's the only thing I'm thinking about. Not to be late whatever happens. To be able to get to the meeting as quickly as possible. I blamed God for not arranging it, I hurled threats at Him for when He forgot it, and now finally I have to beg Him not to delay it any more . . . Beyond this thought, my mind is as empty and calm as a desert. Farewell to the vibrations fluttering around in my brain. I'll be free in half an hour. I'm talking about a real, pure freedom; the freedom of the gods: a world where shame, regret and promises we have to keep have lost their meaning . . . Still, on my way to the reunion I'm five years late for, it's not as if there aren't things I'm curious about: Can conversations under the sea be heard? When we meet, when I say, "forgive me," will she hear me? And most important of all, in the water, will she be able to see that I'm crying?

As we set off toward the south, the coast and the mountains were flowing to the north . . . The long, white trail the motor left behind it had turned the boat into a kite jiggling on the smooth surface of the sea. Furthest to the north, the camel hump of Hisarcık Kayası; to its right, Büyük Ada; in front, Değirmen Dağı, with its ghostly windmills; Küçük Ada; Delikli Burun, like a line forgotten on the canvas; and immediately to our right, Akdağlar, resembling the back of a large fish . . .

I'm not going to say good-bye to any of them. Just as I didn't say good-bye to Sami, or to Çiğdem.

"What have you got in there?" I turned around. The man, who'd crouched down under the tarpaulin as soon as he got on the boat, was looking with restive eyes at the sack at his feet. He hadn't been able to take the silence. "It makes a noise when you shake it."

It was hot, but in spite of that, he hadn't taken off his long-sleeved shirt. "My son," I said.

"Your son?" We were in the waters off the cove after Bodrum, off Saipaltı. The shelter against the short, stubby headland was empty. The trawlers must have left early in the morning to go fishing. I bowed my head. That smile he'd worn like a mask on his strange face beneath his wide-brimmed hat had disappeared. "Are you taking the piss?"

"I'm taking him to bury him," I said.

"We're not going to a graveyard, are we?"

I turned to the right and looked ahead. We were approaching Domuz Burnu. "You could put it like that," I said. "To a graveyard with a view, no less."

"You're a funny bastard." He'd taken a cigarette out of his pocket. "We set off on a trip, and now we're going to a funeral!"

"Or we could call it a reunion. All funerals, in a way, are reunions, wouldn't you agree?"

Instead of replying, he lit his cigarette. I gave the engine a bit more gas, and turned the rudder to the left. I had gone down toward Eşendere Burnu. "When are we going to talk about the hotel?" He was shouting now so I could hear. "In the graveyard?"

I bowed my head. I could have sworn or called him a bastard, but I only bowed my head. His eyes had shrunk to the size of shirt buttons. A bad, unbearable face. God had chosen him to play a role in the final scene; I was helpless; I was going to have to put up with him.

First we went past the headland, and after that, narrow Akkum, which had been thrust like a dagger into the mainland. In the interior of the gulf, tightened by the channel, the sea was even calmer. I took a beer out of the bag. "Half an hour's peace. That's what I expect from you," I murmured to the bottle in my hand.

"Did you say something?"

I reached out the hand I was holding the beer in and pointed to the sack. "When he was alive, he used to hate the smell of alcohol," I said.

He tried to smile, but his eyes were still as small as buttons. It was a waste of effort. Smiling was pointless without his eyes. I turned back to the rudder. Fifteen minutes at most . . .

Fifteen minutes later, we'd passed Boyabağı too; we'd reached the point where the road that passes through the olive groves and links the rich mountain villages with the Izmir highway descends to the coast. As Fındık had described, I looked to the left, toward Uzunada. The juniper tree was there. Approximately thirty feet above the sea, the white limestone, which had been washed all winter long by the waves whipped up by the northeast wind, looked like a green stain on the cliff.

Finally, we had arrived. I was inside that picture I called *Tomorrow*. I put the engine on slow. I was shaking, but it wasn't because of the ants. When the boat suddenly slowed down, its hull fell to the water. We drifted for about a hundred and twenty feet; then I put the engine in neutral, and lit a cigarette. "Thirty fathoms from the juniper tree in the open water . . ." That's what Fındık had said.

Trying to judge the distance, I dropped anchor; the clanking of the chain made a few sea birds nesting inside the cliff fly off. But the anchor remained hanging at the end of the chain without touching the bottom. The water was deep like the old dolphin had said. I had to bring the boat nearer to the coast and try three times before the anchor reached the bottom. I was worn out, half dead, and the rest of me wanted to drink until I drowned, but I bit my lips and ignored the beer. I slowly unwound the rope I'd tied to the end of the chain and brought the boat back to where it had been before. I was pretty much right at the rendezvous point: the edge of the shelf at the bottom of the sea. The tremors that engulfed my hands gave way to a strange numbness.

Once the boat was floating motionless, I put out my cigarette and turned around. The man, who'd spent the last few minutes silently watching what I was doing, reacted before me: "Is this the graveyard?"

He was looking at the land. "Here," I said.

"It doesn't really look like a graveyard."

I pointed out the juniper tree. "Look at that! Do you know what that is?" I replied for him: "A sign. They plant trees at the head of graves so they don't get lost, don't they?"

We didn't say anything for a moment. The man, as if he was alone, started whistling softly and looking around. He took off his hat to reveal his bald head and his strange appearance. "It's quite remote out here," he said, when he'd stopped whistling. "There's no one around."

He was mistaken. I pointed to the road that ran down from the hill to the north. "Look, there's a car over there." He followed the gentle arc my hand traced and turned to the hill. He screwed up his eyes, and tried to make out the road, which resembled a curved pencil line drawn on the hillside. "It's going quite fast too," I said.

"What car?"

"A Citroën," I said. "A 2CV, one of the small ones."

"Where?" asked the man. "I can't see it."

But I could see everything. "It's red. And there's a young woman driving. She's tired."

"There's no car and no woman there."

But there was; I could see the red 2CV swerving from side to side down the road, and I could see what was happening inside the car. At the wheel, there was a woman who was not content with little happinesses, who was looking for something greater, much grander than happiness. "She's crying," I said. "Soon her tears and the approaching darkness will completely prevent her from seeing. And . . ."

"What darkness?" interrupted the man. "It's not even nine o'clock in the morning yet." He was surprised.

Couldn't he see the evening star setting toward the mountain? "And she's lost a lot of blood," I said.

"Is she injured?"

Yes, she's injured. It was me who stabbed her. Twenty or thirty minutes ago. "If she doesn't slow down before she gets to the cliff, she's not going to be . . ."

Raising his voice, the man interrupted me. "You're seeing things, mate." He was pointing to the bottle in my hand. "You must have started early today."

"She's not going to slow down," I said. "She can't see what's in front of her anymore. She's been crying her eyes out ever since she left the hotel, for a whole twelve miles, you see. I guess she's made up her mind."

"Made up her mind about what?" Maybe she hadn't. It was all just a . . . The man's sarcasm silenced my thoughts, which were attempting to deny it. "So you mean to tell me you can see a car and an injured woman from here, do you?"

He'd gotten over his surprise, and now he was trying hard not to laugh. I shook my head and the bottle in my hand together. "And you know, she's in love with me. Madly . . ."

Just then, after I said madly, I fell silent. He asked at the same time: "What's happened?"

"I've lost sight of the car," I said. "But in a moment it'll appear again on top of us."

He opened his hands, annoyed. "There's no crying woman or anything, mate. You're the one crying." Stroking the bottle of beer, I set it down on the wooden seat. "What are you doing with the bottle?"

"I'm bidding it farewell," I said.

At first, he paused as if he was going to ask me about it, then he changed his mind. "Look, let's just get down to business. What should I tell my friends?"

I wanted to talk about being madly in love; he wanted to talk about his shipping-agent friends. Very well, I wasn't going to keep him waiting.

When our eyes met, "Binti, binti, binti . . ." I said, over and over again.

"And what's that supposed to mean?" He was open-mouthed with surprise.

"Go and tell those human traffickers," I said, "that I'll be testifying. Whatever it costs, that bastard who abandoned women and children in the middle of the sea in the dead of the night is going down."

He said nothing for a moment. He was surprised, but he quickly regained his composure. When he got up, he looked calm. He stroked his beard with his hand like he was taking off his mask. He wasn't going to deny it. Good. That would make things easier for both of us.

"Even if it turns out to be more costly than you think?" he asked.

"Yes," I said.

He paused for a moment, finally, as if he'd reached a decision; then he shook his head disapprovingly. "If I were you, I'd think again."

"There's nothing to think about," I said. "As long as I'm alive, I'll stop at nothing to get that poor excuse for a captain and his accomplice banged up."

His voice wavered between disappointment and indecision; then he repeated what I'd said: "As long as you're alive! Is that so?"

"Yes," I said. "As long as I'm alive." There wasn't much time left. I went over to the sack. "And I think that coward will sell out his friends in the tourist sector too."

Our eyes met. The stage was his. It was time for him to play out his role in the final scene.

I turned around and hugged Spot. Just then the noise of the car cascaded onto us from the hill—like water pouring down a waterfall. I hadn't been mistaken; this was our meeting place. The woman who was looking for our heart's most exquisite fluttering had come to take her place on stage.

"Are you sure?" His voice was still indecisive.

He mustn't change his mind! "I'm sure," I said, egging him on.

He put his hand to his waist. Without waiting for him, I went out onto the front of the boat, wound my feet around the rope at the end of the chain and unhooked it. I was one step at most away from that moment when my future, when all futures would become nothing— one step away from the threshold of time, a few minutes or seconds. Hadn't Fındık said heaven is in the sea? He was witness to another kind of life. I had to trust him. But strange, meaningless images were passing before my eyes: the sick cat I brought home when I was five; the glowing refractory bricks inside the cast-iron coal-burning stove

Salim burnt his hand on that I used to watch, transfixed; the blunt razor my father had never used that had been handed down from his grandfather . . .

I could smell rotten vegetables again. The smell of death. Then . . .

First, a red eagle appeared in the distance; then I heard the gunshot; and after a moment, that whisper: "I never thought you'd love me so much . . ."

As I flew through a silence that hadn't matured yet, that had no permanence, I shuddered with joy. I had been afraid for nothing: my voice could be heard under the water. So . . . Together with Spot, who I hadn't been able to watch over, I advanced toward the magnificent eagle who was waiting for us. "Forgive me . . ."

Sami Çetin, August 10, 2004:

"That night—yes, I'm talking about August 21st—everything seemed to be going swimmingly. Kuzey disappeared for a while with Emin in the late afternoon, but as we were starting dinner, he re-appeared. Çiğdem's friends from Istanbul had come, and we ate together. He seemed to be behaving normally. It was only the next day, when he'd disappeared and I'd thought over what actually happened at dinner, that I realized he hadn't been normal. Actually I should have understood something was up: by his own standards he drank practically nothing that night. It was obvious from the tremors that wracked his hands and legs from time to time. He was strangely cheerful throughout the meal. And he did some surprising things: he kissed Çiğdem in front of everyone, and he hugged me, three times no less . . . You know, sometimes you become stupid. You don't notice, you can't see what's happening before your very eyes. I didn't understand he was saying good-bye. Yet it was all so obvious. Çiğdem? She was happy; she kept talking about the future. And if a woman's making plans about the future, that's a sign she's happy . . . I know because my wife never made any plans. And if a woman's happy, she's blind . . .

"Emin said he put the dog bones they'd dug up from a hole on the other side of the mountain in the boat that night—because Kuzey asked him to. So he'd planned everything in advance. He'd promised Çiğdem and me he wouldn't commit suicide, and he kept his word. God helped him; He sent him a killer to do the job . . .

"No one saw or knows what he did or where he went that morning. He must have gone out with the dawn . . . Yes, Kuzey and the boat disappearing coinciding with Osman and his wife vanishing made us think there was a connection between them, of course. Later we investigated, and it turns out the man wasn't from Ankara, and he didn't have a restaurant or anything. No one came forward who knew him. The police and Emin investigated, but they couldn't find anything . . .

"Apparently Kuzey didn't really sleep very much the last evening; after we'd gone in, he sat out on the terrace, and according to what Veli says, he spoke for a while with the man who called himself Osman. And he read the whole night. Poetry. I thought it was strange because I hadn't seen him reading recently.

"And another thing: he also left an envelope with Çiğdem's name on it . . .

"Of course not, there was no miracle or anything! Here's what happened: the day Kuzey disappeared, a rock rolled down from Değirmen Dağı. A rather large rock that looked like the head of a statue when seen from Küçük Ada. Everyone got excited of course. Imagine, a huge rock, weighing at least ten tons, raising up clouds of dust, and rolling six hundred feet down the hillside, passing between so many houses and falling from Delikli Burun into the sea. If you ask Fındık, he'd say that rock was actually a red eagle, and it snatched Kuzey and took him to his grave in the sea. That's apparently what it says in the Register. It's all nonsense, of course. The truth is that four years ago, when the soldiers were making a new road to the hill, they pulled up the bushes on the slope that looks out onto the sea and destroyed the natural structure of the land. And in time the water accumulating on the road and seeping into the ground hollowed out the bottom of the rocks on the hillside. When the time came, the rock rolled down, leaving a cloud of red dust behind it. That's the long and short of it. And that's how the engineers from the local council explained it too . . . Fındık makes up these stories to impress Çiğdem. Why? There must be something that maniac wants from her. And was Kuzey even a snake? Why do I say that? Because

snakes and eagles go together. They're both Zarathustra's animals . . .
Maybe Fındık knows where Kuzey is. But you can't make him talk.
Oh no, he couldn't possibly divulge the secrets of the Register, and if
he did, Kuzey would go to hell . . .

"What was Kuzey like? That's a difficult question. I told you I was
in the business of gathering useless information, didn't I? Recently I've
been into artistic movements. We could maybe compare understanding Kuzey to understanding modern art. As you know, in modern art
the object doesn't express itself; it's the empty space around it that
expresses it. In my opinion, to express Kuzey, you have to understand
the people around him too. But don't forget that a work of art, be it
modern or not, is not exhausted by perception. More than anything
else what makes us similar to each other, what makes us the same
is death. So much so that, as a species, we're even called 'mortals.'
And the immortals? The immortals are those who can design and
choose their own death. If you ask me, this time Kuzey didn't miss
the opportunity he hadn't been able to seize when he was young . . .

"Kuzey said that Çiğdem was a goddess among women, that she'd
go not to whoever she loved, but to whoever loved her the most. He
was wrong about that. Isn't the proof there for all to see? Actually,
we were all wrong about the princess. I'd thought she was looking for
a man who'd never be able to possess her. Because that's how Kuzey
was. But that turned out to be a foolish assumption. In reality, we
don't know what love is, and I think that's why when we do encounter it, we try to define it with other words . . .

"That's right, I'm going to stay. Because I've got nowhere else to
go. Besides, I came here to be buried; the ceremony will be a bit late,
that's all. There's no change, in other words. I pretend that I'm alive; I
put up with the heart-rending existence of life. So you see, my heaven
and my hell are here. No, not because I believe in them. Besides,

one day someone will blow up the stairway to heaven, and there'll be no more heaven or hell . . . Am I crying? I don't notice it. I guess I caught it from Kuzey, like a cold . . .

"The days pass easily. I watch the butterflies and the shadows. I read. Butterflies' tongues are coiled like a spring. And I find the shadows enchanting. You see, they spend the whole day circling the hotel like tame animals tied to a post . . . At night, it's time for the nightmares: memories hurtling around in my head, like horses running riot . . .

"I've forgiven him. Of course I miss him. He was the one living creature on this earth who was the most like me. I'm all alone now. As lonely as the last representative of a species that's becoming extinct, you could say. It's good there's that tiny, miraculous creature. Just let her get a little bit bigger, and I'll tell her what kind of person my comrade was . . .

"It's surprising but true. The hotel's doing pretty well this year. They both objected, but we've taken on an assistant for Şuayip and one for Şükrü. We've computerized everything. We don't owe anyone any money. İhsan Hoca has been staying here since his hovel was knocked down. Emin's here too. He's still working together with the hoca. First they're going to find a way to replace the chairman of the local council, then they say they're going to organize a philosophy conference. From time to time, Handan joins them as well. The association's got a permanent room next to the lobby now . . . Fındık? He still turns up on top of Delikli Burun whenever there's a full moon, like a wolf. But he doesn't bring any fish, lobster or anything anymore. Don't pay any attention to what Şükrü says— you can't say Fındık's mad, because he's humble. Have you ever seen a humble madman? He's pally with Çiğdem these days. Or rather, Çiğdem's keeping him sweet for some reason. He testified in court.

He went with Emin . . . Of course I don't believe what Kuzey said about him being a dolphin. But you can bet there's lots of people on the peninsula who do believe he's a cursed dolphin . . . No one knows what the Register is. And I've never met anyone who's seen it. It's supposedly got secrets in it that would turn this peninsula upside down. Everyone's secrets—I wonder if that means their crimes—are written there one by one. Who knows, maybe it's like you say, and a register is just an attempt to concretize the social conscience and has come down to us from Şeyh Bedrettin's followers. But whatever it is, you can be sure you'll find a complete list of all the crazies, and the half and completely mad there . . ."

"Surprising? Maybe it is. But if I hadn't deceived him, there would have been nothing between us. You could say I was taking advantage of the helplessness of a man blinded and deafened by his regrets. You could even say it was shameful. I know Sami used to think so from time to time. But like I say, I'm not ashamed of what I did. He once said to me, 'If someone turns you into someone you don't know, then it's love.' I was in love with him. That's why I lied, that's why I took someone else's place, and that's why I never even blushed . . .

"How did it begin? Here's how: the day I kissed him, I came downstairs again, long after midnight. I hadn't been able to sleep. It was a hot night, there was a stubborn mosquito in my room, and of course there was what had happened that day . . . As I was going to the kitchen, I heard him. He was moaning, begging in a strange voice. I waited in front of his door for a moment. Invading a person's privacy! That was a troubling thought. First I thought I'd tell Sami, but then I changed my mind and went into his room. He might have needed help. It was dark inside; there was only a faint light coming from the bathroom. When my eyes got used to the darkness, I saw him. In the half-lit bed, he was curled up in the fetal position, crying as though in pain. Because he was tall, he still covered the whole bed. I sat next to him. As I was sitting there wondering what to do, he suddenly stretched out, took hold of my hand and pulled me toward himself. At first I thought he'd woken up or come around, but his eyes were closed. He'd fallen silent too; for ten or fifteen minutes I lay next to him without moving a muscle. Did he kiss me or did I kiss him, I don't remember. After that? We didn't stop after that . . . At one point toward morning he called me Şafak. That's when I understood. I remember how embarrassed, how disappointed I was. I was tongue-tied; I stammered. He started to cry again. He was saying sorry; he kept repeating Şafak's name. In the end, I said, 'Yes darling, it's me.'

"As he cried on my breast, I joined him in his tears. He asked again and again, and each time I told him I was Şafak. After that night, I gave him as much alcohol as he wanted, to knock him out. There was no other way he'd let me love him; if there had been, I'd have tried it.

"For two weeks, I went down to his room almost every night. Mücella was the first to notice. Did she tell Sami, or did Sami find out for himself, I don't know. He was violently opposed to it. That last night over dinner, he was scrutinizing us disapprovingly. Us? Kuzey and me . . . Kuzey held my hand for the first time that night, the first time he was conscious, *and* he kissed me in front of everyone. At one point we went around the back and watched the sky. Like Homer. He showed me the Little Bear then the Great Bear. He explained how to find the pole star. In Nigeria, they call the Milky Way the backbone of the sky. Did you know that?

"His last words to me before I went to bed were, 'Don't let any man love you. Let him be *in love* with you, if he can . . .' Even though a few days earlier he'd told me we should choose love over being in love.

"I couldn't go down to his room that night. Rana was around; then I saw him wandering about on the terrace. Of course, it was surprising he hadn't passed out. But actually I was more pleased than surprised.

"In the morning, Sami brought me an envelope with my name on it. He said he'd found it in Kuzey's room. There were some sheets of paper inside: *The Diary of an Itinerant Drunkard* . . . That was the title of the notes. No, I can't give them to you . . . Maybe you can glance at a few pages. And there's a poem: of course, I read it so many times I learned it by heart:

The ship sailed into the last harbor and anchored to leave no more,
As there was no longer any hope from the wind or daylight,
After the light carried by the dawn had left captain Kuzey,
There buried the ship with a life as short as a day, like a broken wave . . .

"Actually, the captain in the third line of the poem was Captain Eudemos of Olympus; Eudemos has been crossed out and Kuzey written over it.[16] Look, here it is . . .

"For a time I was obsessed about getting to know him: what an empty dream that turned out to be. Who can comprehend a sorrowful man in his entirety? I'm going to love him in his absence. That's what I have to learn now . . . It's practically impossible to find their bodies, but there's still a small hope: Fındık. If I can convince him, maybe I'll bring them both up to the graveyard on the hill, into view . . . There should be a grave where my daughter will be able to visit her father. What's her name? Şimal . . ."[17]

---

[16] The original inscription can be seen at the Harbor Memorial Tombs in Olimpos.

AFTERWORD

Author's note, November 2004:

A few more paragraphs ... then the story will finally be over. But in the middle of September, when I was halfway through the first chapter, between me and the end of the novel there were still problems—problems that could have stopped me from continuing. Would starting off by hearing about people who I didn't know, who I'd never seen, from the mouths of other people who I didn't know, and constructing them with secondhand information make the story less believable? It turns out there was no reason to worry. It didn't make it less believable; on the contrary, it made it lifelike. Because it's not the people we know, it's the people we create that are more real. The pages that followed confirmed this judgment step by step. Fine, but what about attempting to create a world using those pieces of the truth, which I know changes easily, that were able to reach me via word of mouth? How reliable a foundation for the story would that be? Actually, when I was still in the first stage of my journey, begun with an anxious rigor, I abandoned my concerns about whether or not the facts were true. Because what a story needs—as Kuzey screams in his diary—is not the facts of life, but the facts of dreams, is it not? While I was writing, there were times when I felt I knew well the people I was portraying—I prefer to use this word instead of "creating" because it implies subjectivity—and also times when I felt that I didn't know anything about them. And this was natural: writing is an honorable deception or a misconception. It's the transformation of deception and misconception into truth through their interpenetration. And that's what I've been doing for the past five months.

Here's what I've worked out from what I've heard: Kuzey was one of those men who bear their maturity like a stigma. If we were to believe Çiğdem, he was "very sincere, and what you see is what you get." One of those people who are said to be "so natural!" But people like that somehow always make me feel they've got something wrong with them. Because someone who is too good, someone who has completely shed their badness, is a half-person, a gelding. As long as it's moderate, badness is natural; unadulterated goodness, though, is artificial. A personality that has shed its badness, that has been purified, is as unbearable and bland as a body that has not been hewn by sin is crude and formless, and it will eventually lose its direction.

So, how did our hero measure up as a lover? "To be in love is an absolute: it takes everything or gives everything. Other feelings, like pity or compassion, only make it into the outer circle." Kuzey never expressed himself in this way, using the categorical words of one in love. Wasn't breaking up with Şafak for the sake of her future virtuous yet hypocritical, like a rich man praising thrift? By choosing love over being in love, he committed a crime; he sacrificed his badness to his conscience. While someone who is in love can only be free with his passion, someone who merely loves can flee from his heart and take refuge in the depths of his conscience. But life doesn't take sides. He must have sought help from alcohol when his conscience could not digest his sacrifice.

Writing is always a discovery—even if that's not your intention. Arranging the sentences one after the other reminds me of a tour of a swamp where you pluck from the ground, like flowers, truths about people—that will drive whoever finds them to despair. After all these years spent writing, I should explain one truth I've discovered: there's a secret crack in everyone's personality. Kuzey's was his conscience. His regret, which slowly seeped through that crack into his heart—just like water penetrating a rock—eventually smashed him to smithereens.

I guess I've always thought that the Tower of Babel was a magnificent—and, to an equal degree, foolish—proof of the human desire to reach heaven. So, what are we to make of Kuzey wanting to make a grave for himself in the watery depths? After years spent looking for his direction and his girlfriend, did he decide to go to hell? The secret lies in those final hours that no one witnessed. After recognizing the sign God had sent him, he must have spent the night in a sacred madness devising a plan. In our conversation in August, Sami once called him an "itinerant" as he looked out over the channel. I can't say I believe that. Even though he did set off on a journey, he did so in the wrong sea. Because in the end, all inner seas are just lakes.

In spite of his impressive talent for blaming himself, and even in spite of us being related through fate, I was never able to feel close to Kuzey. At one point, I even thought of comparing his heart to an uncut, impenetrable dark wood, full of traps and evil spirits. Nevertheless, I tried to be fair to him while I was writing. You have to respect someone who wants to be "more human," even if you don't like them. All the more so if this person, like you, longs for death, and like you, waits for news from God and fears having to linger on forever. Was him turning toward Şafak a turning toward youth, toward immortality, or was it the temerity of his vital instinct? But it is possible to read in his diary the proof of his suffering and regret. According to what he wrote, the deep and unrelenting pain he felt can only be compared to that of a mother who has lost her child. "There's no such thing as an unstained memory . . ." Was that why he said, "A tragic crime is a crime that no one can be blamed for?" Although to write is to pass judgment, respecting his wish, I shall not be his judge. He himself tied the Gordian knot inside him; he himself undid it. Could it not be that what horrifies us—and for this reason, what enrages us—is that he did it in the same way as Alexander did?

In spite of my best efforts, I wasn't able to get ahold of any particularly satisfying information about Çiğdem's mother, Vildan—or about Vildan and Kuzey's relationship. How did they meet? Did Kuzey ever really love this, as Çiğdem would have it, insignificant woman? Or was Vildan—as Sami intimated—a decorative object who spurred on Kuzey's urge to write? How was their marriage? Why did they suddenly separate? I don't care if they ended their marriage. Is not marriage when two people have to get to know one another, sooner or later? And it is possible they were disappointed with what they found; we shouldn't ignore that.

Winter is on its way. I'm going to tear up my notes as soon as I get the chance. Here's what I wrote about Çiğdem: "A woman so beautiful that her every desire is an order for everyone—except for herself . . . A romantic idolater who worships what belongs to her . . ." At first I thought she was shallow, that she couldn't control her selfishness. Like Sami and Kuzey, I too turned out to have misjudged her. Far from being selfish, she was egocentric. And I should also add that she was generous. That must be why she put such a high price on Kuzey, more than he was worth. Why was she like that? I think she was very pure: so untouched that she hated her purity, and she must have felt the desire to be cleansed of her purity by a dirty soul. A mother, like a dried-up river, who left all her love with the man she'd walked out on. An unhappy father, a creaking marriage, a despotic grandfather . . . That's Çiğdem's background. Still, I must admit that she's the heroine at the center of the story. There's no doubt that this interesting woman was the pillar—as well as the theme—of the story. Şimal, the little girl who keeps crawling around, is the being who made Şafak, Kuzey and Çiğdem real inhabitants of the peninsula; isn't the fact that Çiğdem was brave enough to give birth to her proof of her courage?

Sami: "The man who loves words!" That's the phrase I'd have started with if I'd written him. If a writer is someone who can see a person's dramatic, uncommon sides, then Sami deserves this description, not Kuzey. His disability might have been a hindrance because "He was full of himself like a drunkard." His disability eventually pushed him to the other pole of pleasure, to spiritual asceticism. So much so that the thought did sometimes cross my mind that his feelings too were as crippled as his legs, and that when the time came, he didn't bother trying to take a step and pass beyond the threshold of his consciousness. If Şafak isn't as clearly defined in the story as she should be, I have to say that Sami's to blame for that. Because I got all my information about Şafak, and even more importantly, my impression of her, from him—although I did check with Handan and Mücella. When I was speaking with him, I often got the feeling that there was a side to him that loved gossip. But this wasn't a drawback for the reality I was after. Gossips have more of a natural predisposition to tell stories than others do. While speaking with Sami, I remember there were moments when I had to look away from him embarrassedly. Especially when talking about Fındık. The embarrassment of pretending not to know the old dolphin or the Register is still fresh on my cheeks. The extraordinary, touching relationship between him and Kuzey confirms what friendships like theirs are like: "In long-term friendships, friends eventually become each other's master."

Everyone enthused about him, but I didn't really warm to İhsan, whose conversation was interrupted by the clatter of his false teeth. First of all, in contrast to his "deep words," how much of which he'd actually produced himself and how much of which he'd gathered from somewhere else I didn't know, he had rather "shallow opinions." What's more, he wasn't rigorous either. I deduce that from him sharing himself with all comers. And . . . and he was foolish enough to think that God would denude Himself in front of His worshipers. How could he not understand that what he called "pure goodness" meant God stripping off His badness and being left naked? It's obvious he couldn't strike a balance between doubt and irony, that he couldn't separate one from the other; and I think this confusion lay behind the weakness of his thinking, and him not being able to systematize what he said. He should have been spending his time with his thoughts, not with people, but he was doing the exact opposite. So, what made him bearable? His devotion to philosophy, the childlike sensitivity he hid behind his thoughts. That must be the answer . . . Emin! Because he was inseparable from the hoca, I can't close the subject of İhsan without saying a word or two about him. I only bumped into the captain once. Five minutes was enough for me to realize that nothing would come out of our conversation. He wasn't really there in front of me; he'd never returned from the war he'd gone to. So much so that while writing the story, I used this strong impression of mine and attributed it to Kuzey the night they dug up Spot's grave. By the way, according to what Ahmet told me, he had a son. God came up with a frightful punishment: he decided to make his conscience follow him wherever he went.

And me: now that I've written this story you are reading, I'm not worried about money, Çiğdem's tearful eyes, or creating a literary masterpiece. This effort stretching over hundreds of pages is actually a letter to Fındık, an announcement that I want to make peace with him, that I want to clear up the misunderstanding that has lasted since my father's death; in a sense, it's an appeal for forgiveness addressed to the old dolphin, a peace pipe I offer him so he won't begrudge me the generosity he showed Kuzey. If the death of my father, who I couldn't mourn, has not repaid my debt, I'm even willing to promise: "I will never again try to steal the Register from him. He's the guardian. I accept that you're the protector of the Register; I believe that you can destroy this peninsula with your anger."

Like Kuzey's Kurtz, I've reached the end of the road; the breath in my lungs that would give life to the words is slowly being consumed. The old dolphin ought not to begrudge me the good news he received from God and transmitted to Kuzey. He should know that I too should be able to pick out my rock. Actually we both know which one it is: that altar stone where the night my father died I gave him back the Register, not even a single secret of which I've revealed in all the thousands of pages I've written. A medium-sized, black rock that looks out onto the Gediz Delta, a bit further on from Gazep, on the east face of the headland that shelters Saipaltı from the northeast wind. When it rolls into the sea, it won't make as much noise as Kuzey's did, I realize that. So be it; an eagle, even when flying low, is still an eagle.

And Şafak! The woman who said, "Remembering the end of life . . . It stops me from being content with my little happinesses. What I'm looking for is something greater, much grander than happiness . . ." Did she find what she was looking for? This question, like many others about her, remains unanswered. How, with a passion that drove her to her death, did she end up loving a man who believed not in being in love, but simply in love? Who can know? Maybe what prompted her was the hope of finding that "something much grander than happiness," or maybe it was a repressed sense of adventure. Fine, but that strange evening when, drunk with disappointment, she climbed into her car, what storms were brewing in her soul? We will never be able to find out. But it would surely not be misleading to say that she thought she'd been betrayed, that she'd been let down, and that a dark curtain had come between her and the future. Because to decide in favor of death is only possible once we've completely lost any sense of the future. Even though happiness is experienced in the present, it is always a hope for the future; unhappiness, though, is a loss of the future.

Was it coincidence that Kuzey met Şafak? I don't know; if it was, only life would have been bold enough to devise such a coincidence. Maybe all explanations, reasonings, interpretations about the two of them are pure nonsense. "Sometimes it can't be any other way . . ." This too is probably one of those situations that we can describe like this.

I should finish this story, which actually comes to an end, not last August with Kuzey's disappearance, but six years ago, on that ill-fated evening, benighted by the strange storm that burst out from the mouth of a secret volcano in the middle of the channel and that set about lashing the hillsides, with Şafak getting into her car, with these words Kuzey wrote in his diary before he'd ever met Şafak:

"Disaster reveals the meaningless inherent in life . . ."
What a dramatic prediction.

January 2004–March 2005
Karaburun–Ankara